Jenny Knight studied English literature at university before going on to work in journalism and the publishing industry. For many early mornings alongside this she coached rowing – a job that inspired the initial idea for her first crime novel, *The Fifth Guest.*

Jenny lives with her husband, son and a black-and-white cat.

Find her on Twitter and Instagram @jknightauthor

The Fifth Guest

Jenny Knight

ONE PLACE. MANY STORIES

HQ
An imprint of HarperCollins*Publishers* Ltd
1 London Bridge Street
London SE1 9GF

www.harpercollins.co.uk

HarperCollins*Publishers*
Macken House, 39/40 Mayor Street Upper,
Dublin 1, D01 C9W8, Ireland

This edition 2023

1
First published in Great Britain by
HQ, an imprint of HarperCollins*Publishers* Ltd 2023

Copyright © Jenny Knight, 2023

ISBN: 978-0-00-829758-9

For Shell, thank you.

Excerpt from the *London Gazette*

Most middle-class injury ever!

Just as doctors call for avocados to come with a cutting-injury warning, there's a new health hazard to panic middle-class suburbanites: the humble cheese plate.

At a dinner party in the leafy south-west London suburb of Barnes, a guest was allegedly stabbed in the stomach with an elaborate silver cheese knife normally used for nothing more harmful than slicing a good Brie.

CHAPTER ONE

CARO

Caro was on her way to the gym when the invitation arrived. The postman handed it to her along with a bill and a clothing catalogue. They exchanged their normal pleasantries about the glorious weather and the noise of the builders three doors up. Normally, Caro would have got in the Lexus, sweated her way through Body Pump and then spent an hour in the café sussing out the hierarchies of the post-class cappuccino group and made chat accordingly.

Now, however, she found herself back in the house, sitting on the staircase, third step from the bottom, holding the expensive envelope in her hands while her eyes honed in on the family crest embossed on the 140 gsm stationery.

Her upper lip was sweating.

She turned the envelope over in her hands. Thought about leaving it on the sideboard and heading outside to carry on with her day but she would be too consumed by morbid, itching curiosity to do anything productive. So she opened it quickly and without ceremony, tearing the thick paper deliberately irreverent.

Lady Charles Bellinger desires the honour of the presence of
Mr and Mrs Brian Carmichael,
at the Unveiling Ceremony of the
Sir Charles and Henry Bellinger Memorial
on Sunday 15th July at No. 6
Riverside Gardens, Chiswick
NOTE – THIS CARD MUST BE PRESENTED
TO ENSURE ADMISSION.

Caro stared at the fancy black font for an indeterminable amount of time; it could have been seconds or half the morning, her eyes going in and out of focus.

A memorial unveiling. She could imagine nothing worse than standing on the manicured lawn of the Bellinger family home listening to speeches while waiting for a life-sized likeness of Henry to stare down at her from above like Jesus.

Caro stood up. Exhaled slowly. Henry Bellinger seemed to follow her everywhere she went, existing in her peripheral vision; she saw him in faces going past on the bus or at the airport. She'd see the broad shoulders or maybe the laughing eyes and the dimples. But then he'd stand up and be too short or he'd smile and his teeth would be wrong and that Henry would morph back in to just a stranger getting onto an aeroplane.

Caro leant against the banister, the carved handrail digging into her back, and read the invite again. Riverside Gardens. It was just up the road. She wondered who else Lady Bellinger had invited. If Caro was on the list then surely everyone was; the old witch would never have afforded Caro special privilege. She imagined the Bellinger private secretary having his work cut out tracking them all down.

For a second she considered politely declining, inventing a prior engagement, and felt a moment of relief. But she could never give Lady Bellinger that satisfaction.

The front door opened. It was Mary-Anne, Caro's cleaner. 'Oh, Mrs Carmichael, I didn't expect to see you,' she said, startled by the sight of Caro in the hallway.

'No, no, I was just leaving. Sorry, Mary-Anne.' Flustered at having been caught unawares, especially by her cleaner, as if spotted by the boss asleep on the job, Caro rushed to gather her gym bag and keys and dropped the invitation.

'Is everything all right, Mrs Carmichael?' Mary-Anne asked, moving forward to help.

'No, fine, absolutely fine.' Caro scooped up her things. She caught a glimpse of herself in the hallway mirror. She looked completely fine; a little paler than usual but not of scrap of agitation present on her face. 'I'll get out of your hair, Mary-Anne. Let you work your magic.' Caro slipped out the door.

Outside, the river air and traffic fumes did the trick. She would not be cowed by this, she thought as she strode to the car. She would face it head on. *'Caroline, detachment is easy, you just imagine yourself in a play, acting the part of yourself.'* It was a technique handed down by her mother as a way of sealing off one's emotions. Just one of the many nuggets of how-to advice to secure a wealthy husband. But in this case, Caro felt she might need more armour, something to cocoon her from the furtive looks of other guests, the murmured pity, the sadness of what might have been, or at least, the haughty disregard of Lady Bellinger.

As Caro bleeped the car she thought maybe she could host a dinner the evening before. Recruit some of the key players

5

as reinforcements. She could invite them to stay the night; her house, after all, was the closest to the Bellingers, and that way they could turn up en masse. She checked her diary. Saturday 14th July; her husband Brian and their eldest daughter Bethany would be out at the Barnes Rugby Club dinner. Perfect.

She got into the Lexus, settling herself in the cream leather interior, pleased that a plan was coming together. It suddenly didn't seem so bad. A glorious dinner with old acquaintances reliving their youth. It made her think of humid afternoons spent punting on the river. Honed, toned athletic bodies. Sweet, sticky cocktails and sweat-soaked dancing at college bops. Adoration. Eager, carefree faces filled with hope and idealism. Nights when she didn't wake up staring blankly at the ceiling. All that promise.

Scrolling through her phone she found George Kingsley's number. Last Caro heard of George he'd just moved to Henley-on-Thames, his wife Audrey was expecting a baby and he was working at a middling asset management company in the City. He used phrases like, '*Going great guns!*' He was everything she would have expected him to be. George was the type who kept in touch with everyone.

Caro rewrote the WhatsApp five times before she hit the right level of casual. **George, long time no see. Thinking about a dinner before the memorial – a chance for you to prep me. I've never been to one of these things before! Let me know, am in Barnes so you can stay if you want. Caro x**

She felt better already. She checked her watch; she wouldn't make it to Body Pump but she could still get to the coffee afterwards. Perhaps she'd suggest a glass of wine. Caro tried not to drink during the week. But as one of the mums at the school gate had quipped earlier that morning, Thursday is nearly the weekend.

The Lexus purred along the road. The message from George came back within minutes. The robot voice of the car speaker read it out for her.

Caro! Heard you were back from Switzerland. Dinner sounds great. These things always sad but good – gets very messy afterwards. Travis meant to be staying with me night before so can bring him? TBH would be good to have drink and catch up and not have to worry about baby waking up. G x

Caro pulled into the Virgin Active parking lot considering her guest list. Travis Lawrence-Dixon wouldn't be Caro's first choice, but that was fine, she could squeeze him in.

She opened the car door. The sun was shining. She put her sunglasses on, grabbed her purse from her gym bag and noticed that in her haste she'd brought the invitation along with her. Suddenly it seemed like Henry Bellinger was in the car. His upturned smiling eyes watching from the soft leather seat.

Caro felt her throat tighten. Her skin prickled. She didn't want to be forced back into the past. She had a new life now. One she had pushed and pummelled herself into. Her prickling skin grew hot and itchy; she wanted to yank off her gold chain, her tight Lycra vest. She couldn't bear the reminder of what could have been. Red and sweating, she was on the verge of hyperventilating when a car horn beeped.

Fellow gym buddy Fliss Weschler waved as she reversed her Audi, snapping Caro out of her panic.

She raised a shaky hand. Her thumping heart slowed. She felt the wave of terror retreat. She definitely needed a glass of wine now. Luckily Fliss liked a drink; she'd be up for a chilled Chablis.

Caro reached forward and picked up the invite, stupidly tentative. She turned it over in her hand and read it again. It was just a piece of paper. It couldn't hurt her. Sticks and stones and all that.

As she tucked it into the side pocket of her bag, she noted the Bellinger name embossed at the top and, as she hopped out to greet Fliss, made a mental note that she and Brian should get their own stationery printed.

CHAPTER TWO

LILY

When Lily Enfield got the invite to Henry Bellinger's memorial statue unveiling she immediately booked an emergency appointment with her therapist.

'I don't want to go,' Lily said, straight out. 'The only reason I've been invited is because of my book.' Lily had recently hit the *Sunday Times*' bestseller list with a thriller about a ballsy female fossil hunter forced to play detective when her partner is murdered in inhospitable Antarctic terrain. She often felt herself a disappointment at literary events or, more recently, token parties because any similarity between her and the main character stopped with Lily studying Antarctic fossils for her PhD. 'And then there's this dinner at Caro's,' she added, feeling her panic rise. 'It's too much.'

The therapist looked from the invitation to Lily. Letting the silence settle.

Lily stayed as still as she could under the scrutiny. It was hard to avoid eye contact as there was nothing else to look at in the consulting room. Of course that was probably the point. She often focused on the box of Kleenex on the side table.

Thought about all the clients who plucked a handful of tissues to wipe their eyes while the therapist waited patiently. The idea of crying in there was once so unfathomable Lily could just as easily have stood up and taken all her clothes off. On the floor of the room was a geometric rug. Lily had stared at the pattern so much it repeated in her dreams.

'Remind me which one is Caro?' The therapist took off her glasses. Frameless. Lily had tried a similar pair on in Vision Express but felt far too exposed.

'The princess,' said Lily, then clarified, 'not a real princess. She's the one I met up with in Zurich.' Lily had flown over for a literary festival. Caro had taken her to an ubertrendy rooftop restaurant that was just known by three dots on its sign because, she'd said, who could resist a place that was too cool to have a proper name? Lily Enfield, that was who. Lily was terrified of heights and had to shut her eyes as they were led to the table. Caro had chuckled, sweeping her glorious red mane over her shoulder as she'd turned to say, 'You haven't changed a bit.' Which Lily knew instinctively wasn't a compliment.

The therapist looked back over her notes. 'Ah yes, the literary festival. Where the panic attacks started, in fact.'

Lily watched the spectacles, held loosely in the therapist's thin fingers, bobbing as she spoke. She wondered if she'd actually had to look back over the notes or if it was just a tactic.

'At the time we explored if maybe something to do with the trip was the trigger?'

'Except we decided it was just coincidence,' Lily replied, shifting uncomfortably in her seat. Her trousers were digging in at the waist. Her grey V-neck jumper was too warm.

'You decided,' the therapist corrected. 'I don't decide, Lily. I suggest avenues for you to explore.'

Lily tried her hardest to sit completely still, avoid the all seeing eyes, but that in itself probably told her something.

'And she's hosting a dinner the evening before you go to the memorial?' the therapist checked.

'Yes,' said Lily. 'She must need more girls at the table. Caro's not the kind of person who has close girlfriends. I said girls just then because it feels too formal to say women. I don't want *you* thinking *I* think I'm still a young girl.' Lily sometimes felt she was handing over her neuroses on a plate.

'I thought she only invited you because of the book?'

'No, that was why I've been invited to the memorial. The dinner is different.' Lily's neck started to blotch; she was hot and stressed. 'Or it might be the same. I don't know.'

The therapist neatened her papers. 'I think we're moving away from the point. What do *you* want to do, Lily?'

'I don't know.' But Lily did know. She wanted it all brushed under the carpet and forgotten about. She wanted to live in the quiet anonymity she always had. When she'd seen Caro's WhatsApp about the dinner she'd thought she was having a heart attack and curled into a ball on the floor waiting for either death or her ears to stop ringing.

In her kindest voice the therapist said, 'Why do you think *I* might think you should go, Lily?'

They'd been through something similar the other week. Lily almost put her hand up. 'Because, you think I need to reclaim my story.'

'To go back to where it started.' The therapist sat back and replaced her glasses. 'Take an interest in it, Lily. Explore how it makes you feel. See how *they* make you feel.'

Lily couldn't bear it. The very idea of sitting round the table with them all.

The therapist was staring at her, waiting for the agreement that Lily didn't want to give. The silence ticked on. Sometimes, to distract herself when it got too intense, Lily imagined the therapist suddenly jumping up and doing something crazy. A rendition of 'Gangnam Style' or morphing into a cartoonish villain. Raising her hands to the sky amid burning flames and cackling, 'Lily, this is your chance! Stir things up, find the truth. Let it combust into hellfire!'

In these moments, Lily had to be careful not to let a flicker of amusement show on her face. Instead she just stared blankly back as her therapist actually said things like, 'You're much stronger than you think, Lily.'

And Lily replied, 'I'm not sure I am.'

CHAPTER THREE

ELLE

The embossed invite was waiting for Elle Andrews when she got home from work. She opened it, curled a red lip in distaste and chucked it straight in the bin.

Today she was clearing out her late-sister Sarah's flat. Her head deep under the kitchen sink where it smelt of mould and mouse droppings, Elle found another bottle of Lidl's Rachmaninoff triple distilled vodka. This one half drunk, hidden and forgotten about. She got it out, poured herself a cupful and started to tip the rest of it down the sink.

'What the hell are you doing?' Her brother, who was outside on the phone, leant in through the window and snatched the quarter-full bottle. 'That's good stuff!'

Elle didn't say anything, just leant against the chipped laminate worktop and took a swig from her cup. Wills and Kate were on the side; it was a commemorative wedding cup ordered from some shitty catalogue.

She looked round the room. There was so much to clear out. The yellowing net curtains were so depressing she reached forward and ripped them down. Outside, her brother made a face.

'What d'you do that for?'

Then he got distracted by a neighbour. 'Afternoon, Phyllis. Yep, yep, we're clearing out her place. Very sad. Yeah. Very sudden. No, you're right, she wasn't happy. Okay then. Mind how you go.'

Elle rolled her eyes. He could chat to anyone but did nothing to help. She went to poke her head into the living room to see how her mum was getting on.

'You haven't done anything?' Elle couldn't believe it; the room was exactly as she'd left it. Piles of papers on every table. Cups, glasses. Detritus of life. 'Mum, we need to get this sorted.'

But her mum wasn't listening. She'd found an old photo album, was staring at pictures of them as kids. Her face was all wet with tears when she looked up at Elle. 'Oh, it's awful. I just can't . . . Your child's not meant to die before you.'

Elle sat down on the sofa next her, put her arm around her shoulders, squeezed her tight. 'I know.' Elle had actually fantasized about the day she wouldn't have to rush round here and sit in the dark, holding her sister while she wept. No more hours on the phone to the doctor. No more waiting for ambulances. No more cleaning, cooking, checking. But no matter how bad it was, how ill someone was, however much she thought she'd already grieved for her, her sister not being there was still a shock. She looked between her brother, who was now glued to his phone in the corridor, to her lank-haired mother staring obsessively at the old photos. It was all down to Elle now. The pair of them were useless. But perhaps she should give in to it. Did it matter if the place got cleared out or not? None of it belonged to the sister she knew, it was all just a depressing reminder of the person Sarah had become.

Elle sat back, rested her head on the threadbare sofa, lit a cigarette and got her phone out. She opened the email she'd received from Lily Enfield.

Hi Elle, just wanted to check if you're going to the dinner at Caro's before the memorial. If you are, I was hoping we might be able to go together. Look forward to catching up. Hope you're well, Lily x

Elle scrolled through Instagram, her mother quietly weeping next to her. She stayed behind the scenes on social media. She watched – a detached, yet addicted, observer. She had an account under a false name, belinda.bakes.cakes, with a photo of a smiling woman holding up a batch of cupcakes. Everyone accepted her follow request, she was very non-threatening.

She clicked on George Kingsley's page. He didn't post a lot, but what he did was all selfies and humblebrags. Him on a yacht in the Med, damp hair slicked back, mirrored Ray-Bans reflecting the iPhone, 'Lucky enough to take this little beauty out. Hope I can remember how to sail!' or straddling a bike at the top of a hill, sweating in expensive cycling garb, 'Phew, made it! Not quite as fit as I used to be!' Occasionally George's brown-haired, heart-shape-faced wife, Audrey, made an appearance, usually referred to as 'wifey'. Audrey Kingsley's was an Instagram account Elle would like to get a look at, but as yet her follow request had gone unanswered.

George's latest post showed him and Audrey with their tiny newborn baby, glimpses of the living room behind showing stylishly neutral furnishings. The baby was swaddled in pale blue, its miniature hand wrapped tightly around George's thumb, giant in comparison. The caption read, 'Such love for this little fella. Greatest achievement!'

Elle didn't like to put a name to the emotion she'd felt when she'd first seen the photo. She wanted to think it was all disdain but there had definitely been an annoying flicker of envy. Looking at it again today, in light of the memorial invitation – an event which George Kingsley would no doubt be a key part of – she found the disdain morphing into anger. Sitting among the sad remains of her sister's life didn't help. The juxtaposition of George and his classy off-white lounge with her sister's yellow nicotine-stained wallpaper made her blood boil.

Beside Elle on the sofa, her mum's phone rang and she answered it, saying under her breath, 'Yes I know, yes, I'll be home soon. I'm just dealing with Sarah's things. Yes, yes, I promise.' When she hung up she looked at Elle and said sheepishly, 'Darrell just checking where I am.'

Elle hated Darrell, a controlling conspiracy theorist who believed the world was both flat and against him, cut from the same cloth as most of her mum's exes. Elle considered how poles apart posh, public schoolboy George Kingsley was from dreadful Darrell, yet both had played their hand in making Elle swear off relationships.

Her mum turned another page of the album, sniffing and dabbing her eyes with her sleeve while next to her, her phone pinged with a stream of Darrell texts. Elle couldn't bear it.

The claustrophobia of being with her mum, surrounded by her sister's stuff. The reek of regret and frustration.

Elle got up and went back to the kitchen. Stuck her head back under the sink to see what else was hiding back there. But her heart wasn't in it any longer. She didn't care if they just closed the door and walked away. She sat down on the floor and reread Lily's email about Caro's pre-memorial dinner. Then she flicked onto Caroline 'Caro' Carmichael's Instagram. Her little squares were all highly curated suburban chic. Photos of her on the school run in tasteful navy yoga pants, long red hair loose and glossy like an advert. A corner of her house with a new brass cocktail trolley arranged with vintage glasses against teal Farrow & Ball. Or a nauseating photo of #brunch with lots of little hands reaching for blueberry pancakes in a café with hipster lighting and bad art.

Out of interest, she searched Travis's name and laughed out loud. Pumped and inked, all the photos were of him doing a million different yoga poses with various sunsets in the background and a bio that read: 'Travis Lawrence-Dixon | Strength in wisdom | Book me to speak or teach'.

Elle cradled the cup of vodka. She thought of the statue being erected for Henry Bellinger. Of George and Caro trotting along to the ceremony for canapés and champagne. George taking the mic for a fawning, heart-wrenching speech. All of them at Caro's dinner to which Elle was deemed unworthy of an invite.

Why should people like them get to live how they wanted? All shiny and unencumbered. Elle tried to imagine a world where it was her sister being immortalized in marble or sipping lattes dressed in lululemon, not having drunk herself to death. It drove her mad, the injustice of the world.

She thought how pleasing it would be to put a bomb under their nice tidy lives. But then as one of her stepdads, Neal who lived in Deal, used to say, it's wise to leave the past where it belongs. Elle downed the rest of her vodka. But where would the fun be in that?

CHAPTER FOUR

GEORGE

George Kingsley put his bags down in the hallway. 'Hey.' He was fresh from a week's pre-season rowing training in Lucerne. Tanned the colour of chestnuts from the late-summer Swiss sun reflected off the water. He pulled his shades off, looked around the dilapidated house. 'Not ideal, is it?'

The girl in front of him was mousy, wore heavy tortoiseshell glasses, looked like she came pre-packed with a book in her hand. She wasn't his type by any stretch of the word but when she introduced herself as Lily Enfield, it occurred to him that she could be useful for this year's list. The list was issued every year by the boat club captain; last year the challenge was to shag a girl from every nationality – almost impossible. This year the aim was to work through the alphabet. George was on the fence when it came to the list's moral reprehensibility and had rarely chosen a girl for the sake of it but he did find it pleasing to strike his conquests off against it nonetheless.

Term had only just started and he'd already ticked off J – a nice girl called Jessica from the women's rowing team – and V was looking promising, after he'd flirted his way out of a disagreement regarding his privilege with a girl called Vickie in the Junior Common Room earlier.

'So has everyone already picked a room?' George asked, taking in the sparse furnishings and hastily painted walls. As a fresher he'd had a very nice room with an en suite, almost a home from home. This place, in contrast, was shabby to say the least: swathes of blue paint had peeled off the outside of the old Georgian building, the window frames were rotten and the front room looked suspiciously like it might have been a shop when last inhabited. He peered down the end of the corridor and saw a miniscule kitchen with unappealing brown cupboards. Luckily he'd eat most of his meals in the college dining hall.

The mousy girl, Lily, shook her head. 'Only me and Travis.' Her glasses slipped down her nose. Her cheeks pinked with embarrassment every time she opened her mouth. George could not believe he was sharing a house with this girl. He picked up a bunch of his stuff and followed her up the creaking stairs. As the boat club boys would say, nice arse, shame about the face.

The corridor smelt of paint and damp. The carpet was splattered with white gloss, slapdash brushstrokes covered the edges of the emergency exit sign. George passed an open door on the landing. 'Hey man,' he said to a guy lounging on a double mattress blowing smoke rings into the ether.

The guy sat up, hair all on end, eyes bleary. He seemed to take in George's outfit – his international rowing kit, his massive Nike bag, his dinner jacket in a clothes bag over his shoulder. 'You look way too energetic for me,' said the guy and lay back down again. His room looked to be devoid of possessions except a laptop, speaker and a box set of Harry Potter books on the shelf.

'That's Travis,' said Lily, hovering on the landing. 'His room has a really lovely view.'

George peered across through the six-paned window. Travis didn't strike him as the type to appreciate the picturesque courtyard over the road with its metal finials, the large horse chestnut tree or the ornate Victorian streetlamp visible through the mottled glass. George had met Travis before. He'd helped him out last year when George had bought some steroids off one of the rugby players who'd sworn they were undetectable. But then the guy was kicked out after a mandatory drug test and George had never felt terror like it. He'd sat up all night playing out his dad's reaction were he to face the same consequences. In the end, having worked himself up into a 3 a.m. terror, George asked one of the stoner guys on his course if they knew anyone who might be able to help him. They'd directed him to Travis who charged him fifty quid for some hydrochlorothiazide, a prescription diuretic to mask the drugs in his system. George took it then passed out from dehydration and dizziness the next day at training. And was never drug-tested anyway.

Now, somehow, he was living with this waster.

But did he care? Not really. George was at Oxford for one reason only. A seat in the Oxford and Cambridge Boat Race. That was his destiny. The Kingsleys *were* Oxford. He'd grown up listening to his father's and grandfather's stories of Boat Race glory. Victorious against Cambridge, they had both been granted the honour of becoming Oxford Blues. Their framed certificates hung one above the other in the hallway of the family house in Devizes. A space for George's was ready underneath. In his first year the competition had been stellar and George hadn't made the cut. In a way it was a blessing; meant he could learn the ropes while having a little bit more fun on nights out, enjoy being a fresher without quite so much pressure – getting used to the workload was hard enough. This year, though, it was different, no more niceties. Most of the old guard had graduated and there was everything to play for, this was George's year. He was going to get a place in the Blue Boat if it killed him.

The front door slammed, making the windows rattle. A redhead marched up the stairs in jeans and a cropped top and a cloud of sweet perfume. 'This just isn't right. I don't understand how this is happening. How can they just throw us together? We've paid money for this! My room is meant to have an en suite. What's this place got, like one bathroom? They're ruining our experience.'

She was very pretty. Long flaming hair. Perfect hourglass figure. Pale limbs. Blow-job lips. Oozed confidence from every pore of her being.

The quiet one, Lily, said more dryly than George would have expected from her, 'I think it was the subsidence that caused half the student accommodation to collapse that ruined our experience.'

On the bed, Travis smirked as he lit another cigarette off the previous one. George wondered when the best time was to tell him the accommodation was non-smoking.

The redhead didn't seem to have heard Lily's comment. She

pouted, hands on the exposed skin of her narrow waist. She was directing her attention at George which made his chest puff on instinct. 'What is this place? It's a dump – hardly habitable, they've just splashed paint on the walls of some random old building. Why is it us? Why does everyone else get to be together in the main building?'

George chucked his kit bag and suit into the first available room. 'I don't think they do. I think it's all a mess. From what I heard, the college had to scrabble together as many extra rooms as they could find. Some people are miles out so we should count ourselves lucky.'

The redhead did not look like counting herself lucky would ever be a viable option.

George changed tack. 'They're saying it's temporary. Once they've assessed the structural damage we'll be out of here and back in the main building.'

'Dude, have you seen the damage?' came Travis's mocking voice.

George stiffened. 'No. Not exactly.'

Travis rolled over on the bed, hollow-cheeked, grinning. 'You'd better start unpacking your chinos. We aren't going anywhere.'

Out the corner of his eye, George saw the mousy girl giggle.

The redhead seethed. 'I'm going to speak to the dean. It's so unfair. I can't live with you people.'

The sound of a low whistle made them pause. Then an amused drawl, 'Bloody hell, what a shithole.' The deep, delighted laugh that followed seemed instantly to elevate the stature of the house.

George moved to look down the stairs, drawn to the

effortless confidence of the voice. He almost gasped when he saw it was none other than Henry Bellinger kicking the front door shut and navigating his way past the redhead's stack of matching luggage that was blocking the hall. Slinging his giant duffel bag over his shoulder to climb the stairs, Henry's eyes crinkled with delight as he surveyed the cracks in the ceiling and the woodchip wallpaper.

'Love this place!' He chucked his bag to the floor when he got to the landing, his affable delight making them feel like hipster pioneers in a burnt-out London suburb, not second-year students lamenting the lack of private power shower.

George knew Henry from the rowing circuit. They'd raced against each other since their school days but George barely registered on Henry's radar. The closest George had got to them being friends was last year at the freshers' rowing initiation when Henry was forced to lick up his own sick after downing various lethal and disgusting concoctions from a selection of old wellington boots; George had given him a pat on the back for good luck.

Now George found himself mutely starstruck. A dizzying future whizzed before his eyes where he was suddenly part of Henry's inner circle.

Next to him, the redhead's demeanour changed in an instant. With a flick of her long locks she stepped forward, back arched so the fabric of her strappy top pulled invitingly. Hand outstretched, she said, 'Isn't it *so* fun? All of us slumming it together! I'm Caro.'

Henry's eyes narrowed appreciatively. 'Are you new? I'm sure you should have been on my radar before now.'

Caro giggled coyly. 'No, I'm not new. Maybe you just haven't been looking in the right places.'

From his bedroom Travis snorted.

Henry went over to take a look at who it was. 'Trav! Mate. Didn't know you were here.'

Seemingly Travis's tentacles spread in every direction. The sight of Henry was enough to make him haul himself off the bed, yank up his grey tracksuit bottoms and saunter over for a greeting.

Lily, the glasses girl, stayed firmly in the shadows. She'd raised her hand in a wave as Henry had moved towards Travis's door but it had gone unnoticed by all but George. She was ignored again when Henry went to look up the next set of rickety stairs and said, 'All right if I take a room on the top floor? I like being able to see out.'

'Absolutely!' said Caro. 'Next to mine.' She sashayed up the stairs to claim the other bedroom, adding with a wink, 'We can admire the dreaming spires together.'

Without taking his eyes off Caro's arse, Henry bent to pick up his exorbitantly expensive, discreetly labelled duffel. He clapped George on the shoulder – as if they'd been friends forever – and whispered, 'Race is on to bag the C.'

George felt a rush of delight. He would forgo the entire alphabet of the year's list if it meant being elevated to the ranks of Henry Bellinger's dizzying cool.

CHAPTER FIVE

NOW
CARO

Pre-dinner drinks: Belvedere vodka Martinis

*Hors d'oeuvres: Smoked salmon blinis with
Icelandic black caviar*

Caro put down the phone and considered calling the whole
thing off. JB Watson and his wife had just cancelled leaving
her two people down at the dinner.

Caro's husband Brian, who was in the process of tying his
rugby club tie, said, 'It's not that bad, is it?'

It was that bad. Not only was it humiliating, but it threw
the whole balance off. 'JB was crucial,' Caro moaned, thinking
of the popular rower. JB Watson, an uncomplicated good
egg who, alongside George, would give the party its reason
for being. They were meant to reminisce about Henry and
the good old days and be bonded enough to flank Caro like
bodyguards at tomorrow's memorial.

Brian said, 'I can stay if you want.'

'No,' Caro replied, perhaps a touch too sharply.

Brian looked wounded.

Caro went over and smoothed his tie down. 'Sorry, I didn't mean it.' Really she wanted him out the house so she could get to work salvaging what was left of her dinner party. Lily, Travis and George. What a motley selection.

'I know you didn't.' Brian gave her a little pat on the bottom as he went to get his suit jacket off the chair. She tried to ignore it. Especially when he came back and gave her bum an extra rub, saying of the velvet she was wearing, 'This is lovely.' Then, with his accountant's eye, 'Is it new?'

'Yes.'

'Did you use the Amex?'

They went through this every time. Yes, of course she used the bloody Amex. Yes, of course it was new. But by pointing it out he could brand it with his cautious disapproval. Could never let her just enjoy spending what she felt was her hard-earned money, even though he believed it was his.

Her daughter Bethany bounded in wearing a silver slip dress that made her look twenty-five rather than a gauche teenager. 'Ready, Dad?' she said.

Caro swallowed, readying herself for battle. 'I told you that dress wasn't appropriate.'

Bethany pierced her with a glare of contempt as she held up a baggy grey cardigan. 'And I told you I've got this, *Mother*.'

Caro was still navigating the first forays into teenagehood. She had adored the soft, fresh-baked bread smell of newborns and the wide-eyed neediness of the primary-school days. This stage was more of a challenge; she could recognize too much of herself in Bethany.

Brian stepped between them. 'Come on, let's not get heated. I think she looks very lovely.'

Caro rolled her eyes. Oh Brian, she thought with pity, what do you know about teenage girls?

Caro's phone buzzed with a message and Bethany took the opportunity to drag her dad out the house before Caro could further object.

'Bye, darling,' Brian called.

Caro waved absently, distracted by the WhatsApp which was from Travis Lawrence-Dixon.

Did I mention I'm vegan non-dairy? Will bring own cheese.

Caro grimaced. She'd never wanted Travis there in the first place; now she had to knock him up his own vegan menu.

In the kitchen, she ran through the positives as she drained some chickpeas. Luckily it wasn't raining, they could have drinks on the terrace. She could show off the lawn. The three youngest children had all been packed off to Brian's mother's house. Edward, her second eldest, was at a sleepover with friends. They were all out of the house which was good and she'd made up the beds for Travis and George to stay.

An hour later, the doorbell chimed. Act natural, Caro told herself as she walked from the kitchen, plucking a wedding photo from the hall console table and tucking it into the drawer; she didn't want the details of her life on show. These were just old friends. It was fun, a boost to the ego. She'd be effortlessly in command. Think of all those drinks and parties she'd hosted while they lived in Switzerland. You didn't have to like someone to be friends with them as an expat, you just took what you could get.

Brian had said, when they returned to the UK, that looking

back on their lives in Zurich, it all had an air of unreality. Fun but fake, like McDonald's or candyfloss – nice at the time but just hot sugar and air. She had thought that was quite perceptive for Brian. Although actually, Switzerland had suited Caro perfectly; no one got too close or asked too many questions.

She paused in front of the big mirror in the hall, looked at her reflection. Flawless make-up, exquisite emerald earrings and bracelet set that she'd picked out for her anniversary present, freshly washed gleaming hair. All good. But did her eyes look wary or was that just her imagination? She blinked a couple of times. Better. Would they be impressed with the house? Of course they would. Come on, Caro. She put her shoulders back. She was on edge. Nervous about tonight and the statue unveiling tomorrow. At times she woke up gasping for air. But no, she wasn't going to think about that now. One thing at a time. This was her night. Brian was out. These were her friends.

She stared hard at herself in the mirror. 'You are Caroline Carmichael and no one can break you.'

Caroline flung open the door.

George Kingsley was standing on the step adjusting his shirt, checking his cuffs were straight, taking in all the details of the front of the house. 'Great pad, Caro, gorgeous.' He nodded appreciatively at the stained glass and the black-and-white tiled path that Caro had insisted they have laid. 'Am I late?' He checked his watch. 'Bit of trouble with the trains.' In one hand he had his wheelie suitcase with flowers tucked into the handle, in the other was wine and a paper bag filled with the cheese he'd offered to contribute. 'Brie so ripe in there it cleared out the carriage. Nice to see you, Caro, looking as ravishing as I'd expect.' He put his hand on her shoulder, firm and confident. You could always count on George. Schooled from birth for compliments and easy chitchat.

'Hello darling George.' Caro leant in for the kiss. He smelt of something expensive, musk and sandalwood. Intoxicatingly refreshing when compared to Brian who couldn't wear any scent because it aggravated his eczema. However, he did look exhausted. He was still a good-looking guy but he certainly wasn't in peak shape. The crisp Paul Smith shirt couldn't hide the small paunch. His hair was definitely thinning. And the line between his eyebrows was etched in place. 'How are things? How's the baby?'

'Spawn of the devil.' George laughed. 'Just kidding. He isn't too fond of sleep.'

Caro ushered him in. 'Oh it's horrid when babies don't sleep. I was lucky, mine were always great sleepers. Straight through from almost week one.' It was a lie – both Bethany and Alice, her youngest, had been terrible sleepers – but the nerves were making her overcompensate.

George blew out a breath. 'I hate you.'

Caro laughed.

They both turned to the sound of an Uber pulling up at the gate. The car door opened and out stepped a guy almost unrecognisable from the Travis Lawrence-Dixon they knew. Hair shorn, skin the colour of a raisin, black T-shirt, khaki combat trousers. Tattoo up the front of his neck.

'Wow, Travis, look at you!' Caro was taken aback as he walked up the path.

'Nice house,' he said with a wry smile. After a quick peck

on her cheek he added, 'Wouldn't expect anything less from you, Caro.'

She narrowed her eyes, unsure whether it was a compliment or a sly dig. But she didn't have a chance to reply because George was already slapping him on the back. 'Namaste, Trav, namaste.'

Travis stood back to get a good look at George. 'You look old, mate.'

'Fuck off.'

Travis laughed. 'Who else is coming?'

'Martinis on the lawn?' said Caro, deflecting the question. Ignore and move on was a tactic she had perfected over the years for keeping control of a situation.

Travis said, 'I'd prefer a beer.'

They followed Caro through to the kitchen.

George pointed to the pale green hallway wall and said, 'Mizzle if I'm not mistaken?'

'Spot on!' Caro paused to stroke the fresh paintwork. It was actually called Whirlybird but, as her mother once instructed, men like to feel they know things.

'My life is consumed with paint charts,' George said as they entered the kitchen.

'That's suburbia, mate.' Travis's derision appeared to suck the air out of George. He countered by peering forward and saying, 'What is that hideous thing on your neck?', pointing to the giant tattoo of various twists and lines that snaked from Travis's collar to his jaw.

'It's the Unalome,' Travis replied unfazed, taking a beer from Caro. 'The symbol of the journey to enlightenment. I had it done in India.'

'Then came home and realized you'd made a massive mistake,' George mocked.

'There's nothing wrong with a daily reminder of the twists and turns of life, George.'

'I have enough reminders of the twists and turns of life, thanks.'

Travis shrugged.

Caro mixed the Martinis. 'Go explore!' She waved them towards the bifolds she'd left purposely open.

George stepped outside and gave a low whistle. 'That's a good-looking lawn.' He leant against the veranda railing. 'I mean it's perfect. That must take some doing.' He called back to Caro, 'Have you got Brian out there with his protractor?'

Travis necked a swig of cold Bud. 'Brian?'

Caro was standing by the kitchen island pouring the drinks. She felt her hand tighten on the cocktail shaker.

'You remember Brian Carmichael, Trav,' said George. 'Year above us. Big guy. He was social secretary of the Oxford University Conservatives?'

Travis looked nonplussed.

'Always had a megaphone. Wore a big rosette.'

Travis just managed to save himself from spluttering beer all over the lime-washed decking. '*You* married the megaphone guy?'

Somehow it caught Caro off guard. How the hell? She had prepared for this moment. Had presumed Travis might not know. In her imagination she'd waved the question away with a cool, proud remark about how successful Brian was, how lucky she was to have found him. Not stood there brittle and defensive with her body flaming from head to toe in shame.

In her planning, she hadn't factored in the history. The past knowledge. The imperceptible quirks of the lip and brow that said a thousand words between Travis and George.

Travis covered his shock with a polite, 'He was really nice. Very friendly . . .' but Caro knew what they were all thinking. She knew how their brains worked deep down. Their relationships had been forged before the self-deluding masks of adulthood. She didn't want their sniggers or their sympathy. She wanted their admiration: for the house, for the life she had made. But most of all she wanted not to care.

She went to the fridge to bring out the canapés, purposefully to avoid their smirks. Let them get it out of their system without her seeing.

When she heard George come back into the kitchen to get his Martini she figured it was safe to turn back, sliding the platter of smoked salmon blinis onto the counter. She started to spoon little lumps of caviar onto each one while Travis gave George the low-down on his recent silent meditation retreat.

'Sounds a bit woo-woo for me,' said George.

Caro suddenly remembered Travis was vegan. 'Oh Travis, you can't eat these can you? Damn it.' She hated that he hadn't warned her earlier. It made her flustered. Especially when Travis replied dryly, 'I can assure you I've been in worse situations.' Always able to undercut her with an aside. Little did he realize she'd spent the hour before they arrived desperately trying to concoct a vegan tagine.

She watched him leaning casually against the kitchen table. There was something about his laissez-faire attitude that felt like a fraud. Perhaps it was the fact he was all sinewy muscle – you didn't get that strength from mindfulness and

33

meditation. She'd seen what the guys lifted in the gym to look like that.

Caro smoothed down the top of her velvet jumpsuit. 'Well maybe I could rustle you up some crudités.'

'Honestly, don't bother on my account. But that reminds me . . .' He went into the hallway and retrieved a pack of two *Free From* salted caramel pots from his rucksack. 'Brought my pudding.'

Caro inspected the packaging. 'I read somewhere the other day that veganism is so popular right now because it's the only way people can take back control. We're so inundated nowadays with everything that's happening with the world and social media. It's less about saving the animals and more about not going mad.'

Travis shrugged, non-committal. 'Or maybe that's just what meat-eaters say to alleviate the guilt.'

George popped a blini in his mouth. 'I don't have any guilt. Steak for me, the rarer the better.'

Caro was satisfied that she'd seen the muscles in Travis's neck tense. Her little dig had hit its target. He would hate to be thought of as controlling. Insouciance was his raison d'être. He couldn't fool her, though.

The doorbell rang.

'Oh, that'll be Lily.'

'Lily's coming?' For the first time, Travis looked ruffled.

Caro felt a naughty kick of pleasure at his surprise. Perhaps she might enjoy the evening after all – watching Travis sweat.

'Yeah, of course.' She almost jogged to open the door.

Lily Enfield was waiting, hands behind her back, brown hair tied neatly in a low ponytail, minimal make-up. She was dressed in a grey blazer and the same floral shirt and navy trouser combo that she'd worn for their dinner in Zurich and had on in her author photo. Workwear.

'Lily, darling, come in.' Caro was overdoing it, as much to rile Travis as to try to shake some life into Lily, who was as ramrod straight as she had been when they last met.

'Caro, I have a confession. I know I said I would make a dessert, but I didn't have time so I bought this on the way.' Lily sheepishly handed Caro a Taste the Difference box along with a bottle of wine.

Caro didn't even flinch. 'That's fine, honey, no problem! As long as it's sweet, it's fine with me. Sicilian lemon tart. Mm, sounds delicious.' Sainsbury's? She could have at least gone to Waitrose. Or more importantly, why hadn't she just texted and Caro would have rustled up her Nigella pavlova? That was the problem of relinquishing control, but Lily had insisted she help in some way.

'Lily!' George walked briskly into the hall. 'God, you look exactly the same.' He put a hand on her shoulder, kissed her on both cheeks while adding, 'Aren't you the dark horse? Bestselling author. Brilliant. Don't know how anyone writes a book.'

Caro said, 'Lily, don't let me forget. I've got a stack of books for you to sign for my book club,' while ushering them through to the kitchen.

'So what happens when you hit the bestseller list?' George asked, 'Do you get a badge or something? Like Blue Peter.'

Lily shook her head. It made Caro smile that while Lily's appearance was all neat, plain and impersonal – the shirt, the loafers, the small stud earrings – however hard she tried, she couldn't stop her cheeks pinking at any form of attention.

'No badge,' she said. 'Just lots of talks, interviews, that kind of thing. And then on to the next one.'

George nodded, only half listening as he topped up his Martini. 'Fascinating.'

Caro stood in the doorway, watching with a flicker of glee as Travis and Lily came face to face.

But Travis put down his beer and smiling, said without any awkwardness or hesitation, 'Hey, Lily, how are you?'

And Lily replied, 'Good thanks. You?' Her cheeks were already flushed from George's questioning.

'Good. I'm good.'

And that was it. How disappointing. But who knew what was going on underneath? The pair of them always baffled Caro. Their quirky little in-jokes and ways of silently communicating.

George had stationed himself next to the kitchen island and was steadily devouring the blinis. 'I have a friend who deals in caviar. What type is this?' he asked.

Caro bit her lip. 'It's actually Lidl,' she said with faux-embarrassment.

'Gotta love Lidl,' George grinned, popping another one into his mouth.

Lily said, 'I bought a tennis skirt there the other day.'

'I didn't know you played tennis, Lily,' George replied.

'I don't, but it was only two pounds.'

Travis laughed.

Lily looked coyly down at her drink.

Caro watched with burgeoning pleasure. One of her friends at the gym had said there was nothing that united a dinner party like a Lidl bargain. 'George, could you top everyone up, please? Feel free to move onto champagne. Also from Lidl,' she added.

They laughed collectively.

Caro could finally relax, it was all going to be okay.

CHAPTER SIX

THEN
Trinity term, second year
LILY

Standing by the bar, struggling to bite through an oversized roast beef and Yorkshire pudding canapé, Lily overheard someone say, 'The big question is who Caro will choose out of George Kingsley and Henry Bellinger.' One part of Lily thought the conversations at Oxford would be much more highbrow than this, the other part looked over at Caro in her sparkling dress and wondered the same thing. The flirting in their house had reached a painful peak recently and Lily wasn't sure how much more she could bear.

George's dad had thrown a party at the Kingsley's Knightsbridge flat in honour of his son's participation in the Boat Race. For the second year running, George didn't make the main race. He and Henry were in the reserves crew, Isis, and had schlepped about the house in dark fury at their failure. Lily watched them race; it was very boring. It had been a close race against Goldie, the Cambridge reserves, but they went past where she was standing in seconds and she couldn't really see anything anyway because the people in front were too tall. Sport was not really her thing. At school they could choose Latin grammar or PE. Lily's conjugations were sublime. The party wasn't her thing either. Too intimidatingly flash. The fact they called it the Knightsbridge flat baffled her for one thing, presumably because they had so many addresses it was hard to keep track. Lily's family had one address, Tresores Hill Farm. She thought she'd be used to it by now; since her first day at Oxford there had been talk of bops and JCRs, tabs, sconces, tutes and pigeon post. Their own language to set them apart. Give them their elite standing. But it took more than words to fit in. The self-assurance that came with money and breeding, a school people recognized, an innate understanding of society conventions . . . none of that could be written down and revised under the heading 'Oxford jargon'. Sometimes she just strung random words together to see if anyone corrected her. So far no one had, and while it amused her it hadn't helped on the making friends front.

A string quartet started up in the lounge. She'd heard the party referred to as 'something very casual' and 'a small soirée to celebrate the boys' but there must have been close to two hundred people. Waiters served champagne. Exquisite canapés of quails' eggs and king prawns. It wasn't black tie but everyone was dressed the same. They knew the rules. George and Henry were sweating into the wool of their Half Blue blazers, the white stripe on the top pocket letting everyone know they'd only made it to the reserves crew. The pair of them pretending they weren't in competition over Caro.

Lily didn't fit in there in her green cotton skirt and boots. Nor did Travis. Together they skirted the fringes and watched.

And sometimes they laughed, behind their eyes. She knew what he was thinking. She knew what he thought of them and all this.

Lily never for a second thought she'd be friends with someone like Travis. He rarely went out. Never went to bops, turned his nose up at college balls. He lay in bed and got stoned all night, rolled out of bed for his tutorials and somehow managed to ace his essays. He was too clever for his own good. Never seemed to sleep.

'You're going to kill yourself living like that,' Lily said once when she passed him coming out of his room, white-faced and wired, an essay clutched in shaky hands.

'If I want advice, Lily, I'll go to my fucking mother,' he replied without turning round.

'It wasn't advice,' she called back, 'I just don't want to have to deal with the body.' Then hid in her room. Conflict made tears immediately press at her eyes. Embarrassment made her neck and face speckle red. Her dad said it was endearing. She said it wasn't endearing, it just meant she couldn't talk to anyone and ended up having to be friends with people like Eliza Hattersley-Brown who was so dull she actually bored herself sometimes mid-sentence and just stopped talking. Eliza Hattersley-Brown was probably who Lily would have been living with had the accommodation building not collapsed to the ground and they hadn't just thrown people at random into whatever they could find at the last minute. People like Caro had actually started a petition for an inquest into how they got the allocations so wrong, which Lily was hoping didn't gain traction because it had all worked very much in her favour. Spared her Eliza Hattersley-Brown's invitations to cheese and chess.

Travis came home the day Lily dared question his working habits and went straight to bed. He woke up in the evening just as Caro, George and Henry were meant to be going to a quiz in the JCR, but George was in the shower having just got back from training and Caro was still doing her make-up. Henry, who was always first in the shower, had gone ahead, bored of waiting. Lily was downstairs watching a demented South Korean horror film her brother recommended. South Korean horror wasn't her thing per se but she was feeling homesick.

'You like this film?' Travis's voice asked from the doorway.

'No, why do you ask?' she replied without looking up.

He snorted. Unsure quite whether the deadpan tone meant it was a joke or not. Lily knew that none of them thought there was anything interesting inside her; just because you couldn't see it didn't mean it didn't exist.

Travis sat on the arm of the sofa like he was only intending to watch for a minute then when something made him laugh he slid down onto the seat cushion. Lily tensed at the closeness, felt underdressed in her pyjama bottoms and college sweatshirt.

He got out a joint, lit it, said, 'Do you mind?'

'Yeah,' she said. 'I have chronic asthma.'

He looked momentarily abashed, which she'd never expected from someone like Travis, then said, 'Shit, sorry, I'll put it out.'

'I'm kidding,' Lily replied. 'I'm in the room next to you. You think if I had a problem with smoke you wouldn't know by now?'

'Oh,' he laughed. Took a drag. His hair was sticking up on end from having just got up, his eyes heavy with tiredness. 'You want some?'

She shook her head.

The film got particularly weird and gruesome. Lily felt Travis turn her way.

'What?' she asked.

'Your face moves when you're watching. It's funny.'

'That's what my brothers say.'

'How many do you have?'

'Four.'

'Wow.'

'Tell me about it.'

He got more comfy, rested his bare feet on the coffee table and stretched his arms as he yawned. In contrast, Lily tucked her feet underneath her, unable to fully relax with him there.

As if sensing her awkward self-awareness, he said, 'Do you mind me watching with you?'

'No.'

A second later he stood up. His tracksuit bottoms low on his hips, his shirt done up only on the middle two buttons. 'I'm going to get a Coke. Do you want a Coke?' he asked.

'You just said you were watching the film,' she said.

She could hear him laughing as he went out of the room. When he came back he had a can for her too and chucked it over.

She felt a tiny shiver of pleasure that he'd thought of her but said, 'How did you know I love my Coke all shaken up?'

He cracked his open. 'Had a feeling.'

The doorbell rang.

They heard Caro come down the stairs and answer it. 'Oh, for fuck's sake.' She slammed the door then yelled, 'Travis, one of your idiots is on the doorstep.'

Travis heaved himself up off the sofa. 'Who?' he asked Caro as he went into the hall.

'How should I know? But can you do your fucking dealing elsewhere. I do not want these deadbeats on my doorstep all day and all night.'

'It's not all day and all night. Don't be such a drama queen.'

'Piss off.' Caro stomped back up the stairs.

Travis gave the guy on the doorstep whatever he was buying then came back into the living room. 'Caro, man. She is so uptight.'

Lily laughed, Coca-Cola came out of her nose.

'*Nice!*' Travis sniggered as he flopped into the seat next to her.

She wiped her face with her sleeve. Then reached forward for the pack of biscuits her mum had sent her along with the DVD. 'Do you want a Hobnob?'

Travis made a face. 'I don't know what it is about Hobnobs, why everyone likes them so much. Massively overrated in my opinion.'

Lily said, 'Is that a no then?'

'No, it's a yes but with a statement of displeasure attached.'

She raised a brow. 'Okay, what's your favourite biscuit then?'

'Lily, this is not fresher's week.'

She blushed.

He nudged her. 'Sorry. Okay, pause the film. Right. My favourite biscuit?' He sucked in his breath as he thought. His hair had been cut recently but not very well and one side stuck out more than the other. 'There's this one in Japan. I don't know what it's called but I call it mattress cake. It's all squishy like foam—'

'That sounds like a cake not a biscuit.'

He rolled his eyes. 'Give me strength.' Then took a bite of the chocolate Hobnob. 'God, this isn't that bad actually.'

She grinned. Put the film back on. The sparse living room with its cheap blue carpet and peeling anaglypta suddenly felt like the best room in the house.

They watched two more films her brother had sent back to back, till the birds were singing outside. The two of them, feet up on the table, drinking Coca-Cola, giggling at Korean New Wave.

Travis had been forced to attend George's dad's soiree by his own father, the obnoxious banking supremo Bernard Lawrence-Dixon, who was friends with George's dad and felt his son should put in an appearance if he was going to attend. Travis did not watch the rowing. 'Life's too short,' he said and got the Tube to Brixton to meet a supplier. He turned up at the party hardly able to stand up straight and Lily had to walk him round the block while he drank a Starbucks triple espresso, then he threw up round the back of Harrods and was good to go.

Inside, George and Henry were both flirting with Caro. Trying to outdo each other with witticisms. When some people interrupted to congratulate the boys on their rowing success, Caro swanned off and joined Lily and Travis at the bar that had been set up at one end of the lounge. 'I just don't know which one to choose,' she mused over a fresh flute of champagne.

Unless Caro wanted something, Lily tended to pass under her radar but the reverse was not the case. Lily saw Caro slobbing out when there was no one home to impress. She had some disgusting habits and her room was a tip. Lily's mum would be appalled; it was 24/7 on the farm, sometimes

44

premature lambs kept warm by the Aga, yet it was always clean hands and face at the table. Caro squeezed her spots in the bathroom and then called Lily to see the pus that hit the mirror. But on the outside, there was no denying Caro was beautiful. Statuesque with her long straight nose, high cheekbones and hooded eyes. Her hair was her crowning glory; a sumptuous red glossy mane that she flicked like a disgruntled horse when she was annoyed. Sometimes Lily pondered the unfairness of how bold and striking Caro's features were, like she'd pushed to the front of the queue and taken more than her share. That night, in her sequinned dress Caro was like an Egyptian goddess painted in gold. It was quite something to behold.

Travis had commandeered a whole hors d'oeuvre plate of prawns and was eating them without bothering to shell them. Just pulling the heads off. Lily didn't eat shellfish. She didn't like the eyes. 'They're both exactly the same as each other,' he said, 'so I wouldn't worry too much about it.'

Caro skewered him with her haughty gaze. 'They are not both the same!'

The three of them looked over at George and Henry in their identikit blazers. George, brown hair cut short, solid like he could lift up a car if you challenged him, with a face dominated by a Roman nose, the bridge bent from a childhood rugby break, and a wonky mouth and eyebrows that sloped like he was always sorry for something. Some days it all worked together, others he looked like a bad Picasso. In contrast, Henry was blond, tall, sinewy, with big white teeth in a leonine smile and eyes that tipped up at the corners to make it look like he was always laughing. He was also the alpha of the pair. George his trusty sidekick. Where one went the other followed.

'Henry is better-looking by far,' said Caro. 'But George is sweeter, probably cleverer—'

Travis scoffed. 'He does geography. No one clever does geography. It's only a subject so that people like them,' he nodded towards the rowers, 'can go to Oxford.'

'That's not true,' Caro pouted. 'I found geography very difficult at school.'

Travis raised a brow. Lily looked away to hide her smile.

Caro ignored them. 'Well I think he's kind of clever. And he's the better rower. But he's not as funny or as charming.'

Travis made a gesture of hanging himself and walked away with a prawn to join Henry and George. Caro didn't seem to notice. 'Which one do you think?' she asked Lily, for want of her being the only person there left to ask.

'I don't know,' Lily said, not because she didn't know – Henry definitely, he was the best-looking guy at their college – but because she still found it weird that she was in the orbit of the likes of Caro, Henry and George. It was possible that she would have got an invite to this party simply because she lived with them, but it was her friendship with Travis that really sealed the deal. However much he annoyed them, they wanted to be friends with Travis. He had a certain cachet.

'No, I don't know either,' said Caro with a shake of her flame-red curls.

They went over to join the boys who were sniggering about the fact one of the crew, JB Watson, was currently chatting up a guest called Qiyana, who was in her mid to late sixties, because the rarity of the letter would catapult him up the ranks of their stupid list.

'You're pathetic,' said Caro archly.

'You love it,' goaded Henry.

The laughing stopped abruptly when George's dad, Douglas Kingsley, strode over, proud in his old Oxford Blue tie, clasped Henry and George's hands and patting them both fondly on the shoulder, said, 'Not bad, boys. But the first boat next year, yes?'

'Give them a chance, Douglas,' said another man, taller, more hair. Roughly the same age. It was Sir Charles Bellinger, more understatedly attired in chinos and pink linen. Lily didn't know much about sport but everyone knew Henry's dad, ex-Oxford Blue and five-time Olympic gold medal winner. 'Can't rush these things.'

'With the utmost of respect, Charles, I beg to differ,' Douglas Kingsley replied, obviously annoyed at being undercut. 'They are running out of time if they're going to get a Blue.'

Charles tipped his head, cool and calm to Douglas's reddening face. Lily found herself shrinking back, as one might when dogs started to bay. 'I have faith in them. Don't try and run before you can walk. Slow and steady, remember.'

'They're not bloody tortoises,' Douglas guffawed.

Sir Charles's face tightened. 'Quite so. But a three-line whip isn't going to make them win. Good food, good training and good discipline. It's the only way.'

Henry and George stood stiffly, uneasy about where their loyalties lay as their dads squared off as subtly as they could in polite company.

Travis took a handful of canapés off a passing waitress, chewing and drinking red wine like he was watching a show.

But then another voice cut in.

'At least your offspring have got off their backsides and are doing something to be proud of.'

Everyone turned to look at the short, grey-ponytailed man as wide as bus in a sharply tailored suit, a woman at least twenty years younger than him on his arm.

'Bernard!' Douglas Kingsley greeted him with a hearty pat on the back.

'Great to see you, Douglas,' boomed the grey-haired man, skin clammy with sweat, his fingers never leaving the bare flesh at his girlfriend's waist. 'Bloody marvellous bash. Smashing race boys, but as this chap says, second means nothing in the big wide world. Now, where's my useless wastrel?'

Lily heard Travis sigh. 'Hi, Dad.'

Bernard Lawrence-Dixon gave his son a quick distasteful glance. 'You look fucked.'

'Nice to see you too,' Travis drawled in reply.

Lily suddenly understood better why Travis was the way he was.

Sir Charles excused himself, clearly uncomfortable with the tone of the chat. Douglas Kingsley mentioned something about a share price to Travis's dad who went off on a tirade as his girlfriend stood glassy-eyed with boredom. The boys dispersed as soon as they could, melting into the crowd while Lily got trapped between the bored girlfriend and the grand piano, pushed into the corner by a swathe of passing guests.

She eventually escaped and found George and Travis in the upstairs bathroom, Travis snorting coke off a marble shelf,

George gulping down a pint, while comparing who had the worst father.

George was all mournful, a terrible drunk because he partook so rarely. 'I just wish that once he'd say he was proud.'

Travis made a face. 'Don't be such a fucking cliché. He's never going to be proud. They're such repressed old fuckers they can't show any emotion. Bitching at you is the best they can do. That,' Travis sniffed, smacked George on the arm, 'is how they show you they love you.'

George looked up, all puppy-dog eyes. 'Do you really think so?'

Lily had never seen George look so hopeful.

Travis grinned. 'Course I fucking don't. They're psychotic narcissists who despise everyone but themselves.'

George slumped.

Travis hauled him up by the arm, 'Come on, mate. You're allowed to get pissed about once a year, so you may as well make the most of it. And I've heard there's a Xenia on the waiting staff.'

George sighed, as though the pressures of their list exhausted him. Travis winked at Lily as she trotted close behind, desperate not to lose them again because she'd spent the last ten minutes having to carry canapés when Mrs Kingsley mistook her for a waitress.

George went off to drown his sorrows in vodka shots with his crewmates. Lily saw him again later mumbling sweet nothings into the ear of a waitress who must have been Xenia.

With George otherwise engaged, Henry Bellinger, who didn't seem to have any particular vexation with his father to overcome with drink or drugs, took the opportunity to move

49

in on Caro. Hand on her waist, brushing her fringe out of her eyes. Caro feigning coy surprise at his touch. Lily watched, intrigued by the show, like seeing preening parrots at the zoo. Henry's fingers wrapped around Caro's, drawing her out onto the balcony to look at the London skyline. When they kissed it was like a movie trailer, lit by a golden halo of blazing streetlamps. Both of them acutely aware of their starring roles.

Travis tapped Lily on the shoulder and said, 'Wanna get the hell out of here?'

She popped a quail's egg into her mouth. 'More than life itself.'

They got the train back to Oxford together, eating McDonald's. Lily asked him about the fancy presentation case of Harry Potter books she'd seen on his shelf because there was nothing she adored more than Harry Potter.

'It's a collectors' edition,' he said, chewing on his Big Mac.

'I know, I have the same one at home!'

Travis turned to look at her. 'Well I'll be,' he said dryly.

Lily's cheeks reddened. 'I'm ashamed of my enthusiasm.'

Travis handed her a chip. 'Don't be. It's endearing.'

Lily looked at him like she knew that was a lie.

A smile played on Travis's lips.

After a moment's silence, he nudged her on the shoulder and said, 'I'm a Hufflepuff.'

Taken aback, mouth full of chicken nugget, Lily said, 'No way! *I'm* a Hufflepuff!'

Travis held his hands wide like that was fate.

Lily said, 'Too enthusiastic again, though, wasn't I?'

Travis paused before taking another bite of his burger. 'We Hufflepuffs are nothing if not enthusiastic.'

'I think our traits are actually justice, loyalty and patience. And an understanding of the importance of food.'

'That's me all over,' Travis said, barely able to speak with his mouth full of Big Mac.

Lily laughed. It was the happiest she'd been all evening.

CHAPTER SEVEN

NOW
ELLE

*Starter: Endives and Roquefort (vg. fennel and apple
salad), walnuts and mustard vinaigrette*

Elle was jittery with excitement as she waited for the mock
Tudor door to open. So this riverside mansion was where Caro
had ended up. It was a looming monstrosity that must have
cost millions.

Elle heard the latch turn. She gave her hair a quick flick,
pulled her jacket onto her shoulder, rolled her red lips together.

And there was Caro. Velvet from head to toe. Red hair
too vibrant, as if she'd just had it coloured that morning.
Near perfect flicks of eyeliner. A deep frown line between her
eyebrows at the sight of Elle.

'What are *you* doing here?'

Elle's smile stretched, gleeful. 'That's no way to greet an old
friend.' She took a step forward and lightly touched her cheek to
Caro's, smelt the halo of expensive perfume. 'Hello Caroline.'

She watched Caro claw her emotions back into place and
return the smile as best she could. Elle could see her brain

whirring. Working out if she could she send her away, bar her entry. But rather than cause a scene, Caro said, 'Well isn't this an unexpected pleasure?'

'I thought you might think that,' Elle laughed slyly, slipping past her so she was firmly inside the house.

Caro closed the door. 'Everyone's in the dining room,' she said cautiously.

Elle could sense her wariness and it made her smile all the wider. 'Great!'

The first person to spot her when Elle poked her head into the room with its slate grey walls and glistening chandelier was Lily, who sat up straight with surprise. She was dressed like an admin assistant but her smile looked like a child's at Christmas.

'I hoped you were coming!'

'And here I am,' Elle replied, casting her eyes over the others. A smaller turnout than she'd expected. But there was George Kingsley, standing up from his chair, face frozen in shock at the sight of her. Elle felt a buzz of satisfaction. She pretended not to notice him. Instead she said, 'Bloody hell, Travis, look at you,' and stretched her arm over the table to run her hand playfully over his shorn hair.

Travis gave a bashful grin. 'Didn't know you were coming.'

'Neither did Caro,' Elle winked.

Caro, clearly simmering with fury at the unexpected guest, said sharply, 'Can I get you a drink, Elle? Champagne?'

Elle purred sweetly, 'Champagne would be wonderful.' All the while she could sense George hovering, visibly uncertain.

Elle decided to put him out of his misery. With her smile stretched wide, she turned his way. 'Georgie!'

George's cheeks flushed crimson. Visibly flustered, he held out his hand to shake.

'I think you can do better than that,' Elle said, sashaying over to wrap her arms around his neck and plant a giant red kiss on his cheek. 'Long time no see,' she whispered huskily into his ear.

It took a moment for George to touch her, to rest his hand lightly on her back, replying formally like she was a client in the boardroom. 'Great to see you again. Really great.'

Elle grinned. George sat back down, bashing the table in his haste and spilling his wine. 'Oh goodness.' He fumbled with his napkin to mop it up.

Caro appeared with Elle's champagne. 'Don't worry about that, George. Leave it. I'll get a cloth.' When the stain was dealt with, she set about laying Elle a place in the spare seat at the head of the table.

Elle watched Caro faffing with napkins and matching place mats thinking how old she looked. Too thin. Her hooded eyes made overly prominent by the darkness of her eye shadow. Almost satisfyingly brittle.

When the place was set, Caro pulled back the chair and, clearly still fuming, ushered Elle to sit with such a sharp a jerk of her arm her bracelet almost flew off.

Elle hid her smile behind a sip of ice-cold champagne. She had to admit that the expression on Caro's face when she'd arrived was almost all she needed.

It reminded her of when they'd first met. Caro marching down the stairs of the shared house shouting, furiously, 'Someone's just chucked all my stuff from Henry's room on my bed!'

Elle opened the front door at exactly that moment. 'Oh sorry, that was me,' she said, not sorry at all, looking up at the stunning redhead with a gaze of mock innocence.

Elle had been given the key that afternoon, had gone in and checked the place out. Sussed out the characters from the possessions they'd left behind for the summer. The kid whose room she'd taken – Henry something or other – had already moved out but littered over every surface was someone else's detritus of make-up, clothes, shoes, coats. Elle had picked the things up one by one. Smelt the perfume, tested the lipstick, slipped her arm into the coat. This was all nice stuff, good enough quality but it wasn't the best. It wasn't a patch on the belongings in the room down the stairs: the exquisitely tailored dinner jacket in the wardrobe, the pricey yet functional desk light, the bottle of Bollinger on a shelf next to a stack of medals. No, this girl's stuff wasn't the real thing, almost but not quite. It had been with some delight that Elle had scooped it all into a bundle and chucked it on the baby pink throw adorning the bed in the adjacent room.

'Who are you?'

'Your new housemate.'

Caro eyed her suspiciously, sizing her up as possible competition, clearly unsure what to make of the bleached hair, big boots and shabby little sundress. It had been dislike at first sight as she turned and stalked away, back up the stairs to her bedroom.

George had come out onto the landing to see what the fuss was about. He jogged down the stairs to greet Elle. 'Hi, hi, nice to meet you. I'm George. George Kingsley. And you are?'

'Elle,' she said taking in his open face, white socks, shorts and rowing T-shirt and getting the measure of him immediately.

'And your surname?' asked George.

She tipped her head. 'Nothing you'd recognize.'

He went adorably bright pink.

She extended her long thin fingers. 'Nice to meet you, George Kingsley. I take it I should know who the Kingsleys are?'

George said, 'No, not necessarily.' He was embarrassed. 'My dad's in oil. My mum's on a lot of charity boards. People here, they, you know, our families might know each other . . .'

'Not mine,' said Elle.

'No, no. Obviously not. Well, not obviously. Oh God, I'm really ballsing this up. Sorry.' He laughed, as though he was shocked he'd made such a cock-up. 'I knew we were getting a new housemate, but I suppose I wasn't expecting one who was so pretty.'

Elle bit down on a smile. 'You're fine.'

He grinned, all foppish. 'Let me show you around.'

She followed him, cynical of the flattery but quietly charmed all the same.

Relations never thawed with Caro. Got worse, in fact. Caro still hadn't recovered from the fact Henry Bellinger had put in a last-minute bid to move out for their last year so that him and Caro weren't, to quote him, 'shacked up like an old married couple'. No one was quite sure how he managed to bag one of the much-coveted rooms on the top floor of the remaining accommodation building – big windows, great view. He said it was his infamous good luck but a hefty donation was suspected. Caro, however, overheard him jokingly refer to it as a penthouse shag-pad and hit the roof. It didn't help that when Henry turned up at the house and met Elle, he drawled appreciatively, 'Well, well, well, so this is the infamous Elle, is it? I look forward to getting acquainted!' while Caro seethed in the background.

Although Elle had to admit that sometimes, when Caro relaxed, she could be quite funny. Would sit painting her toenails on her bed listening to the kind of vacuous pop music that drove Travis mad and would therefore result in some back-and-forth banter that made Elle smile as she sat at her desk in the room next door. There had been a few occasions when Elle had even come out of her room to form a triptych of Caro in her room, Elle on the landing and Travis at the bottom of the stairs, the conversation lapsing from witty sniping to easy inanity. Those moments, however, were few and far between because Caro was usually with Henry Bellinger and therefore very rarely relaxed.

Now Elle absorbed the details of Caro's life – her show-home-perfect dining room with its large glossy wooden table dotted with tapered candles, the green marble lamp on the sideboard with its large linen shade and the tastefully abstract art on the walls – while Caro kept glaring at her like she'd ruined everything and said tartly, 'Help yourself to endives. Those ones are blue cheese and walnut,' pointing to a large platter on the table. 'And these ones are vegan. Are you a vegan, Elle?' she asked, slightly accusingly.

'No, no. I'll eat anything.' Elle couldn't help comparing everything in Caro's darkly glamorous home with her sister's dingy flat.

No one seemed to know what to say now Elle had arrived. The awkwardness lay thick like smog. The only noise, a vintage train station clock ticking the slow seconds away.

It was Caro who said finally, 'So where were we? George, you were showing us pictures of your new baby?'

George looked immediately embarrassed. 'Oh no, I don't want to bore you with more of that.' He shook out his napkin and laid it in his lap. His movements stiff and uneasy.

Elle was amused by how uncomfortable she made him. She sipped her wine and carried on watching with impassive contemplation.

Then Travis said, 'I've got something that might interest you all.' And pushing his chair back, he loped out into the hallway.

Caro called, 'What is it?'

'Wait and see!' Travis shouted back. Then a couple of seconds later he came back into the living room brandishing a stack of folded paper. 'I had to stop by my dad's on the way here – he's clearing everything out – and these were in a box in the hallway.' He dumped the stack on the table.

Lily put her glasses on and peered forward to look. 'Oh wow, they're the letters we wrote about each other!'

Caro clapped her hands as if these might just save her evening. 'I'd totally forgotten.'

George looked relieved at the distraction. Elle could barely recall writing one and had no interest in what someone predicted for her future. Instead she let her napkin slip from her lap and when she bent to get it, accidentally brushed George's leg. He jumped. She whispered, 'Sorry.'

Caro had taken the first letter off the stack. 'Oh, it's mine!'

She looked up, eyes sparkling. 'This is so fun. I can't believe you still have them, Travis.' The A4 paper was folded into three and Sellotaped shut. Caro sliced it open with her knife. 'Okay. Caroline Fitzgerald,' she read, '*will be*: something famous. A television presenter or maybe a newsreader.' She held the paper to her chest, looked round the table jovially chastising them. 'Who wrote this?'

No one admitted to it. Elle would certainly never have written newsreader. She'd have written money-grabbing social climber.

Caro went on, 'If she doesn't get fame then it'll be fortune. She'll be a journalist or bestselling writer.' Caro's smile became more forced. 'Well that was you, Lily, not me. I don't have the time to write a book. That's what happens when you have five kids.' She put her hand on George's, united in the empathy of parenthood. Then she looked back at the piece of paper. '*Will live*: Caro will live in a huge manor house in the country with roses round the door, dogs and horses. She'll hold the most magnificent parties. Everyone will head down to Caro's at the weekend. Hers will be the place to be.' Caro nodded. 'That's nice. Very generous. Nice to read, you know, about yourself.' She glanced around her dining room. Then to the table. 'Have more endives. Please.'

George scooped up a couple.

'*Will marry*: Henry Bellinger, of course! Oh . . .' Caro raised her fingers to her lips.

Around the table everyone was quiet. George stretched over immediately and put his hand on Caro's shoulder, gave it a squeeze. 'Oh God, sorry, Caro.'

Elle crunched on her endive.

Caro closed her eyes for a moment, then swallowed. She read on. 'The golden couple, and generations of little Henrys and Caros after them, will reign supreme (NB if Caro can prise him from the clutches of Mother Bellinger!).' Caro half scrunched the paper. 'Oh, for goodness sake!'

Lily took her glasses off and said quietly, 'Are you okay, Caro?'

Caro dabbed her eyes with her fingers. 'Yes. Excuse me, I've forgotten the white wine.' She pushed her chair back and dashed to the kitchen to compose herself.

George made a worried face.

Elle rolled her eyes. 'I'm going to use the bathroom,' she said, having no interest in Caro's histrionics.

There was a cloakroom at the end of the hall but Elle had no intention of using it. Instead, she climbed the stairs and went for a nose about Caro's house.

On the landing she peered round the first door and found a little girl's bedroom with a pink canopy over the bed and fairy lights. The next room had the names of Caro's twins, Tilda and Thomas, carved and stuck on the front.

Elle thought of her own childhood bedroom. The patch of damp that she stared at on the ceiling as her brother snored and her sister wriggled, topping and tailing in the bed with her. Quite often Elle slept on the floor, but then she could hear the mice under the floorboards.

Across the landing Elle found Caro's bedroom. River view, expensively furnished. In the centre was a giant wooden sleigh bed. Dark furniture and heavy brocade drapes. It smelt of Caro's perfume. There was a selection of photos in gold frames on the chest of drawers. Elle picked up the wedding photo in the centre, showing Brian Carmichael nuzzling into Caro's neck. They were on a beach abroad, draped in garlands of lotus flowers. He wore a dreadful cream suit. Caro looked her normal impervious self. Smiling for the camera like a statue. *Why did you marry him?* Elle stared at the incongruous couple then went over to the enormous bed, opened the drawers in the side table. On Caro's side of the bed it was all neat and uniform but on the other side, Brian's side, the drawer was chaos. Elle poked through his random assortment of stuff, found a bottle of diazepam. Yeah, if she was married to Caro she'd need that as well. She considered how Caro had successfully packaged him up into this one little drawer.

Downstairs she heard the front door open and shut. 'Mum, just getting my inhaler!' the voice of a teenage girl shouted.

Chairs scraped. Elle listened to Caro's shoes tap on the parquet flooring. 'Oh Bethany, how could you forget it? Quickly then.'

'Yeah, yeah.' Footsteps thumped on the stairs.

Elle put down the pills and went to stand in the doorway of the bedroom to catch a glimpse of one of Caro's children in the flesh. A stunning redhead flew past her wearing a skimpy silver dress. Elle waited to get a better look at the girl's face on her way back down from the very top floor. Apart from the blue inhaler clutched in her hand, it was like looking at a teenage Caro.

From the landing, Elle watched Caro catch her daughter at the front door for a kiss. 'Okay, bye darling. Be good, yes?'

The girl went, 'Oh, for God's sake, Mother!'

Elle went up to the next floor where there were two more bedrooms, both with en suites. She looked through the daughter's room. Ran her hand over the piles of make-up, revision books, discarded jewellery, the netball jumper with U15s and the nickname 'Bee' printed on the back. She wondered if Bethany 'Bee' Carmichael knew how lucky she was to have this life.

When Elle finally headed back downstairs she found George standing in the hallway waiting for her. Still boy-ishly handsome, he gave the impression of looking casual, leaning against the wall, but as she walked towards him and he pushed himself upright she saw him checking over his shoulder that no one else was around. He ran his hands through his hair then put them in his pockets as if unsure what to do with them. She knew what George looked like when he was nervous.

'Are you all right?' Elle asked.

'I said I needed the loo as well, but you weren't there.'

'I was upstairs,' she said.

He checked behind him again. She wondered if he was drunk. His skin was flushed, there was a splosh of red wine on his shirt.

'I just wanted to . . . you know . . .' He shrugged as though what he was saying wasn't that important. 'With Caro reading that thing about Henry. I wanted to check you weren't going to say anything.'

Elle frowned. 'About what?'

She knew exactly what.

'About . . .' he paused. Sweat beaded on his forehead. He checked behind him again and then, reluctant to spell it out, said in a low whisper, 'What we did.'

She looked at him. Into his sloping brown eyes. Same but

different. Worried; no, panicked. More at stake nowadays. She reached forward, brushed her hand down his cheek. 'No, Georgie, I would never say anything.'

Elle saw her touch throw him off balance. Unable to help himself, he seemed to inhale the scent of her. His breath trembled. When he caught himself he was embarrassed. 'We should go back,' he said, turning abruptly away.

'Yes,' she agreed, following behind. 'We don't want them thinking we've got stuck in the bathroom together.'

'No,' he said quickly, pulling himself together. 'Absolutely not.'

CHAPTER EIGHT

GEORGE

After Henley Royal Regatta in July, George spent the best summer of his life with Henry Bellinger and JB Watson in the Mediterranean villas and English country houses of various Oxford friends. Caro joined them for a week on a superyacht owned by the 6th Earl of Granstead and while Henry and Caro snorkelled around secluded coves, George completed the list's alphabet challenge with a deckhand called Ursula. They all kept up their training. Hired bikes and took part in a gruelling five-hour cycle round Ibiza in the forty-degree heat. When they stopped at the top of a mountain and gazed out at the view, Henry slung his arms around them, panting, and said, 'Look at this. We are top of our fucking game.' George and JB whooped in breathless agreement. 'This is our time, boys. Never gonna be like this again.' Then he whacked JB in the stomach in a pseudo-friendly punch. JB doubled over. George laughed. 'Pussy.' And they all raced down the mountain.

They trained for an Ironman at Henry's manor estate in

the Cotswolds. The ruddy-cheeked housekeeper kept them well fed and watered like a pack of overeager Labradors, while Henry's mother, the infamous Francesca Bellinger, an ex-fashion editor, imposingly tall with cropped white-blonde hair, beckoned them into the drawing room for drinks at 5 p.m. Lounging back on the cream sofas, toned and terrifying, she demanded entertainment from their youthful, boyish banter. George enjoyed making her laugh. Along with her waifish daughter, the beautiful New York socialite Ophelia, who was trying to make it on Broadway but was home for the holidays and spent most of her days stretched out like a cat by the pool and nights getting high in the summer house with her old boarding-school friends. But the real captivation came when Sir Charles Bellinger joined them, regaling the boys with over-modest stories of sporting greatness. George wished enviously that his own father was more like Sir Charles; how different life would be growing up with such calm magnanimity and encouragement.

By the time George, Henry and JB arrived at pre-season training camp they were at peak fitness, all sinew and muscle under copper tans. There were a couple of irritations: an ex-Olympian, Jim Marsden, had enrolled to do a master's and snag some racing kudos before retirement, so he was guaranteed a place in the boat. And one of last year's novices was flying since the summer. But this year was their year. It had to be – after last year's failure it was last chance saloon. And they were the top dogs.

It wasn't till they were at the boathouse, a few weeks into term, that Klaus Schneider, a German fourth-year who'd raced in the Blue Boat the year before, called everyone to attention and declared, 'Boys, today is the day you've been waiting for.'

Henry and George were unloading blades from the trailer. Everyone stopped to listen.

The sun was hidden behind dappled clouds, the willow tree dipped into the glassy water, a pair of swans watched from the opposite bank.

Klaus held his arms wide and said, 'The list is ready.'

A round of sly smiles and knowing looks followed. JB Watson whistled.

Klaus stood serious, framed by the blue doors of the boat-house, waiting for the squad to quiet down. 'We have spent a good deal of time and effort compiling the list for your reading pleasure. All you have to do is keep rank and score. And bag the goods, of course.' Everyone laughed. Klaus went on, 'I would advise you to keep a record of names as we will spot-check at random.'

Toby Fitzgibbon, one of the novices who was sitting on a boat trestle, giggled nervously.

Marco de Poligny, the cox, cleared his throat. 'A word of warning. This list is for your eyes only. If anyone else sees it or it's forwarded or shared in any way, you'll be out. You won't make any boat in this club. Understand.'

They nodded.

'Well, check your inboxes, boys!' Klaus hollered, his broad face splitting into a wicked grin. 'May the best man win.'

As if on cue the clouds parted and the sun glared down.

George looked at Henry. 'Exciting stuff.'

Henry had already whipped his phone out; he always wanted to be the first to know what the list had in store. He snorted a laugh. 'Brilliant.' Then he read out, 'Virgin, slut, royal, married, fat, rich, poor . . .' and carried on listing practically every adjective that could possibly be associated with a female and the score carried by each. He looked to the bottom of the list and scoffed, 'Threesome and orgy. Klaus should be so lucky.'

George said, 'Caro's a princess. She could count as royalty.'

Those in earshot laughed.

Henry, who wasn't good at being the butt of any joke, said, 'Quite fancy my chances with that new girl in your house, actually. Elle, is it? Screw her and I could tick "poor" off the list.' He laughed. 'Maybe her and Caro together – that'd be three birds with one stone.'

When Henry talked about Elle in that way, George had a sudden urge to punch him hard in the face. To pin him to the ground and hiss, 'Keep your filthy fucking hands off her.' Because something had happened to George since Elle moved in. Their old Georgian wreck had come alive. The air sizzled. She wasn't his type at all in her ribbed cotton vests, ripped where the lace attached, and her eyeliner that looked like she'd slept in it. But her laugh was infectious. When George came home from training he would look for Elle's bag in the hallway to know if she was home. He started to learn her timetable; knew when she had hours at the animal sanctuary where she worked on reception, knew when she had lectures, tutorials, went to the dining hall. At the college ball she worked behind the bar and he'd spent the whole time helping her collect glasses. For her, he could endure having his dinner jacket sploshed with other people's beer dregs. He no longer hung out in the JCR with Caro and Henry, looking enviously at

Caro curled up under Henry's arm. Instead, George's jealousy came in the early mornings, when he'd head into the darkness for a training session leaving Elle, who turned out to be surprisingly studious and was often downstairs getting coffee at 5 a.m., chatting to Travis who was red-eyed and bleary after smoking in the living room all night. Nowadays, George found himself leaving later and later to eke out his time spent having a cup of tea with Elle and Travis. Where he used to be champing at the bit to get to the gym, he started to relish those calm, dozy pre-dawn moments.

But on the day the list was announced, as he stood at the boathouse next to Henry mouthing off about a threesome with Elle and Caro, George didn't punch him in the face. He didn't say anything, because not only was Henry his best friend, but also George knew you never told the boys here how you really felt about a girl; especially one like Elle, on whose radar he doubted he even registered. Feelings were weaknesses. They were vulnerabilities. And vulnerabilities were the death warrant of competition. So he laughed along with Henry instead.

Things changed for George the day he missed a course deadline and got summoned to a meeting with his tutor, a trying-to-be-down-with-the-kids man called Redders, who was very sympathetic – in his stripy scarf and natty purple socks – as George explained that life was incredibly stressful at the moment because of impending Boat Race trials. Redders understood, agreed that pressure affects us all, our bodies and brains are only designed to cope with so much, but still he needed that fieldwork report.

That night, George was furiously trying to finish his overdue work then get some sleep before his alarm went off for training when he heard Elle coming up the stairs, back from wherever it was she went out to dressed in a big furry jacket like a tiger and purple suede boots.

'All right?' She paused on the landing surprised to see him awake.

'Fine,' he said, silently praising the Lord for his poor work management as she strolled into his room and sat on his bed. He could barely move with the proximity of her, his senses alert to the smell of cigarettes and Chanel.

'It's bad for a person, you know?' she said, leafing through his textbooks.

'What is?'

'Not having any fun.' She grinned, showing her crooked front teeth.

George shook his head. 'Oh, I have fun.'

She started unzipping her boots. 'If you say so.'

He found himself transfixed, unable to concentrate fully on anything else except each boot falling to the floor and her fingers peeling off the long glittery socks she wore underneath. When she sat back against the headboard and crossed her legs, he couldn't take his eyes off her bare feet, her toenails painted the faintest shade of peach.

He watched her look round his room. Take in the medals and crew photos. On the wall next to her was pinned his training schedule. She leant forward to study it. 'So if you make this boat, what then?' she asked, untying her hair and running her hands through the blonde waves.

George swallowed. Wanted to touch her hair. 'Well then I'm a Blue.'

'And . . .?'

'And what?'

'What, that's it?' Elle replied, her tone both confused and mocking.

George almost scoffed; this wasn't something that usually needed explaining. 'Yeah, that's it. It's a massive achievement.'

She nodded, unconvinced, all the while seemingly laughing at him, eyes sparkling.

'It's something to be proud of,' he went on, trying to make her understand, justify the choices she seemed to belittle with just a glint in her eye. 'Something I'll remember forever. To tell my kids.'

She sat forward, wrapped her arms round her legs. Her perfume pervaded the room. 'It all sounds *very* worthwhile.'

He felt like a fool.

He wanted to kiss her. To press her down on the bed. 'Whatever.' He tried to shrug it off, act like she wouldn't understand. 'It's just a family tradition.'

She moved her foot so her toes pressed against his fingers. 'And you wouldn't want to let Daddy down, would you?' She rested her chin on her knees, her hair tumbling over her shoulders, and grinned, slow and mocking.

George didn't reply. He'd never been around someone who could look so girlish and so knowing at the same time. His eyes were captivated by the coquettish tilt of her head, her rosebud mouth, the glinting fabric of her dress under her fluffy coat. Outside it started to rain. Not a soft autumnal drizzle, but the sort of sudden sleeting downpour that flooded pavements and overspilled gutters.

Elle said, 'Do you want me to let you in on a secret?'

George swallowed.

The sound of the film that Travis and Lily were watching downstairs drifted through the floorboards. The cold, rain-soaked air seeped in through the rotten sash windows.

George couldn't tear his eyes from the whiteness of Elle's skin, the softness of her body.

She looked up from under thick black lashes and whispered, 'I didn't come in here to talk, Georgie.' Then, moving to the edge of his bed, she snaked her hand around his neck and drew him into a kiss that tasted of cigarettes and cherry lip balm and weeks of pure, unadulterated lust.

His hands were under her coat, pushing the faux fur off her shoulders, running along the shimmer of her dress. He pressed himself against her, arm round her back, pinning her to him. He couldn't get close enough, wanted to consume her whole. He yanked at the straps on her dress, pulling it sharply down her body, tugging at her bra strap, kneading and squeezing at the white flesh of her breast. He tore his mouth from hers, kissing and licking her skin down her neck, across her chest while his hand fumbled to get into the lacy skimpiness of her pants.

'George!' He heard his name in the furious haze of it all. Calling him, crying out for him. Then suddenly, slightly sterner, 'Georgie!' and he paused.

'What?'

She moved his head away, held him by the shoulders. 'Slow down,' she said in a voice soft and calm.

'Oh,' he said drawing back, his pride taking a knock as he'd assumed she was in the same intoxicated rapture as he was. 'Right.' No other girl had complained and he'd had the entire alphabet.

Her mouth tilted up in its infuriating half-smile. 'Don't get defensive.'

'I'm not,' he said, suddenly wanting to be off the bed and in the gym, bench-pressing his way to victory.

She curled her fingers into the hair at the back of his neck. 'It's not a race.'

'No, I know, I . . .'

She cut him off with a slower kiss. Reached down to draw his T-shirt up over his head. 'We've got all night.'

George thought, actually I've got training in the morning, but didn't say anything. And soon enough, when he was lying on his back and she was straddling him, taking her time to work her way down his body, he forgot all about training. And when they were locked together, George on a high greater than he'd ever experienced, the rain fogging up the windows, her cold fingers digging into his back, her warm mouth pressed onto his own, the taste of her, the feel of her, he couldn't believe what he'd been doing all these years. He wanted to draw the moment out to eternity. Lose himself forever in the intoxication of her.

The next morning, George raced to the gym, pedalling furiously, careening through red lights on his bike, breathless, exhausted, having overslept and missed most of the training session. The red-faced coach hollered, 'What the fuck is wrong with you? There is no excuse good enough!' No one missed sessions, especially not this close to trials. George could barely believe the direction of his thoughts.

'Look them in the eye and tell them why you weren't here.' The coach pointed to George's teammates. 'Not me, them! Go on! Do it!'

George couldn't. Because instead of dropping to his knees and begging forgiveness, all he could think about was Elle.

'You think they want you in their boat? Can't be arsed? Unreliable? Is that what you'd want?'

The rest of the squad had their eyes to the floor.

George could smell Elle on his skin.

'Answer me!' the coach shouted; his hot breath hit George's face.

He saw the image of her tumbled hair on his pillow.

'No, sir.'

He was a man possessed.

That was why, as he was cycling home with Henry and JB and they pushed for where he'd been, George made the mistake of boasting he'd been having the best sex of his life. He broke his cardinal rule of admitting how he truly felt; couldn't keep it to himself. 'It was just . . . I can't describe it, it was mind-blowing.' He felt incredible, like he'd won a prize that he just had to show off. They lapped it up. They joked and goaded all the way back, stopped off and bought a couple of sandwiches each, scoffing them as they cycled.

George swore to himself he wouldn't get distracted again. He had to focus. But he was back in Elle's bed that afternoon.

CHAPTER NINE

NOW
CARO

Caro was in the kitchen, loading the dishwasher, clattering the plates in. 'Why did I agree to this?' she muttered. The note predicting her future had completely thrown her. And suddenly everything felt enormous underneath the scrutiny of damn Elle Andrews' patronising smirk.

Lily appeared in the kitchen, quietly unnoticed so she gave Caro a shock when she spoke. 'Are you all right, Caro? That letter must have been hard to read.'

'I'm fine.' Caro waved the concern away, 'Lily, did you tell Elle we were having a dinner?'

'No.' Lily looked surprised to be asked. 'Why? Is it a problem?'

Caro didn't know whether to believe her. She never could read Lily; always innocently nibbling on her bottom lip or staring at her blankly like a cow in a field. Caro composed her face, slamming the dishwasher door and going to check on the tagine. Of course it was a problem. Look at Elle in her denim jacket covered in sequined feathers and tight ruched red minidress, making Caro look overdressed and formal in her own home, whispering with George in the hallway.

Caro remembered Elle sauntering through their Oxford house, all boho and instinctive cool. The boys salivating in her wake. Even Travis was hooked. Bastards. Caro had had them in the palm of her hand before Elle turned up.

'So how is everything going, Lily?' Caro fell back into hostess mode as she boiled water for the couscous. 'What else have you been doing apart from the book? Still single?'

'Still single,' Lily replied, accompanied by a resigned bob of her shoulders. 'I have a cat, Patty. She's a rescue, fat as a hippo and only has one eye.' She examined the fruit bowl on Caro's kitchen island, picked up a mouldy lemon that Caro had missed in her clear-up. 'I'm slightly worried that the letter about me is going to say "lives alone with cat". That would be sad, wouldn't it? That that was predicted for me.'

Caro wasn't listening. She reached to snatch the lemon and tossed it in the bin. Trust Lily to find the mouldy fruit hiding at the bottom of the bowl. She went back to her couscous while thinking of her own note. Images of her and Henry. Golden couple. King and queen of Oxford. She tried not to think of what could have been. The life she could have had with him. She remembered the pride of walking into a room on his arm. Knowing everyone there was jealous. Her mother had said, 'The good ones are very rarely the lookers, Caroline. That's the thing with men, they're only good-looking for so long. But a hard-working brain? That pays, I tell you. Aim for the lawyers and the bankers – doesn't matter what they look like, they spend their whole time in the office and you never have to see them. You choose with your head, not your heart.'

Caro remembered their third-year Christmas, her mum and her new husband Lionel – an unattractive investment banker she'd met online and chosen for exactly those criteria – driving up to Oxford to pick Caro up. Lionel didn't like to waste petrol so they were combining the journey with a trip to visit some aging aunt. Caro had made Henry wait on the pavement with her – Lionel didn't like having to wait for the doorbell to be answered – just so her mother could catch a glimpse of him. She made sure they faced the car as it drove up, side by side, Caro holding tight to Henry's hand, presenting him to her mother in all his dimple-cheeked, blond-haired, muscled glory. She knew better than to give Henry anything more than a chaste peck on the cheek though; the ensuing lecture from Lionel if she did wasn't worth the bother. Because while Lionel came with pots of cash, one of his many drawbacks was his dedicated membership of a church who put Christian in their title but seemed to make up all their own rules. 'Money, Caro, always comes with a caveat,' her mother declared, after repenting and converting. And while her mother was prepared to nod along to all Lionel's passionate tirades about the sins of the ungodly while still keeping half an eye on Coronation Street, Caro found him too insufferable and always had to leave the room.

When she tucked herself into the back seat of Lionel's car as Henry waved, Caro caught her mother's eye in the rear-view mirror and gave her a look that said, rich, sane *and* handsome, Mummy darling. He's the whole shebang. Her mother feigned indifference but Caro saw her wince as Lionel huffed and puffed about the weight of Caro's suitcase. When Henry took it from him and effortlessly slid it into the boot, they both knew who they'd rather go to bed with every night.

Caro sighed. Thought of her husband Brian, her own Lionel. The only thing he was happy to spend money on was the house because they were furnishing their 'forever home'. Caro could almost see Brian's brain thinking, let her do it up nicely so she'll never want to leave.

'Caro?' Lily said.

'Sorry, sorry!' Caro shook her head. 'What were you saying? Fat cats . . .' But she couldn't think of a good excuse for having no clue about what had been said. It was only Lily though. 'I wasn't listening at all.'

George came into the kitchen, looking out of sorts after his run-in with Elle in the hallway, cheeks flushed. 'Shall I get more wine for the table, Caro?'

Caro remembered when everyone found out Elle and George were shagging. God, even Henry had been jealous. She'd watch his ears prick up when he heard the bedroom door next to hers close. His eyebrows would raise at the sounds through the wall. Always some wild, exotic laughter and breathless panting. Caro wasn't prim with sex but she didn't tend to make a noise. Too en garde for that, always trying too hard to please. She could tell though, that Henry was drawn to the noises next door so Caro tried her best. George had told Henry that Elle was bare down there, so Caro went for a wax. Elle apparently gave the best blow jobs in the shower so Caro was in the bathroom on her knees. Elle, Elle, Elle. Why had she had to come and live with them? Of course she couldn't blame Elle for the downfall of her own life, but she could certainly blame her for adding to the stress. Whipping them all up. Making Caro take her eye off the ball. Without Elle, Caro would have sailed through calmly as queen bee.

She would have kept her eyes open and her confidence up. When, for example, she had been invited by Henry to his bitch of a mother's birthday bash, the intimidating ice queen Francesca Bellinger, dressed head to toe in exquisitely tailored Dior, had pulled Caro aside to murmur quite casually over a glass of Veuve Clicquot, 'I've always thought women were very similar to horses. You can tell their breeding a mile off. Don't get your hopes up, darling. I know your game!' Caro could have tossed her fiery mane and said, 'I don't quite understand what you're implying.' Instead, she allowed her shock to show, followed by a guilty swallow of acquiescence as if she'd been caught out.

Lady Bellinger's eyes tipped up as she smiled, the emotionless smile of the boardroom.

Scrabbling for a reply that wouldn't make her appear the gold digger she'd just been accused of being, Caro said, 'We love each other.' She still cringed when she thought of it.

'Love!' Henry's mother had scoffed. 'Believe me, young lady, you won't last. Don't even try.' She gave Caro a disparaging once-over, seemed to know instinctively that her dress, while luxury high street, had been half price in the sale. 'My Henry is destined for greater things than you.'

Francesca had swanned off to join her husband, Sir Charles, slipping her arm possessively round his waist as he entertained the doting boys with his stories of Olympic greatness, Henry and George lapping up every word of the heroic gentle giant.

It had taken Caro a calming splash of water in the bathroom to get her act together enough to join them. Stalking back out to the group, clutching Henry's dinner jacket-clad arm and laughing at his dad's jokes a touch too loud and shrilly, all the while avoiding Lady Bellinger's smug, all-powerful gaze. Caro's own mother would have groaned; had she taught her nothing?

Now, in the kitchen, Caro burnt her hand on the oven as she checked on the almonds toasting for the salad. 'Ow!'

Lily hopped off the bar stool. 'Are you hurt?'

'I'm fine,' Caro replied too tersely and Lily backed away.

'Okay, well, I'll wait in the dining room.'

At the other end of the counter, George popped the cork on the Bordeaux as Caro sucked the burn on her thumb. 'Everything okay, Caro?'

'Totally, yes. Completely fine. You?'

'Yeah,' he replied. 'Great, smashing, marvellous.'

CHAPTER TEN

LILY

'I've literally never seen you this excited.' Travis was in the armchair in the living room where he was most days; his head had worn away a patch of the already threadbare material so stuffing poked through.

'I give my deep hidden enthusiasms an outing at Christmas,' Lily said. Then she leant forward to pick up her hot chocolate. 'Come on, it's Christmas. How can you not like it? There's presents, Christmas trees, *Home Alone*.'

'I fucking hate Christmas,' Travis huffed, shifting in his seat to pull his tobacco pouch out of the pocket of his jeans. 'And I fucking hate *Home Alone*.'

'No one hates *Home Alone*.' Lily looked out of the window. It was icy white, there had been frost on the railings for weeks. Travis moaned about the cold non-stop, commandeering George's fancy heater and sitting as close to it as he could bear, but Lily quite liked having to wrap up in a big jumper. Anything to add to the season's magic. So far, the lead up to

Christmas hadn't disappointed. There had been carols and mince pies in the chapel, singing by candlelight. A masked ball at the college – that of course Travis had shunned so Lily had gone with Eliza Hattersley-Brown, proving her theory that Caro and George only invited her anywhere when Travis was attending. The only thing she'd managed to drag him to was the unveiling of the giant tree in the quad, festooned with twinkling lights and shiny red baubles, with hot cider served afterwards in the JCR. Travis had only agreed because the JCR barman owed him money.

Most of the students had already left for the term. Elle had stayed because of her job at the rescue centre, Travis because he had nowhere else he'd rather be and Caro was only leaving now because George and Henry were heading off for Trial VIIIs in Putney which, judging by the tension in the house, were vital to boat selection. Lily's dad had been held up because ice had frozen the pipes at the farm and was coming to get her that afternoon. She'd been all packed up ready to leave for days, case stuffed with presents.

'Oh my God, I think it's starting to snow!' She pressed her face against the cold glass. Caro was standing outside with Henry, waiting for her lift, glued to him like they were on show for all the world to see.

'Okay, maybe I don't hate *Home Alone*,' Travis said, smoothing the paper of his roll-up. 'But I hate snow.'

Elle padded into the room and promptly plucked the cigarette from Travis's fingers, lighting it for herself. 'I love snow,' she said, flopping onto the sofa, wearing an oversized turquoise jumper and old black leggings and still, Lily noticed, looking enviably cool. 'I might go out and build a snowman.'

Travis had begun, uncomplainingly, to roll another cigarette. He looked sidelong at Elle. 'I can't imagine you building a snowman.'

Elle, blonde hair tied in a knot on her head, shrugged and took a drag of the fag. 'No, me neither actually. I don't know what I'm saying.' She laughed, husky and deep, and lay back against the sofa, head tipped to the ceiling as she blew smoke rings that fitted snuggly inside one another.

'What time are you leaving, Elle?' Lily asked, jealous that she didn't smoke, wanting to be part of their little ritual.

'Oh, I don't know,' Elle looked at her watch. 'I have to check the trains.'

'Where are you going?' Travis asked.

Lily knew where everyone was spending Christmas. She had listened as they all told her about their different traditions. Who had turkey, who had goose. Who still put up a stocking – only her. Elle was going to her mum's new boyfriend's for Christmas Day.

'He's okay, actually. It won't last but it's nice for now,' she said, stretching her legs out, putting her furry socked feet up on the coffee table. 'Lives by the coast, Dover or Hastings, somewhere like that.'

'Check before you get the train,' Travis said dryly.

'Thanks.' Elle raised a brow.

Travis ruffed up his hair with his hand and lay back in his chair. 'I'm going to stay here.'

'What?' Lily tore her eyes from the snow. 'I thought you were going home?'

'Yeah. No.' Travis exhaled a plume of smoke. 'I'm going to stay here. My dad rang last night, he's going on a cruise with Cristobel.'

'What about your mum?' Elle asked, shaking a Coke can on the table to check it was empty then flicking her ash into it. 'Can't you go and see her?'

'No,' Travis shook his head. 'She lives in Mallorca. She'll be playing tennis all day. And I'm shit at tennis,' he said wryly.

Lily said, 'My mum made me play tennis – she heard it's good for shyness. It didn't help. Except I do have quite a good backhand.'

Elle laughed.

Travis said, 'My mum is fonder of her twenty-five-year-old instructor, André, than the actual nitty-gritty of the sport.'

Elle pulled a strand of her hair down to examine her split ends. 'Do you see her ever?'

'Not if I can help it. I don't think she wants to see me particularly either. I make her feel old.' He did an impersonation of a plummy woman's voice. *'There's nothing like a teenage son to show one's age.'* I told her the Botox did that well enough but she didn't believe me.'

Lily felt a jolt of sadness. When did one put one's cynicism aside if not at Christmas? 'What will you do on Christmas Day by yourself?'

'Get stoned.' Travis smiled, pulling his hands into the cuffs of his old white fisherman's jumper. 'Perfect Christmas.'

Lily imagined herself at the farmhouse table pulling crackers, her two little brothers yelping about Santa, her mum making mince pies, her older brothers forced off the Xbox to help. How could she enjoy it with Travis here? She knew if it was any other time of year, any other circumstance, she would not have had the guts to say it, but there was something about Christmas for Lily that made her say, 'Come to mine.' The moment the words left her mouth she blushed beetroot.

On the sofa, Elle grinned like a Hallmark Christmas movie was unfolding before her eyes. Lily blushed more. Travis said, 'Nah, it's okay thanks.'

Elle gasped. 'Shame on you, Travis. Who turns down an offer of what I imagine will be the nicest family Christmas I've ever heard of? Have you listened to her talking about it? People don't have Christmases like Lily's unless they're in a book. I'd come.'

Lily cringed. Had she gone on about it that much? She felt like the child in a room of grown-ups, unsure of the inflections on the words. Were they laughing at her? Never had she wanted to rescind an invite more. 'No, seriously, you don't have to come. It was silly of me to ask,' she backtracked, turning towards the snow, pressing her face back on the glass, this time to cool her flaming cheeks.

It was silent behind her. She imagined Travis glaring at Elle on the sofa for pushing it. Lily forced herself to sit with feigned nonchalance. She could see Caro out the window kissing Henry on the cheek while a miserable-looking old man with a grey moustache heaved her suitcase off the doorstep. She heard Elle get up and leave the room.

Lily turned back to Travis. 'Sorry,' she said, 'I didn't mean to make you uncomfortable.'

He shook his head. His hair was long and shaggy over his eyes, needed a cut. 'You didn't. I just . . . I'm not very good with other people's families.'

'No one's very good with other people's families.'

'I bet George is pretty good,' Travis said.

Lily made a face at the idea of George at her farm. 'Well look, there are so many people in my family you can just kind of blend in,' she said. 'That's what I do. You could probably get away with no one actually knowing you were there.' She paused when she saw the look of strained humour on his face. 'Sorry, I'll stop going on about it. I just don't want you to stay here alone. Maybe it's selfish. Maybe I don't want my day ruined worrying about you.' She reached for her hot chocolate again because it had suddenly sounded like she cared far too much about him.

Travis looked down at the pouch of tobacco on the arm of the chair, turned it over in his hand. 'That's probably the nicest thing anyone's ever said to me,' he said, and Lily replied, 'I think that says less about me and more about the other people in your life.'

Travis snorted an unexpected laugh, then he looked up through his too-long hair and said, 'Okay, I'll come. Thanks.'

It was the most magical Christmas of Lily's life. Her mum cooked a turkey and a goose because the neighbours came round too. She and Travis helped her dad get the sheep in off the hillside in the snow, trying to drive the quad bike through drifts, Barney the dog shivering. Lily had never seen Travis out and about in nature, snow-burnt cheeks and wrapped up from the cold.

When they trudged back in, frost on their eyelashes, Travis said, 'I just don't get that thing about Eskimos having hundreds of words for snow. Snow is snow.'

'I don't get that thing about every snowflake being different.' Lily bashed her hands together to keep warm. 'How are there enough shapes?'

Travis said, 'All these lies about snow.'

'Looks good though, doesn't it?' She pointed towards the ice-white hillside ahead of them and the woodland that encased one edge of the farm where as a child she'd disappear for hours until her name was shouted to help.

'It must have been pretty nice to grow up here,' Travis said, wiping the falling snow from his eyes with his glove.

She nodded.

'It makes me jealous,' he said. 'I'd have loved this as a kid.'

Lily said, 'What was your childhood like?'

Travis said, 'That's another fresher question.'

'Asking someone about their childhood is not the same as asking about their favourite biscuit. It's third-year appropriate,' Lily replied.

'Okay.' Travis stopped to pick up a handful of powder, shape it into a ball. 'I would say the main purpose of my childhood was to be a useful asset in my parents' divorce.' He chucked the snowball at the wall of the barn. 'Other than that, they made me an adult when they sent me to boarding school at six years old.'

'Travis,' Lily said, 'that's a very sad story.'

Travis looked at her and grinned. 'I know.' Then he bent down to scoop up more snow and backing away a few paces, hurled the ball straight at her. She shrieked in surprise before making her own to throw back at him. Then her brothers came out and it descended into a full-on fight. It was the youngest Lily had ever seen Travis act. No bravado, nothing. He even allowed himself to be dragged by her younger brothers to snuggle under a blanket on the sofa with hot chocolate and watch Japanese anime.

At mealtimes Lily would catch her mum watching the two

of them, all chuffed and trying to disguise a smile. Lily would glare at her to stop the dopey-eyed look. Travis would catch her glare and grin down at his plate. It was both painful and exquisite.

Then Travis got a text.

Cruise cut short, bad weather. Expect you home for New Year.

He changed before Lily's eyes. Like the light inside him, lit from being at the farm, went out. His face greyed. He went silent.

'I'm going to have to go,' he said.

Lily nodded. 'Yeah.'

They stood facing each other, she could feel the heat of the fire roaring behind her.

Everyone else was in the kitchen.

Travis looked down at the floor. His hair flopped forward over his eyes. 'Thanks for inviting me,' he said, glancing back up. 'It was good.'

They stared at each other. Lily stupidly thought he might be about to kiss her. She even leant in for a second. He stayed where he was. She pulled back quickly enough but knew that he saw.

'I'll tell your mum,' he said. 'Thank her for having me.' He pointed towards the kitchen. Lily followed behind him, cringing.

Her mum reacted predictably. 'Oh my goodness, that's such a shame. It's been so lovely to have you. Are you going with him, Lil?'

'No,' she said quickly, embarrassed it had even been mooted.

Caught off guard, Travis said, 'You can, I mean, if you want?'

'No, I should stay here.' Lily's whole family was in the kitchen listening. She could see her brothers nudging each other.

'Oh don't worry, Lily, don't stay for us, you go, it's fine,' urged her mum.

Her dad said, 'Let her do what she wants.'

Travis said, 'You wouldn't want to come to mine anyway.'

'She would!'

Lily thought she might actually kill her mother.

'Come then, if you want,' said Travis. 'It would make it more bearable.'

They left the warm cosiness of the snow-covered farm, Lily's mum squeezing her into a hug. Kissing Travis on the cheek and saying, 'You look after her.'

'I will, Mrs Enfield.'

They sat closer on the train. Their legs touching sometimes, either by accident or on purpose – Lily couldn't tell. Travis got noticeably tenser the closer they got to London.

At Paddington, Travis got a text from George:

You around for New Year? Party at Henry's if you want to come?

Travis ignored it. 'He just wants coke for his friends.'

Lily wondered if he'd have said the same if he'd got the text while still at her house. Instead, it felt like he was armouring himself up, sarcastic, defensive shield in place. She knew the feeling; she did the same when she got closer to Oxford.

The cab dropped them off outside one of the white-columned Georgian houses in Belgravia. The kind she'd only seen in movies. On a crescent with a private garden. This was wealth she could only imagine.

His father answered the door. 'You need a haircut.' No hello, no welcome hug.

'Answering the door yourself, Dad?' Travis replied without pause. 'That's not like you?'

'Had to give Williams the night off. Bloody employment laws. Who's this?' His dad looked Lily up and down, no question from the expression on his face that he found her wanting.

'A lap dancer I picked up last night.'

Lily looked away. His dad glared, sweaty-faced and mean-lipped. He and Travis squared off against one another in the characterless hallway. All Lily could think of was the huge New Year's Eve dinner her mum would be preparing. The spiced rum and the neighbours coming over to sing 'Auld Lang Syne'.

From the best few days of her life came the worst. Travis's dad put him down every chance he got, needling nastily. For a man with so much money he had very little taste. Lily couldn't spot a single period feature left in the house. The furniture was angular and uncomfortable, the pictures garish, the lighting stark and unhomely. New Year's dinner was miserable. When Lily made an attempt at a joke, Bernard visibly sneered and she felt like a snail pulling back into its shell. When Bernard's girlfriend Cristobel's tiny dog started yapping at her feet, Bernard slammed his hand down on the table and yelled, 'I'm going to strangle that damn rat!' Cristobel fled in tears. They ended up sitting silently in the giant dining room, lights blazing overhead, the scraping of knives and forks echoing over plates of gravadlax.

'Travis, I've lined some work up for you with the bank over Easter,' Bernard said, glugging his white wine.

Travis said, 'No thanks.'

Bernard paused with the drink midway to his fleshy lips. 'Excuse me?'

Lily felt herself tense. She was terrible with conflict.

'I said no thanks.' Travis didn't look up from the cured salmon. 'I don't want to work in a bank.'

'You damn well will,' said his dad, starting up on his meal again as if that were the end of it.

'No, I won't.'

Bernard clattered his fork and knife down. 'You bloody will. You'll learn some responsibility.'

Travis gave him a sidelong stare.

'You're a lazy little shit, you know that?'

Lily flinched.

'Well, anything other than turning out like you is fine with me, Dad.'

There was silence. Bernard's face went red. 'Get out.'

Travis got up and left the room, tapping Lily on the arm to follow. Lily hesitated for a moment then fled after him. Out of the house, she finally felt like she could breathe.

They crossed the road and stood in front of the gate to the private garden. 'I'd let you in but I don't have the key.' He leant against the railing and looked back across at the magnificent white arc of houses. 'Glad you came?' he asked.

Lily shivered against the frosty sleet. 'Best night of my life.'

Travis laughed; it was the first time his face had softened all evening. 'I warned you.'

'I know,' she said. 'I think I just thought you were trying to put me off.' She stopped. 'Not that I mean . . . Not put me off in that respect,' she said too quickly.

Travis pulled his sleeves down over his hands. 'Don't get involved with me, Lily.'

The sleet was turning into snow. Giant flakes falling, blurring vision, settling on their eyelashes.

'Why not?' she asked.

He stomped on the edge of a frozen puddle. The ice splintered into shards. 'Because I'll never care enough. I'm like a vacuum, Lily, completely absent of feelings.'

'That's not true.' She stamped her foot too, shattering the shards into crystals. 'No one's a vacuum.'

'You are if you're a product of that,' he gestured towards the house. 'You can't love if you've never been loved. Ruthless destruction. It's all I know.' He grinned, self-deprecatingly.

Lily kept cracking the ice with her foot. Her eyes were watering with the cold. 'I don't believe you.'

He took a step towards her. 'Don't look for the good in me.'

She glanced up from under her snow-damp hair. 'I can't help it.' Then she reached forward and with her finger dabbed a tiny snowflake off his jumper. 'Look. There's no other snowflake like this one.'

Travis brought her finger closer to his face to inspect it and said, 'I thought we agreed that was bullshit?'

Lily said, 'Everyone's different, Travis. You're not the same as him.'

The snow was dusting their cheeks. Settling on their fingers where they linked. It took all the courage Lily had, but she leant forward and gently, softly brushed her lips against his. She felt him give way. For one second felt the spark and tingle that she dreamt about. But then he pulled back.

'Don't,' he said. 'It won't end well.'

CHAPTER ELEVEN

LILY

Main course: *Ottolenghi lamb tagine with apricot,*
harissa and olives served on a bed of
couscous with hispi cabbage and kalette
slaw (vg. Chickpea tagine with mush-
room and butternut squash)

Caro marched into the dining room brandishing her tagine
aloft as if it were the Saviour. 'We got it in Morocco,' she said,
placing the coned dish proudly down in the centre of the table.
'Shipped it back along with a couple of rugs. They do it all
for you, amazing. Very touristy but we managed to find a few
places off the beaten track.' She started spooning couscous onto
people's plates, talking, busying herself, trying, it seemed, to
keep the dinner party ball in the air. To not allow anyone the
space or opportunity to let it fall.

Lily, however, wasn't there for polite small talk. The whole
point of going to the dinner was to see how being with them
all made her feel. She wanted to get beneath the surface, go
back to where it started. She'd even successfully managed to

get Elle a place at the table. But what was she meant to do now? She wondered if she could nip out and call her therapist from the loo.

The first time Lily had gone for therapy she'd walked out of the waiting room before the session even started. The therapist had called her to enquire as to why she'd fled. Lily had berated herself for picking up the phone.

'Talk to me now, Lily. You're in your home, you're safe. Just five minutes, tell me why you came to see me.'

Lily had looked around at her pot plants, her cat asleep on the chair, her mug on the table. 'I meant to go to the dentist.'

There was a pause. 'Very funny, Lily.'

'I wasn't trying to be funny, it's true. I need my wisdom tooth out.'

'Do you often use humour as a defence mechanism, Lily?'

'All my life,' she said, caught by surprise that someone could see straight to her core down a telephone line.

The therapist let the silence drag on for so long Lily wondered if she'd hung up on her. When she could bear it no longer she said, 'I've started having panic attacks.' Lily could barely bring herself to remember the literary festival in Zurich where she'd stood frozen on the stage, all her slides for the book ready on the big screen, yet her mouth unable to form any words while her mind raced at a million miles an hour and she was convinced she was going to die. In the end the host said, 'Shall we take five minutes?' When her publicist had suggested she talk it through with a professional, Lily had internally scoffed at the notion. It was just burnout. But then came the nightmares. Waking up voiceless, panting for breath, the sheet soaked with sweat. The taste of fear in her mouth.

In Caro's dining room, Travis lifted the lid of a little Le Creuset casserole dish which held his individual serving of chickpeas and squash and asked, 'How long were you in Morocco, Caro? I was in an ashram in Marrakesh for three months, awesome place.'

Caro heaped shredded cabbage slaw onto his plate. 'Oh, just the afternoon actually, we dashed over on the boat from the south of Spain. But we really got a feel for the place. I'd love to go back.'

George took a mouthful. 'Best couscous I've ever had.'

Travis said, 'You should try the stuff in Marrakesh.'

Caro clearly didn't want her couscous compared with that of the Moroccans and changed the subject. 'Shall we read another letter?' she asked, reaching for the stack before anyone had time to reply, tearing open the Sellotape. 'Lily, it's yours!'

Lily took a deep breath. She'd been afraid of this since Travis appeared with the letters. She really didn't want to know what they had thought her future might entail. She imagined whoever had written it staring blankly at the piece of paper thinking, who even is she?

'Okay.' Caro took a sip of wine, dabbed her mouth with a napkin, and started to read. '*Will be:* archaeologist. Very studiously and without causing any fuss, Lily will rise to the top of her profession.' Caro peered over the top of the letter. 'Well, you've kind of done that.'

Lily wanted to bury her face in the napkin.

'*Will live*: when not off finding fossils, Lily will be back on the farm surrounded by chickens and cows—'

Lily was getting hotter, the tips of her fingers tingling.

'She'll have loads of kids. Sweet country bumpkins who take after Lily . . . Oh, how rude!' Caro feigned disapproval. 'And a Farmer-Giles husband who laughs at her terrible jokes and puts up with her dreadful taste in films.' Caro turned the piece of paper over to see if there was anything on the back. 'That's it. Not the most imaginative of predictions. But no cats, eh, Lily?'

Lily was far too aware of her breathing to smile at Caro's little quip. She didn't want people looking at her. She was blinking too much, an annoying tick that came on when she started to panic. She reached to get some water but her hand was shaking so she put it back in her lap. She tried to remember her therapist's advice. *It's just anxiety, Lily, talk to it, acknowledge it, tell it you know that it's there.*

Across the table George had started rhapsodising about the apricots in the lamb tagine. Lily's time in the spotlight was over. But still she could hear the words going round and round, feel the eyes watching.

Caro said, 'Help yourself to more, Travis you especially. It'll be a cold day in hell before any of my children will eat a chickpea.'

Elle, who was toying with her food, knee jiggling under the table, said, 'How old are your kids, Caro?'

Caro snorted, 'How old aren't they? I literally lose count.'

Lily's eye caught the piece of paper Caro had just read from, the one that charted the idealized future of Lily's life on the farm. There was the therapist again: *There are no alternate paths, Lily. There's just what is.* Her office always had the same smell. Lily had looked around for a Glade plug-in but hadn't found one. She spent a lot of time looking at things in that office, to fill the silences that the therapist let run until Lily cracked and had to speak. Like when she said, 'Tell me about your childhood, Lily?' And Lily said, 'It was good. Happy. Lots of brothers. I think I'm pretty typical middle child. Nice parents. Yeah. Good. They've all got kids now; seven girls, two boys. It's a girl-power generation.'

'And how do you feel about all your nieces and nephews?'

'I love them. Couldn't eat a whole one.'

Silence. Nothing. No polite smile. Just that encouraging stare, till Lily was forced to say, 'Jealous. Sometimes I'm jealous of them. That my brothers are happy and settled with kids. But I have my work. My book. It's been really successful. And my cat. She's not successful but I love her anyway. So no, actually, I'm fine. Happy.'

That was the first time the therapist had said, 'You know it's okay, Lily, to feel things. Even envy.'

Right now, Lily just needed a break from being at the table. She wanted to screw that piece of paper up and hurl it over to the other side of the room. It was all overwhelming. The harissa in the lamb was too strong. She could feel the presence of Travis next to her, stronger than before. His smell, the nearness of him. Her eyes were itching to look at him, see the shape of his jaw, his hair, the lobe of his ear. She managed a sip of water but couldn't disguise the shake when she put it down. Her napkin slipped to the floor. She bent to pick it up and the blood rushed to her head. She didn't want to be there, didn't want to take an interest in how being with them all made her feel. Didn't want to feel anything in fact. Coming here was a terrible idea. She sat up, felt dizzy, swayed in her seat.

Travis's arm reached out. 'Are you about to pass out?'

She touched his hand to steady herself. 'No. I don't think so.'

'Are you all right, Lily? Is it the food?' Caro asked.

'No, I just need some air.'

Both Elle and George stood up to help. Lily waved her hand to try to get them to sit, not make a fuss. Her shirt felt too tight. 'I'll be fine.'

'I'll come with you,' said Travis.

'Do you need anything?' asked Caro. 'Are you on any medication?'

Lily laughed, 'No, honestly. I just need some air.'

The others watched as Travis led her out of the room. He held her steady as they went into the kitchen and walked towards the bifold doors. She could probably have managed by herself but the feel of his arm around her waist was quite seductive.

'That was dramatic,' he said once they were outside.

Lily sat on one of Caro's garden chairs, sucked in a lungful of cooler air. 'That's what I was going for. Thought the evening could do with some spice.'

'Fine by me,' said Travis, lounging comfortably. 'Good excuse to get away. I'm with her kids, I can't stand chickpeas. Or endives for that matter.'

'For a vegan you don't like much,' she said, the shooting lines of panic in her vision calming.

'I know.' He ran his hand over his shorn hair. 'Partial to the McPlant.'

She laughed. This was Travis.

He said, 'I've missed making you laugh.'

'Shut up.'

'It's true.'

She sat back, unbuttoning the cuffs of her blue flowered shirt and rolling up her sleeves. 'I can't believe that just happened. How embarrassing. I just need to get my breathing back.'

'Here look, breathe with me.' Travis started to deep breathe through his nose, gaze fixed on Lily. 'I do this for a job.'

Lily knew how to breathe properly, she'd learnt via an app. She'd done everything she could to try to solve the panic by herself. 'Travis, I can't sit here breathing with you, it's too weird.'

'Just try it,' Travis urged. She pretended to follow his breath when actually she was examining every aspect of him. The designer stubble, the veins on his arm muscles, the various designs inked onto his skin. It was him but it wasn't him. She recognized his hands and his blunt fingernails where they rested on the table but he wasn't there in half of what he said. She wanted to reach over and pull off his skin so the real him would pop out.

Travis rolled his shoulders and on a deep exhale said, 'So are you seeing anyone?'

'Is that part of the breathing?'

Out on the lawn the sprinklers clicked on. A sudden burst of rat-a-tat-tat that made them jump. Travis laughed. 'God, only Caro would have her sprinklers on a timer.'

Lily watched the nozzles move back and forth, back and forth, no rest. She wondered whether to tell him about Peter, a guy from her local bookshop who she had coffee with once and it led to a few dates, just to make her life sound more interesting or Travis jealous. But it felt like talking about Bookshop Peter now would sully what she had actually really enjoyed. It would be a waste anyway because Travis wasn't the kind of person to get jealous. 'I'm not seeing anyone,' she said. 'You?'

Travis said, 'No one special.' A moth darted into one of the candle flames then lay motionless in the wax. 'I've thought about you loads.'

'No you haven't.'

'I have.'

She could feel a warming tingle rise up from her feet. 'Really?'

He nodded.

She said, 'That's a long time to be thinking about a person.'

She thought of her therapist again, those silences ticking on and on.

'Can we talk about relationships, Lily?'

'No!'

Now she wanted to go rushing into the stark white office and say, 'I'm sitting here with him, I've laughed at his jokes, what now? I don't know what it means . . .'

Travis tipped his head, studied her. What did he see with his spiritual healer eye?

'How's your family?' he asked.

'Oh fine, same as always, busy. How's yours?'

'As dysfunctional as ever. My dad openly mocks what I do. Wouldn't let me in the house when he saw the tattoo.'

'I'm not sure I would.'

He laughed. 'You love it.'

Lily peered round to examine it. 'It's certainly very bold.'

Travis sat back in his chair, stretched his legs out in front of him; no socks, tanned ankles. 'I think my dad's actually still waiting for an apology for the shame I supposedly brought on him when I got arrested.'

Lily wondered if he brought his arrest up every chance he got or just because he was with her. She could imagine him beefing it up in his motivational talks; how he hit rock bottom and was saved from rotting in jail by the healing power of breath. Not just slapped with a two-year suspended sentence for possessing class A, B and C drugs with intent to supply and labelled by the judge a spoilt, selfish child, naive in the extreme.

The sprinklers paused. Lily looked out at the grass, battered by the torrents of water. 'Did you ever find out who called the police?' she asked.

'No.' Travis glanced at her from under thick lashes.

She remembered asking him way back then whether he'd ever worried about being caught dealing and he'd laughed, 'Nah, police don't care about people like me. They want the kingpins. The ones who run the networks.' She'd never seen anyone look more frightened than Travis when the police kicked the door down.

He stretched, flexing his biceps behind his head. 'But it doesn't matter any more. It changed my life. I did that community service – one hundred bloody pointless hours clearing a patch of wasteland that I don't think they've ever done anything with – and I left. Best thing to happen to me. Took me out of the circle of negativity.'

Lily looked to see if he was using the phrase 'circle of negativity' seriously and whether he was lying about the arrest being a good thing. All she could see on his face was calm neutrality. The sprinklers started again, incessant, firing like guns in the background.

'Whoever it was, they did me a favour really,' Travis said. 'Made me who I am.'

CHAPTER TWELVE

THEN
Hilary term, third year
GEORGE

George was living like Jekyll and Hyde. Every spare minute he wasn't in a rowing boat he spent with Elle. He saw less and less of his friends. She took him places he'd never been: to the Picturehouse where they watched subtitled films about Armenian rock bands. They went to immersive theatre, where George got the giggles but Elle was in full character and refused to reply. She made him skinny dip at midnight in the river. He said, 'If you'd seen what I'd seen in there you wouldn't swim,' pointing to the freezing murky water. She plunged in anyway and George couldn't resist her nakedness. He even found himself enjoying his course work, opening a geography book just so he could sit beside her and study in the relative calm of her sparse room – her dresses hanging from the picture rail, scarves draped over mirrors and a couple of black-and-white movie posters Blu-Tacked to the wall. Elle, with her glasses perched on her nose, shushed him every time he got bored. George grinned as she chastised him to get back to the books. He realised for the first time that the unfamiliar feeling he was experiencing was happiness devoid of wanting more. Life was good.

When they got back from Christmas, he presented her with a little box, wrapped as best as his fumbling fingers could manage. 'I got you this.'

She was unpacking her suitcase. She looked surprised, laughed at the gesture then stopped herself because he knew his face was so serious. 'Oh Georgie, I didn't get you anything,' she said as she took the box. His hands were shaking, he was so nervous. Inside was a necklace, nothing special; he knew she wouldn't want anything too fancy. The sales assistant tried to flog him a big sparkly pendant but he chose just a gold chain with a round gold locket.

'Georgie, I love it!' She grinned, taking it out and putting it on. 'It's the best present I got.'

He nodded, couldn't speak. Felt a mixture of love and stupidity.

'Thank you!' She kissed him.

He said, 'I missed you.' It was an understatement. He'd spent every night of Christmas training camp dreaming about her, the softness of her skin, the curl of her hair, the way her front two teeth slanted back a fraction, the way the lines round her mouth deepened when she really laughed. Being apart had been agony.

Elle squeezed him tight. Then she drew back, looked him in the eye, frowned slightly and said, 'Do you know what, I missed you, too.' She laughed. 'I never miss people.'

From her, the words hit his heart like a golden arrow.

She walked away, went back to unpacking like she had to take a bit of time to think about what she'd just said.

He lay down on her bed, heart thumping because she'd liked his gift. 'Did you have a good Christmas?' he asked, trying to disguise his boyish excitement at having pleased her.

She paused at the question. He watched as her hand reached up to the locket round her neck. Then she came and lay down next to him, on her side, hand tucked under the pillow.

She said, 'My life's not really like yours, George. There's no big Christmas tree and carols round the piano.'

He wanted to say that they hadn't sung carols round the piano since he was ten but instinct told George not to speak.

'I have a mother who is a lot of work and a very long string of stepfathers, some of whom are nice and some who aren't so nice. The current one turned out to be the latter so I didn't stay long. Went back to my mum's flat with my sister and brother and left them to it.'

George thought of his own Christmas, the formal sterility. 'I'm quite jealous.'

Elle said, 'Don't be.'

He couldn't help it; his imagination put everything she did on a pedestal. 'I bet your life has been much more interesting than mine.'

Her hand toyed with the locket. 'Georgie, my life is completely different to yours. They're incomparable.'

George frowned. 'I don't think that's totally true.'

She sat up, looked almost pitying at his naivety. 'Georgie, you've had everything go your way all your life. I've had to fight for every single thing I've ever got.'

He went to protest but thought better of it, stuffed the hand with the new TAG watch further into his pocket.

'That's why I get really cross when you don't do your work,' she said, sitting up, hair falling over one eye, impassioned now. 'Because I've just had to try so hard to get here. I don't have a rich dad who donates to the boat club.'

George blushed. On the one hand, he felt shamefully privileged and lacking in world-weariness, but on the other couldn't get enough of her exotic juxtaposition. Like a butterfly he'd caught in a net.

'But,' Elle went on, 'the one good thing about my mum was that she didn't let up on the value of education. She gave up her chance for my dad and always regretted it. She was like, haul yourself out of this place, don't make the same mistakes I did. And when she was sober, she made us work, really made us work. So I have to thank her for something, I suppose. Just not her boyfriend decisions.'

George's hand reached to touch the necklace where it hung between her breasts. There was something intoxicating about seeing her wear it, like a mark of ownership. 'You've never really told me anything about your life before,' he said.

She paused, seemed to realize that was true and got suddenly bashful and defensive. 'Well, don't tell anyone,' she said, whacking him on the arm.

He pulled her into a hug, inhaling the smell of her hair. 'It feels like the best Christmas present I got.'

George's dad had a favourite saying when they were growing up: *comfort breeds weakness*. He'd say it when they were trudging through the wilderness, packs on their backs, heels weeping with blisters as they put up their tents in the pouring rain. '*Come on, boys, you don't see a lion lounging in a five-star hotel.*' He'd say it when they complained about their rooms at boarding school; the hard beds and the vicious bullies. He'd even use it as an excuse for his style of parenting – every thwack of his belt would be accompanied by some sort of motivational speech: *'Self-discipline, grit and willpower will get you your place in the world.'*

No doubt he would have had something to say had he watched George snoozing his alarm in the mornings to luxuriate for another five minutes in Elle's heavenly bed. And perhaps he would have been right.

It was a day when the sun shone bright but frost was still thick on the leaves and ice cracked on the edge of the river.

'So we're missing Henry today,' said the coach.

George said. 'Why? Where is he?'

The coach said, 'He's had some family news.'

George frowned, remembered the missed calls from Henry that he'd silenced while he was with Elle.

JB Watson was standing next to him. He leant over and whispered, 'His dad's got cancer.'

'Shit, no way?' George thought of Henry's tall, imposing, gold-medallist dad. Henry's hero. Hero to all of them.

The coach was still talking. 'As Henry's not here, Boris will sub in.'

Boris Fazal was a guy plucked from the cafeteria in the first year based on his incredible arm span. He was big and burly but George thought his technique was shit.

At that point, the Blue Boat had almost been selected. Officially naming the crew was just a formality. George had nabbed the 4 seat – the powerhouse, as his dad liked to tell his friends on the phone – with Henry behind him in the 2 seat, the last stroke side place in the boat. George's dad was particularly pleased that it was Henry, not George, in what was commonly referred to as the ejector seat. Had it been the other way round his bragging rights would've lessened substantially.

Unfortunately, while George had been languishing with Elle it appeared Boris had been putting in extra training because during that bog-standard outing the boat flew with Boris on board. The difference was so surprising that it couldn't be ignored. Back on dry land the coaches huddled in the icy wind by the launches while the rowers watched silently from inside the shelter of the boathouse.

George wished he was back in Elle's bed; couldn't face the humiliation and turmoil of what was to come. Klaus was slapping Boris on the back, telling him how well he'd done, while George could feel his insides tighten. Henry and George were pretty much neck and neck. Beat one and you had the other nailed. George might be sitting in the 4 seat but he wasn't stupid, his place in the boat was as vulnerable as Henry's. He knew what the coach was about to say, his face taut and serious. 'Go home, get some sleep. Be prepared for some trials at the weekend.'

George's hands shook. He'd got too comfortable.

Back at the house he went straight to Elle's room where the cold weaved its way in through the shabby windows. She was sitting at her desk in fingerless gloves and a beret snug over her wild curls. When he told her what had happened there were no hugs or words of sympathy, that wasn't her style. She just said, 'Let it play out, Georgie, life is what's meant to be. That's part of the excitement.'

But George couldn't let it play out. 'I've got to win.'

She reached up, turned his face to meet hers. Her fingers were freezing. 'You don't *have* to do anything.'

He felt himself waver, just the look in her eyes was temptation enough. The offer of a different option. The memory of that morning in bed: the warmth, the satisfaction, a tug towards a different way of being. One where points of view surprised him, challenged him, made him consider an option different to the one that had gone before. Where who he became wasn't a dictate of birth.

But then he saw himself carrying the reserve boat down to the water on Boat Race day. Saw the disgusted disappointment on his father's face. Felt the humiliation. It was too much to bear. A better man than him might be able to do it, but not George. It didn't matter how much work he did or how many Armenian rock band films he watched, *winning* was every Kingsley's great love in life. Success was in his genes and he couldn't be the one to break the chain. He looked down at her crooked smiled and said, 'I *have* to be in that boat.'

CHAPTER THIRTEEN

NOW
GEORGE

George hadn't been able to concentrate since Elle had walked in uninvited. Now he found himself alone with her in the dining room. Caro was off fussing with the food that had started to go cold as they waited for Travis and Lily to come back.

'So, married life treating you well, Georgie?' Elle asked, with her wry, intoxicating smile.

The candles on the table flickered.

George was terrified of her proximity. Of the power she held over him, sitting there so gloriously casual in her low-cut red dress. Like a time bomb at the head of the table.

'Yeah, great. Really good,' he said, gulping his wine. 'Little baby Raffy giving us the runaround.'

The things she knew about him could destroy his whole life, ruin everything he held dear, but somehow that didn't just terrify him, it excited him too. Made him feel like an adrenaline-fuelled teenager. When he looked at her, her slinky clothes, her casual movements, her messy yet irresistible hair, he had a growing urge to touch her. To feel her skin under his. How had it once been his right to touch her whenever he pleased? Soft and squeezable. His brain was in overdrive. George loved his wife very much, but he couldn't think of the last time he'd actually wanted to have sex with her. Not just to relieve a build-up but actual desperate passion. Somehow it had got lost with all the planning for the baby. Charts and apps and injections at the hospital. He adored Raffy, would give his life for him, but sometimes it felt like he had. Just the other day, George had passed a hooker in a doorway in Soho, wondered if he should pop in. For the excitement of it. For the shock. But as she beckoned to him, he could see the little girl she was once in the young woman's eyes. He was a parent now. It ruined everything, even sex with a whore. He'd marched away, the smart businessman, aloof as if he'd never seen her.

Now, sitting with Elle – afraid of her, entranced by her – he was getting the shock to the system he craved.

Elle ran her long thin fingers up the stem of her wine glass. He was transfixed by her blood-red nails. 'You have what everyone wants, Georgie. A wife. Family. Money.'

'Yes, yes, I suppose so.' He wondered if she could read his mind. She hypnotized him. He found himself saying, 'It's a lot of pressure. Not that I can't handle it, of course, but it is a lot of pressure.' He couldn't tear his gaze away. 'You've always been so free.'

'How do you know I'm free?' she asked.

'I can just tell.'

'Maybe.' She didn't disagree. She placed her cool hand over his fingers.

He could barely breathe. He turned his hand over so their

palms were touching. She traced his lifeline with her finger; nothing had ever felt so erotic.

They could hear Caro coming back from the kitchen.

Elle leant forward a touch, her dress dipped, he had to stop himself staring at her breasts. 'We can nip to the bathroom and have sex if you want?'

George choked. That was not what he was expecting. Caro was coming closer down the hall. Travis and Lily were obviously heading back too, as Caro was asking Lily if she was feeling all right. Elle was looking straight at him. George didn't know where to look. He wanted to grab her and drag her across the hall but at the same time could see only his wife, Audrey, and baby Raffy. He was a family man. 'I couldn't.'

She shrugged, sat back in her seat.

'Were you serious?' George asked.

Elle smiled. 'You'll never know.'

Caro had zapped the tagine in the microwave. 'Look, have more, this is piping hot!' She gestured to the platter that had taken on a rather gelatinous quality. Lily took her seat, shaking her head at the offer of seconds. George pushed his around the plate. He'd completely lost his appetite. All he could think about was Elle. Of grabbing her hand and marching her away to the downstairs bathroom. Yanking up her stretchy red dress, feeling her legs wrap round him, plunging his hands into her soft silky hair. His whole body ached for it.

A message from Audrey flashed up on his home screen.

Think Raffy may have a temperature but thermometer broken! You were meant to get batteries!!!

This was the perfect excuse to leave. Get up from the table, thank Caro for a lovely night but he had to get home to his sick child.

But George didn't leave. Couldn't leave. Instead he turned his phone over without actually opening the WhatsApp and acknowledging that he'd read it.

Next to him, Elle was saying, 'So Caro, how did you and Brian Carmichael end up married?' while under the table her hand reached across and traced patterns on George's thigh.

Caro skated over the question, lifting up a spoonful of couscous and saying, 'Who wants more?'

George said, 'I couldn't. Delicious though.' His plate was half full.

But it seemed Elle wasn't going to let Caro dismiss her that easily. She said, louder this time, 'Seriously though, what happened? I would never have put you and Brian together.'

Lily and Travis looked sidelong at each other. George was conscious of Caro bristling. He wanted to step in, to stop them squaring off, to keep Elle pacified for his own sake if not Caro's. But all the while, Elle's hand was rising higher up his thigh. He could do nothing more than remember to breathe.

CHAPTER FOURTEEN

THEN
Hilary term, third year
ELLE

The house was empty. Exactly how Elle liked it. She had a shift at the animal rescue centre later and needed to get an essay finished. She'd had a bath to warm up from the aching cold outside and was wearing leggings and a cosy jumper. Face scrubbed, hair up, glasses on. The heating was on full blast and there was condensation running down the windows.

She was so engrossed in what she was doing that she didn't hear anyone come in until a voice in the doorway said, 'I never knew you were so studious.'

Elle looked up. It was Henry Bellinger.

'What are you doing here?'

'Looking for Caro.'

'How did you get in?'

'I still have a key.'

If Elle wasn't so annoyed that he'd kept a key and could freely enter their house, she would have considered quite how good-looking Henry was. Too chocolate-box for her – she liked a quirk of a feature – but he was as close to perfect as a man could get. Even features, straight nose, smiling eyes. Model handsome.

He came in and sat on Elle's bed. She wanted him to leave. She had an essay to write.

'Mind if I sit down?'

'Seems like you already have,' she said.

Henry laughed, dimple-cheeked. 'Sorry.'

'That's okay.' He was difficult to be annoyed with. It always amazed her how much good-looking men got away with. His life must be so easy. Women fawning over him all the time. She saw the ladies in the dining hall giving him extra-large helpings.

'Just a lot for me thanks, Doris.' Henry would quip. *'Looking particularly beautiful today, I might add!'*

'Oh, you are a rogue!'

One of Elle's mother's boyfriends, Cyril – who looked like Richard Gere – would slam her mum's head against the table one minute then dance with her in the living room the next. He got away with anything just on the charm of his smile.

'We've never spoken really, have we?' Henry said.

Elle realized she was not going to get her essay written. She put her pen down, swung round in her chair. 'What do you want to talk about?'

He laughed, deep and easy.

She smiled. His laugh was contagious. She wondered what he saw in Caro with her brittleness and distinct lack of a sense of humour.

'I've had a shit day.' Henry lay back on the bed, legs stretched out in front of him but his feet in his trainers politely hanging off the edge. 'This is comfy. Nice pillows.'

'Thanks.' She twirled her biro. 'Why shit?'

'My dad is dying.' He said it to the ceiling, semi-flippant.

'Oh no.' She got up. 'I'm really sorry.' She sat down again; what had she been thinking of doing? She didn't know Henry well enough to hug him. 'That's tough.'

'Tell me about it. And now there's all this with the Boat Race crew. Man, if I don't race . . . I just want him to see me.'

Why was it that all these boys thought their prowess on the water was so important? Elle said, 'I think you should focus on your dad.'

'I am.' He sat up on his elbows. 'Seeing me race would make him happy. I just want him to be happy.' His voice cracked. 'Shit, sorry. God, I've literally never cried.' He pushed the pad of his hand in his eyes. 'Sorry.'

Elle said, 'Don't apologize.' It was weird to have Henry Bellinger here in her room, all vulnerable, when usually he was head honcho out and about, charming and bantering with everyone he met. She thought it might do him good to cry more often.

He shook his head, as if trying to remove the emotion, and moved so he was sitting on the edge of the bed. 'Jesus, wow, it's tough.'

Elle nodded.

Henry sat with his elbows on his knees. 'Makes me feel like a kid.' He swallowed. 'I'm scared. It feels too big for me.'

She said, 'I've had that feeling.' She didn't share when. Her absolute favourite of her mum's exes, Eryk, leaving them when it all became too much for him to handle. Elle grabbing hold of his coat to keep him in the house and refusing to let go, calling 999, trying to stop the bleeding when her mum slit her wrists in the bath.

Henry closed his eyes tight. 'Sorry.' He stood up, came to stand by her desk. 'What are you working on?'

'Zoology.'

'Blimey. Clever girl.'

'Everyone here is clever.'

Henry was looking at her. 'You look different with no make-up on. Like a child.'

She scoffed. 'Not sure that's a compliment.' Her instinct was to edge her chair away, protect her space.

'No, it is.' He was adamant. 'It's good. You look nice. Fresh-faced. Pretty.'

'Less threatening,' Elle said with a quirk of a brow.

'Easy tiger.' Henry acted like she'd said it more forcefully than she had, raising his hands in defence. 'It was a compliment, promise. You look lovely.'

Elle let it go. The guy had been crying a second ago, she didn't want to be too stand-offish.

Then suddenly he was massaging her shoulders. The strange inappropriateness of it almost made her want to laugh. 'What are you doing?' She jerked away.

'You just looked a bit tense,' Henry said, confused by her reaction. He tried again, hands on her shoulders.

'Don't touch me.' She pulled away again.

'Wow, chill out. I was just being friendly.'

He made her feel like she'd overreacted with his shocked, hurt smile. 'I just don't need a massage,' she said, trying to shrug it off, casual. 'Anyway, I've got to write this essay.'

Henry stayed where he was. His smell, his size suddenly more acute.

'What?'

'Nothing.'

When she turned away, back to her laptop, she felt him run his finger down her neck. 'Jesus.' She jumped up this time. 'You can leave now!'

'Come on, Elle.' He looked put out, offended by her reaction. 'Let's not pretend.'

'Go!' She pointed to the door, at the same time realising that she couldn't get past him; the desk, chair and wardrobe penned her in. A minute ago she hadn't even thought about it, he was just Henry.

'We all know you love it, Elle.' He closed the gap between her and the wardrobe, corralling her like stray cattle. She ducked to the side, his hand shot out.

'Get your fucking hands off me.' She whacked his wrist. Henry's fingers tightened.

He laughed, the dimples less endearing now. 'I think you like it like this.'

She tried to yank her arm away, but Henry's grip was iron-clad, he was a thousand times stronger than her without even trying. 'This is not happening.' It still felt almost like a joke, unreal – he'd hold his hands up and back away. She shouted Caro's name.

'There's no one here,' Henry reminded her. 'Come on. George has been going on and on about how you're the best fuck he's ever had. But you're with the wrong guy. George can't teach you anything.'

'Will you get the fuck out of my room?' She pushed against

116

Henry's chest but it did nothing. She kicked, tried to knee him but he moved his legs back, mouth twitching in amusement.

'That's no way to talk to a guest.' He grinned.

She struggled. He loved it, she could see it in his eyes.

'You're like a wild dog.' He jostled her, moving as she fought against him, his hands pinning her arms to her sides, his chest pushing her back, crushing her with the full force of his strength. All those bench presses. He had her cornered, shoved her up against the wardrobe. She had pepper spray in her bag but that was over by the door. 'What about Caro?' she said, all the time looking round, thinking, eyes darting, trying to work out what she could hit him with.

'What about George?' he replied, as if they were in this together.

She thought of her mum once saying, 'Don't struggle, it only makes it worse. Just let them get on with it.'

'Get off me!' She kicked again, tried to free her arms. She wasn't her mother.

Henry only held her tighter, hands like a vice, the wardrobe handle pressing into her back. 'You're fun.' He grinned; she could smell the coffee on his breath. 'Come on.' He started kissing her neck, sucking warm and wet. 'I need cheering up. I need something to help me forget.'

The wardrobe handles were cutting into her skin now with the weight of Henry against her. She could feel the trail of his saliva as he ran his tongue up to her ear and gritted her teeth, struggled, writhed, stamped on his feet. She'd got out of worse situations than this and she wasn't going to let this smug, entitled bastard have her. She tried to calm herself down. Henry had her hands clasped in one of his and the other was up her top, squeezing painfully on her breast. Think about who he is, she told herself. Don't give in to the panic.

She could see her laptop. The indent on the pillow where he'd just lain. He was unbuttoning his jeans. Then his hand moved to her leggings, yanking them roughly, his fingers in her pants. She winced. Henry drew his head back, looked down at her, wanted to see the expression on her face. She slowed her breathing, looked up at him, met his gaze, the casual satisfied grin.

'You love it,' he said, pushing himself against her.

She stared up, eyes expressionless and said, 'You have something in your teeth.'

'What?' The second Henry lessened his grip, Elle jabbed her fingers in his eyes, exactly as the dwarfish self-defence teacher, Mr Lardy, had taught them in high school. Henry jerked back. 'What the fuck?' Hands over his eyes.

Elle grabbed hold of her chair, got enough grip to lift it from the ground and hurl it at him. He was too strong for it to do much good, but it was enough force to make him stagger to the side to regain his balance.

'You're a fucking psycho,' he shouted, reaching to grab her arm, just missing the fabric of her sweater as she sprinted to the door, to her bag, where she had her pepper spray. He was on her, grabbing her with powerful fury now, no jollity. But she had the spray and she wrenched herself round, held it close up to his face and said, 'Get the fuck off me, you arsehole, or I will blind you.'

Henry let her go. He took a step back, swallowed.

She was breathing hard, prepared for him to lunge again, anything.

He glared at her. She could almost see his brain working.

But then he laughed. Aloof and perplexed like everything was suddenly overblown. 'All right, calm down.' He rubbed his eyes, blinked. 'Jesus.' Opened them wide. He exhaled. 'That was crazy. I think you *have* blinded me.'

Elle's heart was pounding. She could still feel the imprint of his hands on her, the throbbing bruise on her back from the wardrobe handles, the waistband of her leggings pulled down round her hips.

'Get the fuck out of my room.'

Henry was doing up his fly. 'You're insane. What is wrong with you?'

She didn't speak, just braced herself with the pepper spray against the possibility of him charging at her like a bull. Hands shaking less now. She refused to give him the satisfaction of knowing how scared she was.

Henry righted the chair she had thrown. Laughed again as he stood it upright. 'You should have just said.' He took his time, straightened his plain, beautifully cut sweater, checked his teeth in the mirror.

She'd known vanity would be his weak point.

'You need to leave my room, now,' she said with robotic authority. Her heart slowed. She could hear the clock on the wall ticking. The room seemed too normal. Henry too casual, like it had never happened. She wanted to stab him to death, wished she had blinded him, she wanted him snarling and furious instead of this patronising attempt at misunderstanding. She wanted the police to storm in and snap his arms painfully into cuffs. But that wasn't how it worked. She knew that. She could just imagine the case against him. '*Tell me,*

Miss Andrews, what is it that you claim my client actually did?' 'He pressed me against the wardrobe.' It was laughable. His expensive lawyers would rake through her family's past, use phrases like extremely vulnerable, deprived area and three children with three different fathers. Compare it to Henry Bellinger's life – son of a five-times Olympic gold medal-winning national hero who had just been diagnosed with a life-threatening disease. Henry, the slippery bastard, would win public approval with his good-looking, dimpled face on the front of *The Sun*.

Elle glanced around her room, all completely ordinary. Just two regular people. Just a day like any other. 'Give me the key,' she said.

Henry turned to look at her with kind, almond eyes. 'Don't be angry. It was just a bit of fun. I really like you.'

He walked closer, she held the spray higher. 'Don't come near me.'

'Okay, okay.'

His smell, the sight of him, his smile, disgusted her. His loping informality. She swallowed, breathed the feeling down. This twat wouldn't get the better of her. 'Just give me the key,' she repeated.

Henry chucked the key on the bed. Ran his hand through his hair, looked momentarily hurt by the situation, then turning to face her said, 'Sorry if I, er, misread the signals.'

Downstairs they heard the front door open, Caro coming in with George. 'Oh my goodness, don't worry about it,' Caro was saying as they walked up the stairs. 'There's a kid in the first year, writes my essays when I don't have time. And doesn't actually charge that much— Henry, what are you doing here?'

Caro stopped abruptly on the top-floor landing, taking in the scene of Henry in Elle's bedroom.

Henry turned on cue, his big white-toothed smile in place. 'Came to see you.' He strode out of Elle's room with unfettered ease and took Caro's face in his hands to kiss her.

George was looking at Elle who'd lowered her hand and pushed the pepper spray up into the sleeve of her jumper. 'Elle?'

'Yeah?'

'What's going on?' he asked.

'Nothing.' She retied her hair.

Next to George, Caro bristled. She looked at Henry. 'What's wrong with your eyes?'

Henry shook his head. 'Just upset.' He rubbed his eyes. 'About my dad.'

'Oh darling,' Caro wrapped her arms round his neck.

Elle needed some air. Adrenaline was making her shake. She'd beaten off the pawing advances of her mother's exes before, so why had Henry's attempt riled her so much? She grabbed her bag. 'I've got to go to the library.'

George looked confused. 'I thought you had work?'

Elle didn't reply; the three of them merged into one being in front of her. As she pushed past them, Henry said, 'Thanks for the chat. I appreciate it.'

Elle threw him a look of disbelief. That was why it riled her. That lazy entitlement. The cocky swagger. The ease with which he could turn on the charm. This was his turf, where he was comfortable. He hadn't had to scratch and claw his way here, carve out his own niche, he belonged without question. He took what he wanted in life and knew exactly what he could get away with. That power would follow him wherever he went. She jogged down the stairs, shaking with fury. George came down after her.

'Elle? What are you doing? Why are you leaving?' He caught her arm. She whipped round, yanked herself away.

'Sorry!' George stood back.

When she looked at him, all she could see was Henry. The same injustice of his entitlement. All their pathetic rowing crap, their demeaning lists, their cocky banter. She forced her expression to soften; she couldn't let the venom infect her relationship with George. She should just walk away from them all, that's what she'd always told her mother. But she couldn't. She liked it here. She deserved to be here. She had worked damn hard to get here. George had got under her skin with his exuberant naivety, his puppy-dog adoration, his amazement at what she could show him, teach him. She'd got used to being loved by him. Addicted to how she looked in his eyes. Maybe was even a little bit in love with him herself. 'I'm just going to pop to the library,' she tried to make her voice sound normal. 'I won't be long.' Within those seconds, she pulled herself back together. She was stronger than this. She had hauled herself through worse.

George looked uncertain, thick brows drawn together, wary that perhaps she was holding something back. He said, 'Do you want me to come with you?'

'No, it's fine.' She took a sip of water from the bottle in her bag. Put her shoulders back. Smiled. 'It's all fine.'

George said, 'Okay, well I'll see you later.' He kissed her on the cheek.

She had to stop herself recoiling. 'Yep.'

Then, unwilling to let her leave, George drew her into a hug.

Elle felt like she might cry. She didn't want to be touched but at the same time there was part of her ready to crumble into his arms. For a second she squeezed her eyes tight, wondered whether to just give in to it, but when she opened them she caught sight of her reflection in the hall mirror. Hated the tinge of fear she saw on her face. She took a deep breath. Stared into her own eyes and thought Henry Bellinger would fucking rue the day.

Elle pulled away from George. 'I have to go,' she said.

He nodded, reassured but still puzzled by what had just happened.

Outside, the icy air immediately cleared Elle's head. The fear became red-hot fury as she pounded the pavement. She crossed the road without looking and nearly got run over by a bike. 'Sorry, sorry,' she muttered stepping back, and took a moment to lean against the honey stone of the nearest building, look up at the carved chimneys, the all-seeing gargoyles, the stained glass of the church at the end of the narrow road, and ground herself. Her brain pulsed with should-have scenarios. Furious that she hadn't pepper sprayed him, hadn't smashed him over the head with her bedside light. She berated herself for not doing him some serious damage when she'd had the chance. But she knew it was impossible, his strength, her fear, would always make it flight rather than fight and then he'd somehow normalized it all with his casual attempt at crossed wires. Elle stared into the blank stone eyes of the gargoyle above her, its mouth open in a silent scream. She clenched her fists, face set; he would pay for this. She had never hated anyone more in that moment than Henry Bellinger.

Elle was two streets away when she heard the sound of running, high heels on the pavement.

'Elle! Stop!' It was Caro, breathless. 'What's going on? What happened up there?'

Elle paused, wondered if she saw beneath Caro's over-made-up face a genuine whiff of concern. Panic even.

But then, without waiting for a response, Caro ordered, 'Whatever you did, keep your hands off him, okay, Henry's mine!'

Elle almost laughed. Of course, any concern of Caro's would always be for Caro herself. She curled her lip and said, 'You're fucking welcome to him.'

CHAPTER FIFTEEN

NOW
LILY

Sitting quietly at the dining table, Lily was suffering. It was killing her not to step in and try to change the subject as Elle needled Caro about her marriage. She saw everything, she felt everything. All the egos that needed quieting. She could feel it all on her skin like spiders. But she had to sit back and let it collapse around her. As she told anyone in the audience who was listening at her book tour speeches, 'The truth always lies behind the facades.'

At the head of the table, Lily could sense Elle was up to something. Eyes darting this way and that, flicking her hair, fingers drumming the table.

Fussing over the gelatinous tagine, Caro looked about to blow, so wound up she was practically twitching. Lily wasn't sure Caro had recovered from being handed the Sainsbury's lemon tart. Lily had been intending to bake. But then she'd sat on her bed in her pyjamas, her brain refusing to move as it ran through various directions the evening might take.

Across from her, George was clearly on edge. Drinking

too much. Flinching every time Elle spoke. Caro was heaping more couscous on his plate even though he'd said no to more.

Only Travis was keeping his cool. Sitting next to her calm and detached. A walking advert for his own brand of mindfulness.

Lily glanced at the stack of letters and seeing Travis's name on the top said, 'Maybe we should read the next letter?' but no one listened. Status, she'd heard, could be determined on whether people stopped when you said something.

She cleared her throat. Said louder, 'Shall we read another letter?'

On the opposite side of the table, Caro glanced over in acknowledgement. 'Yes, let's open another letter. Come on everyone, let's read another letter,' taking the idea and twisting it as her own. She reached over to the pile. 'Travis!' she read the name with a big smile, as if holding all the secrets of his life.

Travis sat back, hands in his pockets, black T-shirt taut across his chest. 'Well, I'll be interested to hear what this says,' he said, his chin lifted haughtily so the Unalome tattoo stretched the full length of his neck.

'Okay, here goes.' Caro peeled open the Sellotape. '*Will be*: Travis won't be able to resist the lure of his family's money. As soon as he's done with Oxford, he'll fall into line and end up working for Daddy—'

Travis shook his head, mouth open in outrage. 'Who wrote this? Elle, was it you?'

Before Elle could reply, Caro cut in with, 'No one ever tells!'

'Well, it's complete rubbish.'

'Oh Travis, don't be silly,' Caro chided, tone as if she were talking to one of her children. 'It's fun.'

'Hilarious,' he huffed, crossing his arms over his chest, revealing arrow tattoos on both undersides of the tanned flesh. 'I can't believe that's what you thought of me.'

Lily could see the muscles in Travis's neck tense. Knew how much he'd hate this. She almost reached a conciliatory hand to his arm but stopped herself by toying with her fork.

The change in Travis, however, had piqued Elle's attention at the end of the table. She leant forward, stroked a finger along her pale jaw and said, 'So you haven't taken his money then, Trav?'

'Not a penny. I renounced my possessions in Tibet,' Travis replied, humourless and aloof. 'I want for nothing and no one has a hold over me. I'm at peace in my own company.'

George was quick to joke, 'Christ, I'd go mad stuck with just myself and no possessions.' Desperate to keep the tone light.

But then Elle turned her hawk-eyed gaze to him, resting her chin in her hand and saying, 'So you don't like being alone with your thoughts, Georgie?'

George swallowed. 'No . . .' He tried to laugh it off but it came out thin and forced. 'I just really bloody love my BMW.'

Polite laughter resonated round the table.

Elle waited a beat to watch George squirm before turning her attention back to Travis. 'So you're saying that when your old man carks it you won't take a penny?'

'I don't even know if anything'll be up for grabs,' Travis said, arms still crossed defensively over his chest. 'The bastard's probably written me out of the will. But as I said, possessions mean nothing to me. Consumerism is based on want, not need.'

'You keep telling yourself that, Trav,' Elle joked.

Caro bashed the table making Lily jump. 'Can we please not interrupt the letters?'

Elle reclined languidly, satisfied that she'd disrupted the peace while also making Caro look sufficiently uptight.

Lily bit her lip. Waited. It intrigued her how much she wanted to see Travis lose his cool.

Caro smoothed down the velvet of her jumpsuit and carried on reading, 'Travis will lie atop his millions in tax-haven luxury—'

Travis cut her off. 'I don't need to hear any more. That's me done.'

Caro said, 'I have to finish it, Travis.'

'No, you don't,' he replied, standing up and reaching forward, past Lily, to snatch the paper from Caro's hand.

Lily flinched. Could smell his scent of lemons and sweat. Goosebumps trailed over her skin. Deep in her belly she felt an unexpected rush at his annoyance, a delighted thrill at seeing him mad, his emotions fired up. She wanted to stand up and shout, 'Aha! That's where the real you is!'

'It's complete bullshit!' Travis ripped the letter into pieces and stuffed it in the pocket of his khaki combats.

'Very Zen,' quipped Elle, tipping back on her chair.

Lily sat silent, basking in a momentary high, wondering if maybe all she'd ever wanted to do was unmask the fraud; prove he did have feelings hidden somewhere deep inside.

CHAPTER SIXTEEN

THEN
Hilary term, third year
LILY

Lily never wished for anything more than not having to get the train back to Oxford with Travis after the disastrous New Year. She had tried to kiss him. The memory made her insides curdle. Travis acted like nothing had happened. His focus seemed to be on getting away from his father. When he announced he was going back to Oxford early, all Lily wanted to do was scurry back to her parents' farm, but then they would worry the trip had been a disaster, so she went with him.

'No slacking this term, understand?' Travis's dad said when the taxi to Paddington arrived.

Travis replied, 'You know when you ask me to do something, it makes me want to do the exact opposite.'

For Lily, it was too much like watching her little brothers bicker. When Travis got into the cab, muttering, 'He's such a dick,' she said, 'Does it ever occur to you that you're playing into his hands with this stuff?'

'What stuff?' he asked, deadpan oblivious, but she knew he knew.

'Nothing.' She couldn't be bothered. Too tired and deflated. Instead she voiced it in her head. How it would take more courage to be a success rather than a constant source of irritation. How she knew that underneath all the bravado he was afraid. That his petulant act was the only way he knew to get attention from his dad.

Lily would never say anything like that to Travis's face. But she knew, as they sat silently side by side in the taxi, there were other ways of communicating. She was pretty certain her every thought was radiating off her rigid body.

They didn't really speak on the way home. Not when the train pulled into Oxford and everything was covered in a layer of frost so thick it was like a city wrapped in cotton wool. Or when they walked through town, past the glowing shop windows, snow teetering on the intricate carvings of the gothic rooftops, and the delicate spires shimmering as the late afternoon sun hit the ice.

When they got to the house, Lily went straight to her room. She didn't cry. She never cried. She clicked on her old fan heater, sat at her desk and worked. It filled her brain like a balloon, squashing everything else to the corners. Her mum would say, 'Lily, I'm sure it would help you to get all that emotion out.' But she found it preferable to push it right down inside herself. She was more like her dad, out in the fields from sunrise to past sunset. The only time she'd seen him show any emotion was when foot-and-mouth struck and he had to burn all their cattle. Nothing wrong with any of them, but the farm next to theirs was infected. He stood watching the pyre all night, the

130

smell of death engulfing the air. In the morning, Lily watched him from her bedroom window, doubled over, retching by the barn. He didn't speak to anyone for a week after that. Occasionally, if it got too much, Lily too made herself sick. But other than that, work was the answer.

It took over a week for Travis to knock on her door. She'd avoided him as much as she could by hiding out in the library or when she was in her room keeping the door firmly closed. She heard all the noises of the house. The others arriving back from their holidays. Travis getting up from his bed when the doorbell rang, muttering about the cold. George ranting and raving about his stupid race. Lily could tell who they were just by their footsteps. Caro always paused on the landing to check her make-up. Elle sometimes called to see if Lily wanted a cup of tea. But Lily knew, when the knock came, it was Travis outside her door. She knew he would come. He was like one of the stray cats on the farm. Act like she didn't care and it would eat out of her hand eventually.

'It's me,' he said, like she didn't know, like she hadn't been waiting for that knock for days. 'I'm going somewhere that I think you might like.'

She rolled her eyes. That was as close to an apology as Travis would ever give. She opened her door a crack. 'Where?' she asked.

'You'll see,' he said. To her annoyance, the sight of him made her go a bit giddy. His hair, still a little too long. Three days of stubble. Cigarette behind his ear. Dark circles under his eyes. Green woollen jumper, frayed at the cuffs. All the feelings about the brief kiss that she hadn't allowed herself to think about came flooding in at once, like a tidal wave inside her head. She looked at the floor to stop herself staring.

'So do you wanna come?' he asked.

'No,' she said.

He laughed. 'Please?'

She sighed. 'If I must.'

He said, 'It'll be cold.'

The idea he worried about her getting cold made her smile inside. She got her coat off the back of her door.

'Okay, let's go.'

Lily had to do her best to remain aloof and not skip after him.

Outside it was bitter. A glacial wind stung her cheeks and made her eyes water. Bikes had frozen to the railings. A leaking drain coated the pavement with a river of ice. Next to her, Travis turned up the collar on his coat. 'Nice weather for it,' he joked, looking her way through eyes slitted from the cold. Then he said, 'Are you talking to me?'

She said, 'Only if it's an emergency.'

He nodded, pleased, she thought.

They headed towards rather than away from the college buildings. Crossed the quad that glistened with frost, past the bare rose bushes, the arched windows of the dining hall, the boards advertising baroque music by candlelight that Travis couldn't help but scoff at, then up one of the paths that led to the accommodation building which had collapsed from subsidence at the start of their second year. Lily had been quietly pleased when only Henry put in a request to leave their house. They all had their reasons to stay – George didn't need the distraction of moving on top of the stress of the Boat Race,

Travis a combination of laziness and the ease for his clients, Caro the fear that she'd be relocated to the rooms on the far edge of town that had been hastily leased to make up for the lack of accommodation, Lily simply because they all stayed; but mostly because of Travis.

Travis stopped beside a wire security fence that circled the fallen building and, flicking his cigarette onto the frost-tipped grass, said, 'In here.'

'We're not allowed in here,' she said.

He grinned. 'I thought you were only talking to me if it was an emergency?'

Lily read out the sign that said, 'No unauthorized entry. Unsafe structure. Danger of death.' She looked at Travis. 'I think that could count as an emergency.'

Travis laughed. 'It's fine, I promise. I've done it loads.' He pushed through the slashed gap in the fence, his jacket snagging on the wire, then beckoned her to follow. 'The sign's just a deterrent.'

Lily shook her head, she couldn't believe she was even considering it. She didn't want to get caught and jeopardize her course. But when he smiled at her, half reassuring, half daring, she followed him inside because it was Travis and she found she couldn't not.

They picked their way past the building-site detritus. The ice-encrusted stacks of wood and giant bags of sand. They ducked under scaffolding and ignored more signs that forbade entry to climb in through the newly built frame of a lower-floor window. In the dark and the gusting wind, it felt like a haunted house. Lily was torn between being terrified and wondering if this was a date.

Inside, the ceilings were held up with a maze of steel props. Travis had a torch and the beam skated over ladders and cables and piles of rubble. 'Fun, eh?'

Lily said, 'I'm worried something's going to fall on my head.'

Travis rolled his eyes. 'We can go right up to the top floor where there's a hole in the roof. You can see all the stars.'

She held in a smile as she followed him up the partially constructed staircase. It was the most romantic thing he'd ever said to her. It really felt like it might be a date. She wondered if he'd been thinking about their brief almost-kiss. Had he realized that she was the one to thaw his frozen heart?

'Travis?' said a voice when they reached the landing. Everywhere the joists were held up by scaffolding. Lily stepped unsteadily on floorboards that creaked under her feet.

'Hey,' Travis nodded to a couple of guys skulking in the shadows, dressed in their suits ready for a Formal. Out of place and awkward but trying not to show it. In comparison, Travis looked like some mafia don.

Lily's heart deflated. He'd just brought her along on a deal.

Travis said, 'I'll be one sec,' and left her at the top of the stairs like a lemon as he went with the boys into one of the rooms off the landing.

Lily stood against the wall shivering, wishing she wasn't there, or rather wishing those boys weren't there and Travis had thought only to take her to look at the stars. What a pathetic, love-sick fool she was. She deserved to be standing there alone as punishment for such outright idiocy.

They were ages. She wanted to leave. She would never leave. She tried to take her mind off the cold by using the torch on her phone to look around. Under a layer of dust in the corner she found an old poster for the speleology club, a remnant from previous residents. She thought about her dad looking at it and saying, 'Why don't they just call it caving?' And her saying, 'That's just semantics, Dad.' He'd say, 'What's semantics?' And she'd glance to check that no one had heard. That was why she never let them visit her here; shame did funny things to a person. It was shame that kept her on the landing. Shame at daring to think she was the main event when really she was the afterthought. Someone like Elle would have left.

It was so cold. Finally, they appeared in the dark doorway. The guys were laughing, trying to play it cool, gloved hands pulling up the collars on their smart black overcoats, their shiny shoes incongruous in the dust. Travis had a fag in his mouth and was stuffing a fold of twenties into the back pocket of his jeans as he watched them go.

'Thanks, Travis,' one of them said.

He tipped his head.

Lily kept her eyes on the floor as they hurried away.

Trav said, 'Sorry about that.'

She wanted to say, 'It's not okay.' But the disappointment was so huge inside her that she didn't think she could speak. She wanted to be back in her room. Back to the moment when he knocked on her door and there was still all that anticipation to play for.

So she said, 'I have to go, I've just remembered I have an essay.' Travis looked perplexed but she didn't give him a chance to say anything, just turned and ran down the stairs.

It was the fourth step from the top where, in her hurry in the darkness, she missed her footing. She lost her balance, thwacking backwards, trying to reach for the temporary scaffolding handrail but already bouncing down the stairs. Her head bashed against the steps, her shoulder jarred. She heard Travis shout as she landed bruised and ungainly in a painful heap, wondering if she might be dead.

Travis was there in a second, crouched beside her. 'What the fuck, Lily? Are you okay? Do you need an ambulance?'

She pushed her hair back, looked around dazed, checked that she could feel all her limbs. Her ankle was throbbing, her head ached, her palms were cut and bleeding. 'I'm okay,' she said, shaken, embarrassed.

Travis exhaled. 'Fuck, I thought you were going to die.'

She winced as she tried to move her ankle.

Travis sat on the floor next to her.

Lily tried to ignore the different aches and pains ricocheting through her body. Didn't want Travis to see the blood on her hands.

He shook his head. 'I honestly thought you were going to die. My God. I just . . .'

Lily looked back at him, nervous, not sure what to say, wanting the attention to stop. 'Well at least now I can talk to you. It's a real-life emergency.' She tried to smile but it hurt.

He pushed his too-long hair back from his face, said, 'Lily, I'm so sorry.' And then he did what she least expected in the world: he cupped her face in his hands and he kissed her. The kind of kiss she'd hoped for the entire time she'd known him. Soft, impassioned, gentle. She could have happily died then and there. When he pulled back, still holding her face, he rested his forehead on hers and said, 'I'm really glad you didn't die,' and she said, 'Me too.'

He said, 'I take it you don't want to go up to the roof any more?'

She would have gone to the moon right then if he'd asked. But she wasn't sure she could walk. She had to show him her ankle. He winced at the swelling. Then he turned around and said, 'I'll give you a piggyback.'

'Really?'

'I'm stronger than I look, Lily.'

'I'm not quite sure how to take that,' she said, feeling suddenly quite self-conscious.

'You're ruining the moment. Just get on my back.'

It transpired he could only carry her up one flight. The rest she limped, holding onto his arm like a crutch, but she thought less about the pain and more about the fact he'd referred to this as a moment.

'That's the room with the view.' Travis pointed to the far end of the top-floor hallway.

Inside, the room was an obstacle course of scaffolding but as he promised, if you stood in the half-constructed shell of the new dormer window and looked up, above the lights of the glowing city, the bare trees, the icy rooftops, the spires and the domes, all you saw were a million stars in the dark, navy sky.

Travis disappeared into the hallway and came back with an armful of old packaging from the building works. He piled it in a heap on the floor under the window and said, 'Lie down.'

'Travis, I . . .' Lily felt suddenly nervous lying on the makeshift bed with him.

He grinned. 'It's just to look at the sky.'

She lay down. Too hyper aware to relax. He lay next to her, nudged his arm under her neck and curled her in towards him.

'For warmth,' he said, and when she let herself be drawn into him, her cheek pressed against the soft wool of his jumper, she thought she felt him kiss her hair.

'Travis,' Lily said, 'What are we doing? What does this mean?'

He lay back, eyes fixed on the sky. 'I'm not sure. Let's just see how it goes. Yeah?'

'Yeah,' Lily said. 'Take it slow.'

He said, 'Slow, Lily, is something I excel at.'

She laughed. Allowed herself to relax more into his hold.

His arm tightened. 'We've got all the time in the world.'

They lay there for ages. Till their fingers and toes went numb, but Lily didn't care because her hopeful heart was warmth enough. She ignored the ache in her ankle from the fall. She never wanted to leave. She wanted to stay in that moment for the rest of her life; no one else, no expectations, no disappointments. Just Lily and Travis. And the stars.

CHAPTER SEVENTEEN

NOW
CARO

Caro was itching to clear the table and move on, but George was still politely picking at the couscous she'd forced on him in her panic to avoid Elle's questions about how her and Brian met. Not that Caro desperately wanted to serve the dessert. Under normal circumstances, she would save the evening with a sumptuous pudding, but Lily kyboshed that possibility with her cheap Sainsbury's lemon tart. When she'd first handed it to her, Caro had tried to remember if she had any meringue nests left over from her summer barbecue, because if she did, she could Mouli up some frozen raspberries, whip some cream and she'd have an Eton mess to serve alongside. Who didn't love an Eton mess? But now she just wanted the evening to end. Travis had ripped up his letter like a petulant schoolboy. Elle was still asking bloody questions about bloody Brian.

Who wanted to talk about Brian? Certainly not Caro. She spent most of her life trying her best to ignore him. To focus on the children. If Caro had her way she'd have a hundred more kids to pour all her energy into but her body couldn't handle it, not after the twins. But goodness, there was nothing nicer than a fresh little bundle in her arms, smelling all soft and sweet, and consuming every second of life Caro had to offer.

'Brian must be doing very well,' Elle said, looking round at the décor, her perusal somehow making everything seem showy and ostentatious. 'You don't work, do you, Caro?'

'No,' Caro replied. Just the tone of Elle's voice put her back up. *Don't let her get to you.* The last person Caro wanted to get into whether she worked or not with was Ms Self-Sufficient Elle. It was too complicated. Caro couldn't explain that if she worked then she wouldn't be able to pick the children up from school, make their packed lunches, volunteer with their clubs, be chairwoman of their school PTA, sit with the little ones at the kitchen table as they learnt their times tables or try to persuade Ed and Bethany to revise as they stomped up the stairs glued to their phones. Her children were the only thing that gave her life meaning.

'You met Brian when you were in Zurich, didn't you?' Lily asked, straightening up her dessert spoon and fork.

Caro wanted to shout, *Can we please stop talking about Brian?!* But instead she sipped her white wine and said, 'Yes. It was so fabulous in Switzerland. Expensive of course but an amazing lifestyle – so much to do, hiking, swimming, and literally a couple of hours from the best ski resorts. And such a lovely community of friends.'

'I find the expat life really strange,' Travis shook his head, disapproving. 'Living somewhere and having no part in it politically or culturally.'

'Well, aren't religion and politics the two subjects to avoid at dinner parties?' Caro quipped. Deflect and move on.

'Yes, it's much more fun talking about you, Caro,' Elle purred, annoyingly saccharine. 'What made you go there in the first place?' She leant forward like she was really interested. 'How did you and Brian meet?'

Shut up! Shut up! 'I got a job offer I couldn't refuse. Marketing for a luxury department store. Very high-end. You know the kind of thing, just the best there is.' On the back foot, Caro knew she had a habit of going too far.

'Really?' said Elle, eyes widening impishly, wisps of hair falling free round her face. 'That sounds *amazing.*'

Caro narrowed her eyes, unsure of what Elle was up to. 'It was. Really amazing. My perfect job actually. They offered it to me and I couldn't refuse.'

Elle ran her finger round the top of her wine glass, stopping just as it started to sing. 'So it wasn't because you were pregnant then?'

'I beg your pardon?' Caro sploshed her wine in shock.

Across the table, Travis drawled, 'This might go on the list with religion and politics.'

Elle lounged back in her chair, glass dangling between her fingers. 'No, I was just curious, because I was upstairs and I saw your daughter as she was leaving—'

'What were you doing upstairs?' Caro could feel the tips of her cheeks start to speckle. She didn't want Elle snooping around her house.

Elle ignored the question. 'She was very pretty, just like you, Caro. But much older than I expected. And then in her room, I happened to see a sports jumper with U15s on the back. You must have had her very soon after you left Oxford. Made me wonder, that was all.'

Travis leant forward, one tanned finger tapping against his lips, enrapt by the accusation.

'Are you serious?' Caro was incensed, her brain boiling with self-righteous indignation. She glared at Elle. 'How dare you! What kind of person comes into someone's house and accuses them of . . . I don't know, what are you accusing me of? Of having Henry's illegitimate baby? Would you say that if Brian was here?' Caro could feel the anger choke the words at the back of her throat. 'How dare you!'

Next to her, George stammered, 'That does seem a . . . er, a little below the belt, Elle.'

'I was only wondering.' Elle shrugged, careless, the strap of her dress slipping down her arm. 'Seemed quite a fitting explanation.'

On the far side of the table, Lily was clearly looking anywhere but at the ensuing conflict. Her eyes fixed on a black and gold calligraphy print that Bethany had got Caro for her birthday which read, *We'll go dancing. Everything will be all right.*

Caro scrunched her napkin in her fist. She'd had enough. 'Why I married Brian is nothing to do with you. What I would say is that what you are referring to was one of the most difficult times of my life. My eldest daughter Bethany was born premature and with pneumonia. She had less than a 50 per cent chance of survival and I spent almost two months in the hospital with her hooked up to different machines and tubes and it was awful.' Caro struggled to get the breath in through her nose while holding back the tears that sprang to the surface without fail every time she spoke about the trauma of Bethany's birth. 'Awful. The worst time of my life.' At least

Elle had the decency to look a little abashed. 'So next time you want to drop in one of your attention-seeking little quips, have a thought about what else might have been going on at the time.' Caro threw her napkin on the table, pushed her chair back and stormed out of the room.

CHAPTER EIGHTEEN

THEN
Hilary term, third year
GEORGE

Today George Kingsley and Henry Bellinger would race for the last place in the Oxford Blue Boat that would compete against Cambridge in the Boat Race. Best friends, archenemies. For two years they had both missed out on the top boat. They had one more chance to achieve their dream and they would go head-to-head that day.

Rain pummelled the water like hammers beating iron. George had never been so psyched.

Henry was in the changing room, swapping his top to a dry one before heading out on the water. 'Good luck, mate.'

George nodded, 'You too.' He walked to the door on legs shaking with adrenaline.

'George,' Henry stopped him.

'Yeah?'

Henry shook his head. 'Nothing.'

But George could tell he had something to say. 'What?'

'No seriously, it's nothing.' Henry's eyes were red. He looked like he either hadn't slept or was about to burst into tears.

George stepped back into the damp sweaty room. 'What is it?'

'It's nothing. It's just—' Henry took a breath. 'I spoke to my mum this morning. They think my dad's got weeks. That's it.'

'Oh mate, I'm really sorry.' George reached out, put a hand on Henry's shoulder.

'It's fine.' Henry said, but his chin wobbled.

George couldn't imagine seeing Henry cry.

Henry sat down. 'Fuck.' He put his head in his hands. 'I don't know what to do. I'm a mess.'

'You'll be all right once you get on the water.'

Henry shook his head. 'No. I know I'm going to lose.' He wasn't being over dramatic, it was a valid fear. While Henry and George were pretty even, George had a maverick quality on race days that, if he was on form, meant Henry was beatable.

George was itching to get outside. He didn't want to be having this conversation standing among discarded wet kit, the acrid smell of stale sweat choking his throat. His crew were about to put the boat on the water. 'We need to go, mate.'

Henry nodded but didn't move. Above them one of the lights flickered.

'Come on,' George beckoned.

Henry said, 'Would you do one thing for me?'

'What?'

'Would you let me win?'

George laughed on instinct. 'Are you serious?'

Henry squeezed his eyes shut. 'I'm really sorry to ask.

I know I shouldn't. I know it's unfair. But my dad's dying and all he's ever wanted was to see me in that boat.'

George felt his whole body tighten. 'I can't, Henry. You know what it's like. This is my—' He couldn't find the words. 'This is everything.'

'I know. And I wouldn't ask. But he's dying, George. He's fucking dying.' Tears rolled down Henry's cheeks. He was a big guy, formidable usually, but weeping, he looked like a schoolboy.

George didn't know whether to stand firm in outrage or go over and put his hand on Henry's shoulder in the hope he might wipe away his tears and apologize.

But when Henry did eventually look up, to George's surprise, he said, 'Elle understood.'

George tensed. Elle. Why was he bringing her into it?

George had been insecure since the day he'd caught Henry in Elle's bedroom. And she'd been acting weirdly ever since. Distant and detached. Her words not quite matching her eyes. She didn't listen as intently as she used to, was often distracted when he spoke. Like her feelings for George might have changed. The more he fretted about the race, the more irritated she got. Either to test her or just simply out of insecure desperation, he'd told her he loved her that morning. He'd wanted to say it for ages.

Elle had lain still. The sound of the rain filled the silence. Then she rolled over to face him, put her hand on his cheek and said, 'Good luck, George.'

He'd felt his stomach drop with disappointment. It felt like a slap in the face.

George had nodded. 'Thanks.' He took a breath. Psyched

himself to leave her bedroom and not let the disappointment affect him.

Elle lay watching, mascara smudged under her eyes, cheeks pale. Then she sat up too, holding the duvet tight against the cold. 'I will never love anyone, Georgie.'

He shook his head. 'Why not?' he said, sounding plaintive and boyish.

'Because it's who I am,' she said.

'No. It's just self-protection. I know people have hurt you in the past, but I won't.'

She lit a cigarette, movements languid, hair piled in a messy blonde bun on top of her head. 'Georgie, everyone lets you down in the end.'

'No,' he said, adamant. 'I won't.'

She had turned away. The rain battered the glass. He wanted to get back into bed with her, bury his face in her skin. She looked back, kissed him on the shoulder. 'Have a good race.'

George couldn't bear the idea of losing Elle. Especially not to Henry Bellinger. Yet here was Henry, sitting in the sweaty changing room, implying Elle supported the idea of George throwing the race in his favour. Had she said that because she was under Henry's spell or because it was the right, moral thing to do?

Or was this mind games? George wouldn't put it past Henry. He always knew which buttons to press.

George stared at the changing-room floor, befuddled. He couldn't imagine throwing the race. What would his dad say? His grandfather? What was right? Should you let the friend with the dying father win? Throw away your ambition? He wouldn't have even considered it before. But what *would* Elle say? Would she think sacrifice was better than self-interest? Or was she the most self-interested of them all?

Oh God, he was so confused. He felt the giant weight of unfairness on his shoulders. He wanted to shout. To smash the wall. 'Henry, I . . . I don't know. I'm sorry.'

Henry held up a hand. 'No. It's fine. *I'm* sorry. I should never have asked.' He wiped his eyes on the damp T-shirt he'd just taken off, then he stood up, gripped George's shoulder. 'I shouldn't have said anything. Shouldn't have put friendship over competition. I'm sorry. Good luck, buddy.' He sucked in a breath. 'Let's do this.'

They jogged out into the sheeting rain. 'George, let's go!' Klaus shouted.

George's mind was spiralling. His hair plastered to his head like a drowned rat. His killer instinct replaced by a desire to crawl back under Elle's soft white duvet. He looked over at Henry, wondering if he would have asked the same were the roles reversed.

The trials went on and on. George's muscles burned, the copper tang of blood filled his mouth. His body struggled with his lack of focus. His brain kept chipping in, upsetting his concentration, reminding him how much this hurt. Finally, the coach called, 'That's it. Take it home, boys.'

George was too exhausted to look up from the changing-room bench when the results came in.

Henry Bellinger had beaten George Kingsley to the final seat in the Blue Boat by just over a second.

George didn't know if he could breathe. He saw sparks in the corners of his eyes. It felt like his world had ended.

Henry took a seat beside him. Slapped him hard on the back. 'Sorry mate. Good race.'

George stared, horrified, at the floor.

'Apologies for asking you to throw it,' Henry added, giving George's shoulder a squeeze. 'Glad actually it was a fair race. Makes it more real.'

George didn't reply, just grabbed his bag and bolted. Didn't care what the others might think.

It was still raining. Never-ending cascades of water. Elle watched, smoking, from the bed as George kicked the bedside table making a cup fall to the floor and smash. Shards of cheap ceramic littered the carpet.

'Argh. Fuck!' The action of kicking the table had done nothing to relieve George's fury. Instead he felt momentarily embarrassed as Elle stubbed out the cigarette and silently got off the bed and started clearing up the broken cup.

George bent to help. 'Sorry.'

She climbed back on the bed, long creamy legs tucked underneath her. Looking round the room, she said, 'Are you going break anything else because if you are, tell me now and I'll put the good things away.'

George felt like a fool. He moved to the bed, crumpling in on himself.

She put her hand on his head.

He felt like a small child, stripped bare and hopeless. He squeezed his eyes shut. 'What am I going to do?'

She toyed with her lighter, turning it over and over on the bedside table. 'Do you know that animals rarely compete against one another, especially if they suspect they are going to lose. Even stags. They don't want to fight, it's a waste of energy—'

George stood up, started pacing the floor again. 'I don't see what that's got to do with this.'

She stared up at him, all dishevelled and beautiful, calm. 'Well, if you'd let me finish . . .'

He lay on the bed on his back and stared up at the ceiling. 'Go on then, what do animals do?'

'When they don't want to fight?' she said. 'Well, they adapt. They find another way. So one lizard developed sticky feet so it could feed higher up the tree when another bigger lizard came along and invaded its territory. Or there are bats that agree to eat different food from one another so they don't compete. It's amazing what animals do.'

'Sticky feet are not going to get me in the boat.' He screwed up his fists. 'I can't actually believe Henry asked me to throw the race. And then he was such a smug twat afterwards. All supercilious.' George couldn't control the sense of impotence, of injustice. He felt tricked and manipulated. 'I fucking hate him.'

Elle uncurled her legs, shimmying down the bed so they lay side by side. 'Maybe you should kill him,' she said.

'Elle!' George recoiled. 'You can't say things like that.'

'That's what meerkats do to get rid of the competition. The females eat the babies of other meerkats.'

George made a face of disgust. 'Well, luckily I'm not a meerkat.'

Elle laughed, pulling a pillow down under her head, tucking her arm underneath it and getting comfy.

They were face to face. George could see the flecks of dark

blue in her eyes, each individual eyelash, the tiny freckles like a flick of paint that smattered over her nose. 'Do you know I've been worried there might be something between the two of you, you and Henry?' he said. 'You know, because of him in your room that day. Before the race he said you'd think I should let him win.'

Elle stared at him. He knew her well enough by now to know she was deciding whether or not to tell him something.

'What?' he asked, dreading that admission of an affair was coming. He didn't want her to answer. He wanted to draw her in tight, smother her against his chest so she couldn't speak.

Elle licked her bottom lip. 'He tried,' she said. 'The other night.'

George held his breath. 'But nothing happened?' he clarified.

Elle shook her head. 'Nothing happened.'

George sank back on the pillows. Stared up at the ceiling, exhaled the weight of the world. 'Thank God.' He breathed out again, his thoughts reconfiguring. Relief became outrage 'Fucking Henry! How dare he!' he snapped, sitting up, furious. But when he looked at Elle she was her usual calm and unreadable self, and George suddenly worried that she was lying. 'You're sure nothing happened?'

'I can assure you, Georgie,' Elle curled her lip, surly suddenly, like a teenager, 'there is nothing whatsoever between me and Henry Bellinger.'

George felt a shiver of pleasure at the intensity of her reaction. He stroked her hair. 'I can't believe he tried it on. What a twat.' And yet it was completely believable. The guy had no scruples.

Elle brought his hand round and kissed his palm. George

wanted Henry to see, wanted to have him by the throat up against the wall and spit in his face, 'She's mine!' Instead, he shifted down the bed so he was right up next to her, could smell her skin and perfume, and sighed. 'Well now I do want to kill him.'

Elle smiled.

'Even though I know it was just a joke. We're not going to kill him.'

She raised a perfect arched brow.

'I mean, it's ridiculous,' George reiterated, because now the seed was planted there was something strangely exhilarating about the idea of wiping the slippery bastard off the face of the earth. And to think George had worshipped the guy.

Elle grinned, her face so close their noses were almost touching. 'Georgie, you can't fool me. I know exactly what you're thinking all of the time.'

'No you don't.'

She reached out and traced his jaw. 'Yes I do.'

At training the following day, George couldn't look Henry in the eye. Felt the pulse of humiliation as Henry said, 'Can't talk, Georgie boy, Klaus is all about sticking together as a crew.' George watched the eight top rowers and the cox close ranks, suddenly greater than the sum of their parts, an elite, arrogant machine. He wanted to tear the skin off his body in jealous rage.

George had never felt anything as intense as that; his hero-worship of Henry had morphed overnight into an all-consuming hate. On the water in the reserve crew, George's every stroke was petulant and irritable. Off the water, he hung his head during a one-to-one with the assistant coach; they didn't even get the main man any more. 'I've been there George, I know what it's like not to make it to the top. I know what you're going through.'

George stared at the assistant coach in horror. Watched his thin lips as he reeled off more platitudes. His flyaway hair. The stomach stretching against the fabric of the Musto rain jacket. He couldn't be aligned with this guy. This was not his destiny, to spend a lifetime shuffling along in second best.

That night George lay in Elle's brushed cotton sheets. Soft like a baby's blanket. The window was open and the air smelt of cold rain. She was working, reading papers by the glow of a sidelight draped with a red scarf.

George watched her. Her lips moving as she read. On instinct she seemed to realize he was staring and turned to look his way. 'All right?' she asked.

He nodded.

Her brow creased in thought. She put the papers to one side. 'What's wrong, Georgie?'

George locked on to her bright blue gaze, he had no idea what it held in its depths. Just an understanding that she was different to everyone else that he knew. And at the very least she was unshockable. 'I need to get rid of Henry,' he said.

Elle tipped her head. Her mouth widened into a smile as she came and sat down next to him. 'You know, I had a feeling you might say that, Georgie.'

'You did?'

She nodded. 'I thought I'd look into it. Just in case.'

He frowned, wary about what she had in mind. 'Into what exactly?'

She got a cigarette out of the pack. 'Into a way to get rid of Henry, just for the race.'

George sat up, slicked back his hair, immediately intrigued. 'Go on.'

She tapped the ash into an old seashell ashtray balanced on the covers. 'Have you ever heard of the drug Xylazine?'

'No.'

She nodded. 'It's a veterinary sedative. It's used for cattle and horses but also on cats and dogs before they're put down. I can get it from the animal charity where I work.'

'Right . . .'

'It's not authorized for use in humans but that doesn't stop people taking it – they mix it with coke and heroin to make speedballs. On its own though it sends people to sleep. From what I've read, effects can last for anything up to *seventy-two* hours, Georgie.'

George could feel his heart pumping faster. Her pupils had dilated. He wondered if his had done the same. 'Is it dangerous?'

She sucked on the cigarette, blew out, waving the smoke away with her hand. 'In the wrong dosage it is. But we wouldn't give him the wrong dosage.'

George's hands were tingling. He squeezed them into fists. He couldn't believe how lucky he was to have someone as cunning and enigmatic as Elle as his girlfriend. 'And what if Henry wakes up?'

'He'll feel like shit,' she said. 'Whether he sleeps for ages or not, whatever happens, when he wakes up he'll feel dreadful.

There's no way he'd be able to race. You get black-outs, memory loss. They call it the zombie drug, Georgie, people wander around completely out of it.'

'But then people would know that we'd given it to him.' George was feeling suddenly less excited by the idea.

She shook her head. 'Georgie, they don't test for it. We mix it with something. Does Henry take anything that you know of?'

'Only Valium sometimes to sleep.' They nearly all took something when the nerves got too much. George's preference was melatonin, his dad got it for him when he was in the States on business. JB Watson swore by Nytol Herbal.

'Well that's perfect! It's his word against anyone else's that he wasn't just trying to get a good night's sleep pre-race.'

Outside, the sounds of the city rumbled on, the brakes of bikes, a can rolling in the wind, groups of footsteps on the pavement. The moon peeked through the dark rain clouds. 'How would I stop people thinking I had something to do with it? Don't you think it'll seem too fortuitous for me?'

'Who cares? They can think what they like. They won't be able to prove it. And technically, why would you poison your friend?' Elle stretched and yawned. 'Why not the other guy?'

George paused. 'Why not the other guy?' While he wanted to get his own back on Henry, it would be much less obvious to take out Boris or even Klaus.

Elle pulled her hair up on her head and tied it with a band from her wrist. 'I think it actually gives you more of an alibi if it's Henry. It's a pretty shitty thing to do to a friend.'

It seemed laughable that George was ever worried Elle

might like Henry too much. 'Yeah.' He nodded. It was equally unimaginable that until so recently he'd have called Henry his best friend. 'You're right. Less obvious. But what about when he doesn't wake up in the morning?'

She blew out a smoke ring, then another. 'He'll feel rough and they'll think it's a sickness bug.'

'What if they test?'

'Who's going to test?' Elle stubbed her cigarette out, yawned again.

'Officials.'

'What officials?' she laughed. 'It's just a guy who wakes up feeling shit. At the very, very worst, Georgie, a test will show there's Valium in his system. He won't be able to prove he didn't take it himself. And by then the race will be long over and done with.' She lit another cigarette and relaxed back against the headboard. 'If he tried to blame you, you'd be within your rights to say he was trying to frame you for his own mistakes. You wouldn't be friends again. Not that I think it would get to that. He'll just seem knocked out with a bug.' Elle was all practical, hair tied back, no make-up on, while George felt giddy as a schoolboy inside. 'And when would we give it to him?'

'Well that bit's not so great.' She scrunched up her face. 'Ideally it would be by injection. I think we'll have to put it in his drink but it's going to have to be done as late as possible to make sure, basically, that he's out of it.'

'We'll work something out.' George bit down on a growing smile. 'Elle, you're a genius.'

She shrugged. 'We haven't done it yet.'

'Yes but,' he leant forward, took her face between his

hands and kissed her on the lips, 'we will. And it will be amazing.' He tipped his head back up to the ceiling and smiled. 'You are so, so clever.' Then he looked back at her. 'I'm going to be in the race.'

'You're going to be in the race. If it all goes to plan,' she caveated.

'*If* it all goes to plan.' He thought for a second. 'We've got the same water bottle actually, came free with a six-pack of Heineken. They're our lucky bottles. I know that sounds cheesy. But . . . Well, anyway, maybe I could go see him in his room, swap the bottles, swap them again later, that kind of thing.'

Elle frowned. 'No. Because then you'd have been seen in his room the night before. That's a terrible idea.'

'Oh.'

'Let me work on the logistics, Georgie.'

He nodded. 'Right, yeah, okay.'

Elle rolled her eyes.

George grinned, felt a desire to punch the air but never would in front of Elle. He couldn't believe it. He would never have had the courage to do such a thing without Elle in his life, yet now it seemed almost obvious. A game. The forehand thwacking the ball back to Henry's earlier backhand.

He lay back on the bed, hands behind his head, all his excitement for life flooding back. 'I love you more than I can say, Elle Andrews.'

There was something in the coy look in her eyes as Elle stood up and said, 'I have to get back to my essay,' that made George sit up and dare to hope he was winning her round in the love stakes. The plan had brought them closer together; united them against the world. It made him fizz with excitement.

Just before he settled down again, he said, 'And it can't, you know, kill him or anything like that?'

Elle looked over from her desk. 'No.'

'Great. Brilliant. You're a genius.'

CHAPTER NINETEEN

NOW
CARO

Caro wanted Elle gone from her house. She took a moment to steel herself in front of the hallway mirror, straightening the little buttons on her velvet jumpsuit, pushing her bracelets up her arm, giving her chin a haughty lift, trying to convince herself she was above it all.

George popped his head out of the dining room, then came to stand next to her. 'You all right, Caro?'

Caro turned to face him, arms crossed over her chest. 'George, I married Brian for the security. I don't deny it. We have a kind of understanding.' She did a bitter half-laugh. 'Well, I have an understanding, I don't know if he does so much.'

George nodded profusely, as if he completely understood. 'You don't have to explain it to me, Caro.'

'I do,' she said, wanting to draw him firmly away from Elle's camp into her own. 'I married Brian so that I never had to face the lack of security I had growing up. My mother put up with Lionel in order for me to go to bloody North Wales on holiday, have orange squash, and live in a 1930s semi.' Caro rolled her eyes at the memory. 'Did you know I didn't want to go to Oxford? I wanted to be an actress but my mother wasn't having any of it. "*You'll be the first one of us to go to university, Caroline.*" She employed this horrible tutor who came round practically every night to get me into not just university, George, but *Oxford*.' She paused, concerned that perhaps she'd given away too much from the look of pity on his face. 'Well, when we graduated, I had nothing. Henry was gone. I had no comfortable family home to go back to. My mum and Lionel, they had their life, they didn't want me in their house. My uncle lives in Switzerland, he sorted the job for me. Lionel paid for the plane ticket. Brian happened to have a very good job out there in a bank, I bumped into him quite by chance. He's always been, how do I put it . . . very adoring. It's no more juicy or salacious than that.' She looked up at the ceiling then back to skewer George with a direct stare. 'I won't be antagonized by Elle in my own home, George.'

'No, no, I completely understand. I think she just—'

Caro cut him off, didn't want to hear any mumbled defence of Elle. 'George, do you think you could ask her to leave?'

George looked reluctant at the suggestion. 'Just ignore her, Caro. Rise above it,' he said. 'You're better than that. You know it's not worth it.'

Urgh. He was so weak.

Caro sighed. 'Fine.' As always she was on her own.

With a flick of her hair and a quick check of her make-up, she marched back in.

In the dining room, Lily was stacking the dinner plates.

Elle was wandering round the room, picking up and putting down objects on the sideboard.

Travis was saying, 'Just say it is Henry's kid and she's covering it up by playing the sick baby card, that's some seriously bad karma—'

'Excuse me?' Caro stopped in her tracks.

Travis froze, mouth half open. Looked immediately guilty. 'Nothing, I was just saying—'

'I heard what you were saying,' Caro hissed.

At the end of the table, Lily was trying to quietly carry on stacking the plates, not get involved.

'You have no idea what I went through!' Caro felt her hackles rise at Travis's karmic judgement bullshit. Him standing there all aloof with his tattoos and his tan and his absolutely no responsibility in the world.

'We've all been through things, Caro,' he said, tone irritatingly patronising. 'It's how you choose to face them that sets us apart from one another.'

Over the other side of the room, Elle was watching fascinated, one of Caro's delicate glass candlesticks in her hand.

Caro snorted a laugh. 'Is that the kind of smug judgement people pay you for?'

Travis closed his eyes, as if rising above the petty playground slanging match with an inner mantra. 'Okay,' he said, raising a hand in the air, showing the tattoo of an arrow elbow to wrist on the underside of his arm. 'I think there's a bit too much emotion in the room. Let's take a break.'

Caro scoffed. 'Too much emotion?' She felt the others watching. She was not going to be the one called out for too much emotion. Uptight Caro unable to keep her cool. 'I'll give you too much emotion. You know why my baby couldn't breathe when she was born, Travis? Because I had chlamydia, which can cause pneumonia in babies in the womb. And you know who I got that off? You! You were fucking responsible for my baby nearly dying.'

Travis reared back.

Elle placed the candlestick back very carefully.

Lily stopped stacking the plates. Her cheeks prickled red like raspberries.

Caro felt the instant satisfaction of a direct wound. *We all have fucking arrows, Travis*, she thought.

Over the other side of the table, Travis took a moment, silently flummoxed. Caro could almost see his brain working. Ditto Lily, both racing through timelines in their heads. She folded her arms, lips tight. She wanted to look over at Elle, all blonde, cool and self-satisfied, and raise a brow as if to say, you didn't think I had it in me, did you?

Then Travis put his hands on the table, arm muscles tensed, and said, 'I didn't have chlamydia. It was nothing to do with me.'

Caro narrowed her eyes. 'No? You sure about that?'

'So hang on a minute,' Elle cut in, voice laced with disbelief. 'Let's get this straight, you and Travis were sleeping together?'

Caro tossed her hair. 'I wouldn't quite call it sleeping together. But yes, on occasion we had sex. I know Henry wasn't a saint either.' She glared pointedly at Elle.

Elle narrowed her eyes. 'Why are you looking at me?'

At the table, Lily was staring fixedly at the pile of dirty plates. Caro took a moment's pleasure in watching Travis try to catch Lily's eye. That would teach him to judge her.

Then Elle sashayed forward to the table, red dress hitching as she walked. 'So it could be Travis's baby?'

Caro slammed her hand on the table. 'It's no one's baby but Brian's!'

'But you're happy to blame me for the STI?' Travis was visibly furious, lips thin, jaw clenched. He glared at Caro. 'You are something else. As far as I remember, we used protection every time. You have no idea who gave you what, you just wanted to bring that up. To get at me. And Lily.'

Caro shrugged one shoulder. 'We didn't use protection right at the beginning.' She couldn't bring herself to say, *Yes, that's exactly right, you smug bastard. Don't think you can judge me without consequences!*

Sex with Travis had always been her grubby little secret. The antidote to all those moments when she'd come home from having to be Perfect Caro for Henry. Avoiding questions from horsey rowing girls at socials about what school she went to while trying to keep Henry's eyes off the gymnasts drunk on half a sherry. Dressed in the best labels she could find from hours scouring the rails of TK Maxx. Her Barbour she got from a charity shop – seven pounds! – for the weekend Henry took her on a mock hunt with some of his course pals – *'Totally actually a real hunt, just don't tell the protesters!'* She'd had to feign a childhood back injury for the fact she couldn't get on a horse. Every Thomasina and Kiki trotting along on their palominos.

One of Caro's favourite hobbies nowadays was to go to TK Maxx, see which designer brands were in stock, and then try to spot who was wearing them at school pick-up or at the gym; see who wasn't quite as rich as they said they were, who was passing off bargains as full-price boutique finds as she used to have to do at Oxford. It was a little thing that gave her a thrill. Maybe she should get a job, maybe she had too much time on her hands.

But back then, keeping up the Caro that stood by Henry's side – the prom queen to his king – was exhausting.

And she was already exhausted from doing battle every day with all those learned Oxford professors, all from the same entitled backgrounds as her peers. It took confidence and resilience to argue back if you didn't know the social codes. Didn't have the blind self-belief instilled from birth. Just walking the hallowed halls, crossing the beautifully manicured lawns, donning her robe for three-course dinners with ingredients she'd never heard of, knowing which hand to pass the port with, all of it kept her permanently on high alert. Caro was treading water the whole time, battling, gasping, fighting every single day.

The days it became too much, she'd blow out an afternoon's work and walk home alone, fast along the cobbled streets, head down, the looming yellow stone buildings solid and unwavering, oppressive in their perfection, and go straight up to her room. She'd put on her Primark pyjamas, put her hair up in a bun, and depending on what mood she was in would either slob out in her room and shove a whole packet of Maryland Cookies into her mouth. Or go and see Travis. Who obligingly was nearly always home.

Caro remembered the day she'd caught Henry and Elle together in Elle's room. She was determined not to be made a fool of. When everyone had gone, she'd stormed into Travis's room out of anger. 'Just do it,' she'd said, hitching her skirt up before Travis had even hauled himself off the bed. She remembered the feeling; fury and humiliation.

Then Travis had said, 'I don't think I can.'

'Excuse me? What do you mean you don't think you can? What's wrong with you?' She didn't have time for this. She went over to the bed, started to straddle him as he heaved himself up.

But he had the audacity to place his hand on her stomach, to keep her back. 'It's just I don't think we should.'

'Why not?' Caro would not be refused.

Travis looked pained. 'No reason, it's just . . . you know . . . me and Lily . . .' He winced, embarrassed. Couldn't quite say it.

'You and Lily what?' Caro snapped.

'You know?'

'Oh, for fuck's sake, Travis, now is not the time to get a conscience. I have no interest in your little love affair.'

'It's not a love affair,' he protested, rubbing his bleary eyes.

Caro knew exactly what made Travis tick. 'Fine, whatever. I won't tell your girlfriend anything.'

'She's not my girlfriend.' Travis bristled at the word. 'We haven't even done anything.'

Caro smiled slyly. 'Well you can relieve your frustrations now.' She slapped his hand away and this time straddled his legs. 'Just get on with it.'

Sex with Henry Bellinger was all Caro contorted into whatever position Henry wanted. She was always scrubbed and buffed, made sure there was a pout on her lips and made all the right noises. With Travis she did not give a shit. It was always sweaty and fast and the room smelt of weed and dirty sheets and Caro never had a shower beforehand. She would dig her nails in his back, groan, really let herself go. He didn't care. And she could chat, say things like, 'Elle, the bitch, I think she might have shagged Henry – and he wants to have a threesome. Who do you think I should ask? Can you go a bit faster, I've got a lecture?'

When they were done, slick and exhausted, he'd light a joint and she'd allow herself one puff then trot off to the bathroom to shower and change and put Oxford-Caro back in place.

Now though, Travis did care. He was all holier than thou. Glaring at her across the dining table like she was sharing a sordid secret he took no part in. And more than anything, she realized, she wanted to break his whiter than white, possession-renouncing aloofness. She had struggled so much, given so much of her self away, and there was Travis, calmly having walked away from everything that Caro aspired to. *That,* she thought, was the luxury of privilege; the ability to renounce something simply because you had experienced it. To drift along as people like her clawed their way to just a glimpse of that flippantly relinquished lifestyle.

Across from Caro, Lily had her eyes fixed firmly on the table, arms tight to her sides, shoulders curled inwards, as though she were trying to physically take up as little space as possible. When she reached for the remaining plates, Elle noticed and shifted them away to stop her. To make Lily look up.

Caro was braced ready for whatever Travis had to say. She wanted to hear it. Wanted to fight. But his face changed to pity across the table as he said, 'I feel only sympathy for you.' And Caro felt herself instantly deflate. Then he walked out of the room, past Lily, touching her on the arm as he went. 'I need some air.'

CHAPTER TWENTY

THEN
Hilary term, third year
GEORGE

Elle had no problem securing the Xylazine.

'And no one noticed?' George asked when she pulled up on her bike and took the bottle out of her bag, a little too blasé for George's liking. He'd been waiting for her in a side street on his way back from the gym.

'Christ, no. They've got bucket loads of the stuff. And if you saw the chaos there you'd be surprised *all* the drugs hadn't been nicked. The amount of people who let their cats just wander off and get pregnant . . . it's just so irresponsible, and we've got all these sick kittens . . .'

George usually cut her off when she went into a diatribe about cat welfare but he was more concerned about someone seeing the bottle. He pushed her hand back into her bag as he checked no one was around.

For George it still didn't quite feel real. Like they were about to play a childhood prank. But Elle was very serious about it, trying to iron out the plan as they walked together, pushing their bikes. 'Travis says it's easy to get into the condemned building. From there, on the scaffolding, you can get to the parapet and Henry's window.' Henry's room, of course, had skyline views and a makeshift balcony where the parapet wall joined the tiled roof. 'You'll have to unlock it when you're in there with him the day before or something.'

George sniggered.

'Why are you laughing?'

'It's exciting. It's like we're in a movie or something.'

Elle scowled and stopped walking. 'It's not exciting, George. It's serious, we can't mess it up.'

'Sorry.' Chastened, George gave her handlebars a little tug to make her start up again. They walked on in silence, over the Magdalen Bridge, tourists in punts being chauffeured along the water, trees reflecting in the stillness, until George said, 'We're not actually going to be in Oxford though. The whole squad moves to Putney in the lead up to the race.'

'Oh, Jesus Christ! George!'

He made a suitably guilty face. 'Sorry.'

Elle stopped abruptly under a chestnut tree and said, 'Well, how will I get into a house in Putney?'

George shrugged. 'I don't know.'

She closed her eyes for a second in disbelief. George waited, feeling like a fool for not thinking to mention it. Wondering if his Boat Race dreams were about to crumble before his eyes. But then, after a calming breath, to his relief she started to push her bike again. 'Right. What kind of house is it?'

'They're really nice houses, actually,' George said, 'Victorian. Big gardens. The owner cooks for us and does our washing and last year her kid played PlayStation with us.'

Elle glanced across at him, brow raised at the luxury and pampering. 'You lot. It's like you all think you're gods.'

'We are, kind of,' George said.

Elle shook her head. 'No you're not.'

The plan, in the end, relied on an unconventional tactic the coach was trialling. Rather than the crew sitting together the night before enjoying a carb-loading dinner and the traditional glass of pre-race port, the coach wanted each rower to prepare based on a personally tailored psychological plan. Some liked being alone, blocking out the world completely. Some liked being together. JB, Henry and two of the other crewmates were gamers and would burn their nerves off on the PlayStation.

George's plan came down to *Call of Duty*. More specifically, a new instalment of the series that wasn't due to be released till later that year. Unless, of course, your father was Douglas Kingsley and had tentacle connections that stretched into every pocket of commercial industry.

Through Douglas, George managed to secure an early prototype of the game. On the eve of the race he messaged JB who hated getting psyched up and would willingly throw open the doors of the Blue Boat house to anyone bearing such bounty.

Three of the reserve crew, including George, went round and were surreptitiously ushered upstairs so as not to alert moody Klaus, who was taking a nerve-calming bath. JB shared a room with Henry. Henry was sitting on his bed, a big TV on the wall in front of him, waiting to be immersed in violent on-screen enemy pursuit. His lucky Heineken water bottle was on the carpet next to him. The same water bottle as George's. The same one that Elle had so defiantly pooh-poohed when George had suggested the idea of a swap, a memory that, when George successfully switched the bottles, made him feel all the more triumphant.

The moment was short-lived, however. George was so desperate for Henry to drink that he could barely concentrate on anything else. But Henry was entrenched in the game and didn't sip his water once. It was on the tip of George's tongue to say, 'Stay hydrated, guys,' but even he knew that was too obvious, having never said it before.

When JB yawned and said, 'Reckon I need to hit the sack,' the *Call of Duty* spell was suddenly broken. George knew they had to leave. 'Yeah, we should go,' he said, hesitant, irritated, knowing he needed to swap the bottles back before he walked out of the door. 'Just going for a piss,' he added, to kill a bit of time.

George stood in the bathroom trying to work out how he could force Henry to drink. Fear traced up his spine. What if it didn't work? What if he would still end up racing in what his dad now referred to as 'the losers' race' tomorrow? But then it occurred to him that of course it wouldn't work. What was he even thinking? How could he possibly have considered this plan? It was utter madness. He suddenly craved the order and regime of school. His parents' Sunday dinner table. Oh to have old George back who didn't question, just did what he was told and sat in whichever seat he was allocated.

He had to rest his head on the cool bathroom tiles just to get his breathing back to normal. *Calm down, you dickhead. Calm down. Just get the bottle and go. It's over.* It felt almost a relief. The shutting down of the insanity that had overcome him. This wasn't the way a Kingsley behaved. Face up to the fact you lost your seat.

George walked back into the bedroom feeling a little more himself, only to be confronted by the sight of Henry glugging back his water from the Heineken bottle. The only vague reference that anything might be amiss was the look on his face as he replaced the cap.

'The water here tastes like shit.'

George was momentarily paralysed. Was this good or bad? He could hear Elle in his head saying, 'Just get the bottle!' That was the easy bit; he'd dumped his bag and sweater next to where Henry was sitting so, as he collected his stuff, he switched the bottles back quicker than one could say, 'Fuck, I've actually just poisoned my friend.'

CHAPTER TWENTY-ONE

NOW
LILY

Outside on the veranda stood one of the Martini glasses from earlier. A wasp had drowned in the alcohol. Lily watched its floating body as Travis spoke.

'I'm really sorry,' he said. 'I know it was years ago but I feel like you've just found out I cheated on you.'

Lily couldn't take her eyes off the wasp. 'You did cheat on me,' she said. It was a fact. Her therapist once said, 'You like facts, don't you, Lily?' And Lily said, 'Is that a trick question? Surely everyone like facts? They're what keep the world working.'

Undeterred by Lily's deliberate obtuseness, the therapist replied, 'Absolutely, I'd just like to see the same interest devoted to your emotional self.'

Travis was pacing, clenching and unclenching his hands. 'Christ, Caro can be a bitch sometimes.'

Lily didn't want to hear about Caro. She wanted to hear about Travis. About the times Caro had gone to his room or vice versa, or wherever they had their liaisons – probably in a bed underneath the stars. She wanted to know if they'd laughed about her. Mocked her inexperience. If Travis had said things like, 'God, it's so much less hassle with you, Caro.'

Lily dug her fingers into her palms. Dug and dug till she left half-moons in her skin. She wanted to go into the kitchen, get a knife out the drawer and run it clean along her arm.

When the therapist had glimpsed the scars on Lily's stomach, unwittingly as her jumper got caught in her T-shirt as she pulled it over her head, she had said, 'There's a difference, Lily, to feeling things physically and feeling them emotionally.' Lily had tucked her top tight into her jeans and said, 'I one hundred per cent agree with you.' The therapist said, 'You don't have to fight me all the time, Lily. I'm not the enemy. You're allowed to just relax and talk.'

Now on the veranda, Travis took a step closer. Wide shoulders, broad back. She stiffened. She felt like she could smell Caro on him. Had there been others? Or was Travis so lazy he'd just taken what rocked up on his doorstep? She felt like such a fool. He reached out a hand and rested it on her upper arm. She could feel the warmth of his fingers. Could see the lines on his box-fresh T-shirt. Not like the scrawny, scruffy old Travis.

'I'm really sorry. I should have told you at the time. That wasn't the way I wanted you to find out.'

'No, it certainly wasn't optimum.' Lily tried to make light of it, overly aware of his grasp, her skin burning under his touch. She wanted to wriggle free, run with her hands clamped over her ears across the sprinkler-wet lawn. She hated what was happening, what was being said. He would never have told her had Caro not.

'No, not optimum at all,' he said, sensing her discomfort and letting go of her arm, stuffing his hands in the pockets of his cargo trousers. 'You were the best thing about Oxford. I just didn't appreciate it enough at the time. I was an idiot.'

'That I'll agree with.' She forced herself to smile. In the dusky outside light he looked more like the boyish Travis she had known. The shadows obscured the ugly tattoo up his neck and masked the shortness of his hair. He stood watching her, saying nothing.

Lily didn't like being watched. Nor did she like silences between people. She found herself saying, 'Why did you sleep with her? I mean I know why, it's Caro, she's beautiful. I mean, why, as in, why when you were with me?'

He thought for a moment. She could imagine him working out the answer that would please her best. 'Self-sabotage,' he said in the end. 'Like everything.' Beside them, moths darted towards the low light making tiny thrumming noises as their bodies burnt. Travis glanced over at her with big puppy-dog eyes. 'I did always say to never get involved with me.'

Lily surprised herself with a laugh. 'You're surely not still falling back on that one?'

Travis hung his head with an impish grin, his whole demeanour the chastised schoolboy. 'That was a stupid thing to say. I'm sorry.'

Lily nodded. 'It *was* a stupid thing to say.'

He came closer. 'If it's any consolation, I really regret it. I regret it now and I regretted it then.'

She stayed, unmoving, unsure what was about to happen. Feeling a sprint across the damp lawn beckon, she forced herself to pretend she was glued to the seat.

'Can I hug you?' he asked.

Could he? Absolutely not.

He watched, big Bambi eyes.

She thought of her therapist encouraging her to flex her physical barriers: *Become interested, Lily, in what things might feel like.*

Lily looked up at Travis and forced herself to nod.

Tentatively he put his arms around her. There was no denying it was an awkward moment; Lily bolt upright, rigid under his touch. She could smell him, the sweat, the fabric of his T-shirt. His skin. The same but different. She closed her eyes. Felt like she was on a boat, up and down in the waves, desperate to grip something to steady herself. She felt him smell her hair. Her therapist had once said, 'Tell me about the relationship with Travis, Lily. Tell me how it made you feel at the time.'

'It felt like one of the most important things in my life,' she admitted.

'And how does it feel now, looking back on it?'

Lily hadn't wanted to tell her, as if admitting it were to smash it open on the floor, but of course the therapist knew that Lily hated silences by now and let the quiet stretch on and on until Lily said, 'Like the end of everything.'

CHAPTER TWENTY-TWO

THEN
Hilary term, third year
GEORGE

Today was race day. George's alarm hadn't gone off yet. Outside, grey clouds made it impossible to tell what time it was. He was overcome by a strange feeling not unlike Christmas Day as a child. Had Santa been? Was it all a dream?

He looked out at the garden and wondered if anyone had tried yet to wake Henry. His heart beat fast with a mixture of excitement and dread.

He imagined Elle back in Oxford. Should he text her an update? He picked up his phone. No, she'd be furious if he wrote anything down.

On his phone there was a message from JB.

Henry in hospital. Coach heading your way.

Holy fuck.

George threw the phone on the bed. Had to get it away from him. He stared at it like it was alive. He'd fucking poisoned Henry. Henry was in hospital. George was going to jail, no doubt about it. Shit.

Out of the window he saw the minibus pull up outside the house. George was sweating. Liquid dripping down his back. The time it took for the coach to get out of the van, slam the door and head to the house were the worst minutes of George's life to date. What had he done with the water bottle? He searched the room. His heart was going to burst out of his chest. He imagined the court case. The judge. His father. Oh God, his father.

Fear made him hyperventilate. He ran to his en suite, splashed water on his face. Braced himself against the sink. He needed to think of a lie, fast. He needed to find the water bottle. What if they tested Henry? Of course they'd test him. What if he died? What if he *was* dead already? George would be tried for murder. The water bottle was on the side of the bath. He'd left it where he'd washed it out the night before. But now that didn't seem enough. He stood at the sink scrubbing and rubbing at the plastic trying to rid it of any trace before he heard the coach's heavy knock.

George paused before opening the bedroom door, tried to wipe the panic off his face. He focused on how he would act if he knew nothing about what he'd done, if this was just his friend in hospital. He tried to imagine it was JB instead of Henry. He'd be horrified. He'd be shocked.

Coach didn't seem that interested in George's facial expressions, however, and looking pale and ragged himself, his cap in his hands, he said, 'Mind if I sit?', gesturing to the desk chair.

George nodded, sweat beading his brow. 'Of course.'

'You know what's happened?' Coach asked.

George shook his head. 'JB said Henry was in hospital.' *Stay fucking calm.*

Coach sighed. 'It seems at about midnight Henry got up for some reason, got his stuff and got in the car. Which he then promptly crashed into a tree.'

George didn't have to fake his confusion. 'Why?'

Coach sighed. 'Who knows, George. I think that's what the police are trying to find out.'

'Is he okay?' George tried to surreptitiously wipe away the sweat.

'Yes, he's bloody okay.' Coach ran his fingers through what was left of his hair. 'You'll have to forgive me, it's been a very long night.' One of George's crewmates walked past the room on the way downstairs. 'Hawkins,' Coach shouted, 'get someone to bring me a coffee, would you?'

The pulse pumped in George's neck. *Just finish the story,* he urged silently. What was going on? It was too much. He wanted to shout – I did it, I poisoned him!

Coach turned tiredly back to George. 'The doctors believe Henry's confusion was possibly caused by one too many sleeping tablets – there was a packet in his bag.' He shut his eyes momentarily. 'Also in his possession, George, were a variety of other banned substances. Winstrol and Trebolone to name but two.' Disappointment was writ large on the coach's gnarled, weather-beaten face.

George leant fractionally forward. 'Sorry?' Had he heard that right?

'Steroids, diuretics and amphetamines, George.'

Hawkins came in with the coffee. George watched as the coach sipped gratefully from the steaming mug. George almost smiled. Almost laughed. But stopped himself in time.

'Suffice to say,' the coach sighed, 'you'll take his place.'

George nodded, head hung, went through the motions of solemnity the situation required, as if he were stepping up to the task purely for the good of the team. This was no time for whooping and cheering even though his body was fizzing with so much adrenaline his arm almost jerked of its own accord as they ran through the logistics of the day.

But as soon as the coach was out his room, George closed his eyes, raised his arms to the sky and allowed his brain to rejoice in a Hallelujah chorus. Henry Bellinger had been taking steroids. Of course he was. That's how he'd won the trial. The cheating bastard. They'd all been slyly doing what they could to make it. 'Well, well, well,' George muttered. 'Not such a hot shot, eh, Henry?'

George grinned as wide as the Cheshire Cat. He lay back on the bed experiencing a strange euphoria that lifted him out of his body. The plan had worked better than he had ever hoped. Not only was Henry out of the race, he was exposed as a sneaky doping cheat and George could take his place in the Boat Race fair and square. He wasn't the substitute, oh no, he was the rightful owner. He didn't even have to feel guilty about what he'd done because in doing it he had exposed a much worse crime, one that robbed an innocent man of his place in the boat. One could argue that George had been forced into wrongdoing to preserve the fairness and integrity of the race. Now justice had prevailed. George wanted to hold on to the moment forever, victory like rolling waves on a warm beach.

*

Race day was majestic. George was in his element. TV cameras. Interviews. Posing for photographs with his serious race face. Striding down to the water's edge like a hero. Women cheering, calling his name. He was a celebrity. And he lapped up every second. It was everything he ever dreamed it would be.

The two crews raced from Putney to Mortlake, an hour and a half before high tide when the current was at its fastest. Oxford raced on the Middlesex side, Cambridge on the Surrey side. The clouds had vanished and the weather was glorious. Bright, crisp sunshine that bounced off the water in glimmering starbursts. The Tideway was a millpond. The tang of river water infused the air. Spectators jostled on the banks. George was so pumped he was on the cusp of delirium when the umpire's starter gun went off.

The crews were side by side the entire race. It was a gruelling, hellish barrage of effort that didn't let up for a second. But George barely noticed the searing pain in his muscles nor his gasping desperation for breath. He relished every stroke. He fed off the attention of the flotilla of film crews, the relentless hollers of the cox, the umpire yelling for the boats to stay apart. Spittle flew from his lips. Weeks, months, years of training came down to this. They were river gods, brothers of Neptune, their trident oars spurring them to victory. News helicopters and drones buzzed in the sky. Hammersmith Bridge. Chiswick Eyot. Landmarks he'd rowed past since he was fourteen years old. As they went under Barnes Bridge, past the heaving pubs and the rowdy cheers of a million onlookers, George started to feel exhaustion ripping his muscles, cramping his legs. He imagined Henry watching distraught, aflame with envy, from his hospital bed and it gave him the lift he needed. A surge of righteous glee pumped sumptuously through George's aching legs. Every stroke now edged them away from the Cambridge opposition. George knew he'd reached the pinnacle of his life.

When they crossed the finish line, the dark blue Oxford boat was ahead by a length of clear water. A stunning victory for a crew who'd lost a boatman the eve of the race. George was doubled over, heaving for breath, hands shredded and bleeding, limbs wrecked, but his whole body singing triumphant. They were winners; untouchable in their glory. On the bank they were sprayed with champagne as they hugged and backslapped knee-deep in the river. With microphones thrust in his face, George briefly wondered if he was the star of his own film, the plan having come together so beautifully. He didn't think life could get any better. Then his dad stepped out of the crowd, accompanied by his grandfather, the eminent tycoon Piers Kingsley, slower on the slipway with his walking stick. It was the first time in his life George had seen a smile crack the lines of his grandfather's imperious face. Douglas Kingsley pulled his son into a hug, thwacked him on the back, and while happily posing for pictures, said, 'Bloody good work out there. We're proud of you, son.'

That was it, that was the pinnacle.

CHAPTER TWENTY-THREE

NOW
CARO

*Dessert: Sainsbury's Taste the Difference Sicilian
Lemon Tart, crème fraiche and raspberry
coulis (vg. Gü Free From Salted Caramel
Cheesecake)*

They reconvened for dessert. Tension trailed through the room
like the smoke from Caro's snuffed-out Jo Malone candle. Elle
had gone for a fag. Travis didn't look at Caro. Neither did Lily
for that matter. Caro didn't care. Leave him to sulk into his
vegan Gü pot.

She'd pimped up the Sainsbury's tart with icing sugar, slices
of fresh lemon and a quick raspberry coulis. Nigella always
advised having frozen raspberries to hand. She served it up now
with brisk efficiency. Anything but succumb to the squirming
chill in the air.

Ever the well-mannered guest, George opted for politeness,
'Did you make it, Caro?'

'No, Lily bought it from Sainsbury's,' she replied frankly.
Lily blushed.

George said, 'Well, it's a lovely tart, Lily.'

Caro almost laughed, felt on the edge of hysteria. It was funny how someone could blush about bringing a mediocre dessert when the host had just said they'd been shagging your boyfriend.

Elle sauntered back in, blonde hair swept casually to one side, reeking of Marlboro Lights.

'Next letter?' George suggested, mouth full of lemon curd.

Caro leapt on the idea. 'Yes!' She snatched up the letter on the top of the stack. 'Oh, Elle, it's you.'

Elle raised a brow with faux delight. 'Can't wait.'

Caro ripped it open, her emerald bracelets clattering together in her excitement. 'Elle Andrews,' she read, hoping for something that might wipe the smirk off Elle's face, '*will be:* something much less quirky than you'd imagine!' Caro paused to let the words settle, couldn't resist an amused purse of her lips. 'After graduation Elle will succumb to the path of convention, she won't be able to help herself. She'll do an MBA or take up a place on a graduate scheme at PwC and go on to marry someone you'd never expect, like Miles Saunders-Clark.'

'Sounds like I got your one, Caro!' Elle quipped.

Caro's momentary satisfaction vanished and she glared at Elle over the paper. How did she manage to reroute everything so it became a nasty little dig at Caro?

To prevent another spat, George cut in with: 'I bumped into Miles Saunders-Clark the other day.'

'Oh yeah, how was he?' Caro asked. Miles Saunders-Clark was the kind of ex-Oxford guy that everyone remembered and everyone knew. Larger than life in size and personality.

Went to every party, knew everyone, loudest voice in the room, craziest on the dancefloor, geekiest in the tutorials.

'Did you know he got done for plagiarism? Never graduated?'

Across the table, Travis said, 'He can join my club,' while digging into his little pot of salted caramel.

Elle declined dessert. 'That's what happens if you get someone else to write your essays for you.'

George said, 'Never did me any harm.'

It got a laugh. Precisely why he'd said it, keep it all light and jovial. But Elle's scorn was apparent in the expression on her face.

Caro rolled her eyes. 'Oh, for God's sake, don't be so sanctimonious. Everyone did it.'

Elle scoffed. 'No they didn't. Some of us actually *did* the work.'

'Well, weren't you perfect?' Caro replied, relishing the opportunity to goad Elle for a change. Elle sat back, arms crossed over her red dress like her outfit no longer suited her mood, shaking her head with clear disapproval.

Caro wondered whether to say what she was about to say. She'd never told anyone. But the chance to be the reckless one in the face of Elle's priggishness made her blurt out, 'They hauled me in after Henry died, actually, because of similarities in essays. I was petrified.'

'They didn't?' George paused, his fork of lemon tart at his lips.

Elle's curiosity had been piqued enough for her to cock her head and listen.

'They did!' Caro was feeling smug now at the attention. Puffed up with pride that she had the ears of the table. 'I almost got away with it. Played the sympathy card. Told them everything I knew, thought a bit of quid pro quo might get me off with a warning. But—' She made a guilty face. 'I didn't graduate either. They didn't let me take my final exams.'

George frowned. 'But I remember you taking them.'

'Well, I went through the motions, George, because I didn't want anyone to know. But I didn't *actually* sit the exams.' Caro felt positively impish.

George sat back, stunned. 'I can't believe it!'

Caro slapped her own wrist playfully. 'Naughty Caro.'

Elle's lip curled in a sneer. 'And you're proud of that?'

Caro shrugged like she couldn't care less. Fiddled nonchalantly with her earring. She felt great at having subverted their expectations. She was the cool, rule-breaking one now. 'It's never done me any harm. I tell everyone I got a First from Oxford. No one's ever challenged me on it.'

They all laughed. Except Elle, who sat disgusted at the head of the table twirling her wine glass and said, 'I suppose that's what happens if you marry for money and never have to get a job.'

Caro made the kind of fuck-you face she told her twins off for making.

Elle arched one icy brow in return.

The room fell into silence again.

George said, 'How about we read the next letter? Should be mine, I think.'

CHAPTER TWENTY-FOUR

THEN
Hilary term, third year
LILY

When Lily was younger, her nan read Mills & Boon romances. She subscribed and had hundreds of them. They were in boxes in the attic and lined the shelves in various rooms. When she got older and lost her sight, she would say, 'Read to me, Lily.' They weren't Lily's kind of book. Lily was one of those kids who'd read everything in the library and had them order in more. She read a lot of non-fiction; books on biodiversity in agricultural ecosystems that made her mum sigh as she and her dad got into what she would call one of their deep, dull discussions. But Lily also read loads of crime thrillers; her whizzy brain loved a puzzle to solve in its downtime.

When Lily first started reading romance fiction to her nan, she was very disparaging. Laughing at the titles of her beloved books and trying to skip over all the naughty bits. Lily was always the clever one in the family and reading romance was not for an academic like her. But then, when her nan nestled back with her cup of tea and the blissful expression appeared on her face, completely unselfconscious, Lily started to relax, let go of her sardonic snobbishness and allowed herself the pure indulgence of those sweeping romances in far-off places with brooding heroes and plucky young heroines. She came to adore them. Whether it was the cosiness of the house, her nan's exquisite happiness or just the utter escape from her frenetic brain, those reading visits became the best time of her week. She left high on the promise of true love and happy endings, a joy that fast deteriorated when back in the thick of fights and tantrums with her brothers.

The time Lily spent with Travis after that night under the stars was like her very own Mills & Boon. Although their relationship wasn't perfect – Travis still too emotionally closed to fully commit and Lily too self-consciously shy – she was higher than cloud nine. They had perfected a delicate balance of pretence that they were nothing more than friends while waiting for one another outside lectures, but snogging like crazy when no one was looking. When they walked home Travis said things like, 'Mind if I rest my arm on your shoulders, it's really aching. Slept on it weirdly.' And Lily said, 'Yeah I have that problem sometimes. Go ahead,' while internally grinning.

Spring was in the air, daffodils and daisies scattered over the lawns as they sat stretched in the sunshine staring up at the pale blue sky, their fingers interlaced. At night Lily would go to bed way before Travis. The first time they slept in the same bed she came out of the bathroom in her pyjamas and he was hanging around on the landing. 'I was just . . .' and then he grinned and Lily went bright red, but then he came into her room and he kissed her and it was like in the books, except he tasted of cigarette smoke and smelt of weed and whichever one of their shower gels he'd nicked in the bathroom. His lips were soft and gentle. His hand pressed the base of her spine. His fingers threaded through her hair. Sometimes Lily wondered if he'd read the same romance books to his nan, he knew so perfectly what to do. And he lay next to her, their bodies pressed together, the beat of their hearts as one, until Lily fell asleep and he went back downstairs to get stoned.

A calmness settled over the house while George was away for the Boat Race. It was Easter vacation. Caro had gone to London a couple of days beforehand to stay with friends. Lily loved it, just the three of them: her, Travis and Elle. But then when Elle got the messages from George about what had happened to Henry, the car crash and the steroids, the scandal was addictive. They all decided to get on the train to London with Elle to cheer George on, even Travis. There was a thrill to being in the thick of things. Nudging their way to the front of the riverbank crowd, Elle in her big pink scarf and vintage denim, her waft of cigarette smoke, pint sploshing, Lily, wearing Travis's jumper because it was chillier in the shade than she'd anticipated, felt the high of being part of something. She got a buzz from knowing all the facts when she heard gossipy speculation from bystanders about what had really happened with Henry Bellinger and George Kingsley. No longer on the fringes, Lily was a bona fide member of the in-crowd. Travis stood beside her, blinking like a mole in the daylight, disgruntled at being out and about (and now inappropriately dressed for the cold), dropping acerbic asides that made the spectators flinch and Lily giggle as she stood close to him to warm him up.

Back in Oxford, post all the race hullabaloo, George strutted back into the house, kit bag over his shoulder, talking on the phone, his booming cut-glass voice filling the hallway. When he came into the living room and chucked his bag on the sofa, Travis looked at him and said, 'Your head's so big I'm surprised it fits through the door.'

George guffawed, clearly unable to contain the enormous smile on his face. His skin was grey-tinged from all the celebrations but his eyes shone. Drained of sleep but wired from his win. His phone had a constant stream of messages. People knocked on the door for him to ask about the race, to find out what had happened. Suddenly everyone knew him. He was giving interviews to newspapers. Asked to pose for a feature in a Sunday supplement.

Elle seemed to watch it all with detached bemusement. As if her child had excelled in something she didn't quite understand but was happy for them all the same.

When finally George's phone stopped ringing, he collapsed on the sofa, feet up on the coffee table covered in empty Coke cans, ashtrays and Lily's textbooks because she was working on an essay. 'So my dad's insisting on throwing a party to celebrate the race. You're all invited. He'll slap a whack of cash behind the bar. Free everything. It's gonna be good.'

Elle was drinking a cup of tea, curled up in the corner of the sofa. She didn't look enamoured by the idea. 'Do you need another party? Didn't you already celebrate?'

Lily, Travis and Elle had hunted George down after the race but they didn't stay long. He was too distracted by all the attention, sticky from champagne. Elle said, 'This is my worst kind of George.' And they left, back to Oxford where the leaves were out on all the trees and the familiar buildings enveloped them in a cosy sense of home. They strolled the narrow backstreets to the pub, ate pie and mash, lost the quiz, then watched films all night.

As he lay sprawled on the sofa, George stretched his arms out, toyed with Elle's hair. 'This is more than a one-night celebration, Elle, my darling. This is the stuff of lifetimes.' You could see he was high on it all, pumped from the attention, the drama, the race, the adoration. He sat with his legs spread wide, like a king. Out of place in the living room among the ignorant peasants. To Elle he said, 'I'll take you shopping for something to wear, buy anything you like.'

Elle laughed. 'I don't want anything, Georgie.'

George dismissed her refusal. 'You can choose anything. Anything you like! Money no object.'

Elle thought for a second then said, 'There is actually a pair of leather leggings I quite like.'

George said, 'What about a nice dress?'

Elle raised a brow while finishing off her tea. 'I think you might have got me confused with someone else, Georgie.'

Travis, who was sitting in the armchair absorbed in pulling a loose thread on his shirt till the button fell off, laughed. Lily was on a cushion on the floor at his feet, pretending to work at the coffee table but distracted by the chat. She could feel the laughter vibrate through him.

George looked momentarily put out, his machismo and adrenaline-fuelled arrogance finding no place there.

Lily listened, considering the strange juxtaposition that existed inside herself. The idea of someone offering to buy her a dress for the ball, something exquisitely expensive that might make the whole room stop to whisper, 'Who's that girl?', was so bang on the fairy tale she felt a ball of envy tight in the pit of her stomach. Yet in reality she couldn't imagine anything worse; she didn't like being looked at, didn't dance and would stick shyly to the fringes for the whole evening feeling overdressed in her showy gown.

With Elle mocking his offer, George seemed to remember where he was, who he was with and laughing said, 'Fine, yes, absolutely, have your leggings.' Then he heaved himself up. 'I'm going to have a shower. I stink.'

Travis had started rolling a joint. He looked at Elle and said, 'That party sounds like hell.'

Elle tipped her head up to the ceiling, blonde curls trailing down her back. 'Tell me about it.'

Lily looked between them, wondering how the hell she'd got herself in with people who out-cooled the varsity gang. Who didn't need a gown or a ball, actively shunned it in fact. This was the real fairy tale. Sitting there, cosily curled up next to Travis, Elle all languid and insouciant by the window, was all Lily actually wanted. It was almost too good to be true.

CHAPTER TWENTY-FIVE

NOW
GEORGE

The letter in Caro's hand had George's name on it. He was actually pretty excited to hear what had been predicted for him. He pretended he wasn't, sat back with a couldn't-really-care-less expression on his face, but he expected something along the lines of what had been written for Caro: big house in the country, lots of parties, couple of horses, Rolls-Royce. Something he could take home and show his wife Audrey, and she'd say, well they weren't far off, were they?

Caro straightened out the paper and read, 'George *will be*: in an office.'

George snorted a laugh. He was indeed in an office. A very nice corner one overlooking the river.

Caro flicked her hair back off her shoulders, took a sip of sparkling water and carried on, 'One of those ones in films where everyone has their own grey booth. A photo of their wife and their own mug that says something like, "I'd rather be playing golf". He hates his job, despises his colleagues and wishes he made more money but his boss has said he's perfect middle-management material.' Caro snorted a laugh, didn't seem to be able to help herself.

George tried to maintain his relaxed lounging pose but it was a struggle. He *was* middle-management. He wouldn't always be but it was important to move around departments, experience the full range, if one was going to make it to CEO. He tucked his shirt in a bit tighter, straightened the napkin in his lap.

Over the other side of the table Travis was smirking into his Gü pot. He could talk, George thought irritably, he hadn't even been able to listen to his.

'Oh goodness,' Caro said, fanning her cheeks, a little embarrassed as she carried on. 'George doesn't have time to get to the gym so all his muscle has turned to fat . . . Who wrote this? It's very mean . . . His suits are too tight and – oh no!' She cringed. 'He's thinking about shaving his head to hide the fact he's losing his hair.'

George's hand went immediately up to his head but he stopped himself just before he could touch the thinning bald spot at the back. He wanted to tell Caro to shut up but couldn't. Thought of the Peloton bike he'd wanted to order but hadn't got round to. He was so tired from broken nights with the baby that the idea of cycling and not getting anywhere was too much of a mockery of his former life. One where him and a bunch of mates chose a scenic cycle route every weekend with a good little gastro pub along the way.

Caro went on, casting George a sad glance and a sympathetic pat on the leg. '*Will live*: George will live in suburbia. Any one of those places at the end of the train line. He'll have two children, a dog, a mortgage, a pension—'

He couldn't look at Elle. Couldn't bear that she was sitting alongside him listening.

There was nothing wrong with any of those things, for goodness' sake. Yet why did each word feel so damning? So average? Was that what they thought of him? Average George? Was that who he was? Audrey was already talking about baby number two. A guy at his work, Frank, had told his wife that she could have as many as she liked as long as he didn't have to do anything to help, which she'd apparently been fine with. George certainly felt a twinge of envy as Frank regaled him with stories of coked-up Friday nights and lads-only trips to Copenhagen, but knew such a life wasn't for him. Audrey was not the kind of wife who would take kindly to a similar suggestion; that was one of the reasons George had married her. His dad would say things like, 'Better in our day, men didn't have to do a thing.' And Audrey would glare at him across the table.

George had been very proud of that glare. Kudos to anyone who could stand up to his father. And George loved the time he spent with baby Raffy, reading him *The Gruffalo* and marvelling at his tiny fingers. But right now it all felt banally textbook.

He sat up, rested his elbows on the table, steepled his fingers and listened, as if this were the most riveting, amusing of tales.

'George will marry a nice but dull brown-haired girl called something like Bonnie who has a nice smile and good teeth but never quite loses the baby weight. They'll stay together for the sake of the children.'

What had he wanted? For it to read that George was a three-time Olympic gold medallist who now splits his time between houses in Barbados and Mayfair and is married to a supermodel? Yes! Yes, anything but the mundanity that his life had actually taken. Could there be anything worse than being predicted average? For people not even to believe you might veer from the norm?

'Golly,' Caro folded up the paper, took a sip of wine to hide her embarrassed pity. 'Bit harsh.'

'Harsh but fair,' Travis laughed; he'd got his sense of humour back.

George tried to laugh too, but it sounded false even to his own ears. At the head of the table, he could feel Elle's gaze. He made the mistake of glancing over. Saw the amusement in her expression. He wondered if she'd written it. Had been the one to predict him so accurately. He felt disgusted with his life, ashamed even. He felt both embarrassed and protective of Audrey's post-baby weight. He would never wish his child away but . . . God, he was so boring. He'd once been someone who was so driven by ambition he'd poisoned his fellow athlete in competition. He'd won the Boat Race! Got a degree from Oxford. Run the Marathon des Sables. None of these people had done that. Where was that George? The one who took risks? Dated women like Elle? Lay with his head on her breasts and inhaled skin that smelt of cigarettes and Chanel?

He found himself having to control his breathing. Steady in and out. The others were talking, he didn't know what about, he had zoned out entirely. Elle was staring at him. She hadn't joined in the chat. Her eyes were locked on his, enticing, daring. He felt his lip draw back, his teeth bare in annoyance. He saw the paper with his name on it casually discarded on the table by Caro, his whole life summed up in a few derogatory lines. He had to be worth more than that. More than the sum of his pension, his boring job and his brown-haired wife.

He closed his eyes. He opened them. Elle was half smiling. She knew, she'd always been able to read his every thought.

George lifted his napkin from his lap, wiped the corners of his mouth, stood up and said, 'Excuse me,' then he walked as calmly as he could from the room, every fibre of his being knowing that she would follow.

CHAPTER TWENTY-SIX

THEN
Trinity term, third year
GEORGE

George felt like a different man after the Boat Race. He wouldn't compare himself to Christ out loud, but in his head this was the start of his Anno Domini years. Even Elle's wry take on his swaggering pomposity couldn't bring him down. The story of his last-minute addition to the boat – plus an elite doping scandal – meant journalists had clamoured to interview him and George even appeared, bare-chested and brandishing an oar, on the front of the *Sunday Times Magazine*. There was nothing more exhilarating than walking down the high street seeing his own golden muscles gleaming back at him as people relaxed with a cappuccino and the paper. His father had a framed copy in the Knightsbridge downstairs loo.

Henry Bellinger was discharged from hospital with bruising to his face and chest. Apparently, it hurt to breathe and laugh. But he wasn't doing much laughing. Back at Oxford he stalked about like a newly caged tiger awaiting his fate.

If George was honest, seeing Henry brought him down – the

puffy face and the self-pitying sullenness – but his role as the victor meant he could afford to bestow magnanimity when Henry came to offer an apology flanked by his dad, Sir Charles, who was mid-treatment for a particularly aggressive cancer and looked grey and thin as he waved away George's offer to come inside for a cup of tea. 'Can't stay long,' Sir Charles said. 'Just wanted you to know that we are sorry.' Henry looked at the pavement. Sir Charles went on to add that there was no place and no excuse for performance-enhancing drugs in sport, said he couldn't apologize enough for what George had been through. George felt his face colour, both boys in the end staring at the floor as Sir Charles spoke.

As they were leaving, Henry muttered something about going on a bike ride later. Seemed to imply that he wanted George to come but clearly the apology had taken as much of his self-respect as he was willing to sacrifice and he couldn't bring himself to ask outright. It was the sad hope on Sir Charles's face that George bore them no ill will that led him to say he'd join him. He just hoped Henry's injuries meant they wouldn't go very far. They barely went a mile before Henry stopped cycling. He pulled over onto a grassy verge and sat with his head hung, shoulders moving up and down slowly. George had a horrible feeling that he was building up to something; maybe an accusation in George's direction about what had actually happened that night. But when George got closer he saw that Henry was crying, great wracking sobs.

George swallowed his own paranoia and reached out to rest his hand on Henry's shoulder. 'Come on, it's okay, mate.' He beckoned for Henry to abandon the bike and sit down on the grass.

Henry wiped his face with his sleeve. 'Fuck, this is embarrassing.'

George said, 'No, don't worry. It's fine.' Quashing the little buzz it gave him to see Henry reduced to this.

Henry pressed his hands into his eyes. 'They stripped me of everything. Every medal. Everything.'

George knew Henry and Sir Charles had been at the disciplinary meeting that morning. 'Coach just sat there. Two-year ban. Won't row here again. Nothing.' Henry's jaw clenched. 'And my dad hearing it all, it was so humiliating.' He squeezed his eyes shut. 'He's dying. I only did it for my dad, and he's dying.'

George didn't like to think of Sir Charles dying. How could such a titan shrink to nothing; where would all that energy and strength go? 'It'll be okay,' he said. 'He's having treatment.'

Henry shook his head, plucked handfuls of grass from the verge. 'He won't be okay. And I've let him down.'

'He'll forgive you,' said George, feeling quite uncomfortable about the fact the party his own father was throwing to celebrate George's Blue was later that evening. 'He loves you. And he's a good guy.'

Henry turned to look at George, expression doleful. 'He couldn't even look at me.'

George thought of Sir Charles's face when he'd stood on the doorstep. His thin, tired body emanating shame at what his son had done; like Henry had shaken the very foundations of everything Sir Charles had worked for in his life. 'It'll be okay,' George said again, but not with quite the conviction he'd hoped.

Henry bashed the dry ground with his fist, then sat with his head in his hands.

George focused on a ladybird climbing a blade of grass and tried not to think of the water bottle laced with Xylazine and his own part in the debacle.

Later that evening, as he was getting ready for the big party, George said to Elle, 'Henry should have thought of what the consequences of getting caught would be before he decided to cheat. Yeah?'

Elle looked at him and laughed. 'You're joking, right?'

George buttoned up his new shirt. 'I'm just saying—'

'I know what you're saying, Georgie,' she grinned.

George was aware of an underlying tension at play between them since he'd made it into the Blue Boat. When he was with Elle he was reminded that the self-righteousness he'd cultivated since being selected was built on shaky foundations. A reality he was less fond of acknowledging.

Elle was lazing on his bed in her pyjamas, her blonde curls, damp from the shower, tumbling over her shoulders. She was flicking through the magazine with his face on the cover, her wet hair dangerously close to the pages. He wanted to warn her not to damage it.

'Shouldn't you be getting ready?' he asked, deliberately changing the subject, pulling the tag off the new socks he'd bought. Everything he was wearing tonight was new. New trainers, new shirt; he wanted to look good and smell good. Tonight was his night and he didn't want anything to detract from it. Everyone was going: the hockey team, the gymnasts, the rugby boys, all the rowers. But George was star attraction, his dad was paying for everyone's fun. It was the kind of party he would remember for the rest of his life.

Elle chucked the magazine onto his desk. George straightened it out. 'Are you sure you need me there?' she asked, 'They're not really my people and I'm wondering if I might just get in your way.' Her tone, as if she were doing him a favour, immediately annoyed him.

'Yes, I need you there,' he said, yanking on the socks, trying not to sound irritated. 'Come on, it's one night!'

'I know, but it's just going to be a load of rowers who haven't had a drink for a year getting wasted.' She made a face of distaste. 'I have so much work to do this weekend.'

Why did she do this to him? He couldn't go to his own party without his date. Elle was one of the best-looking girls in the whole of bloody Oxford, he wanted to show her off.

'People will think it's weird if you're not there.'

'Travis isn't going,' said Elle by way of excusing herself.

'Travis doesn't go anywhere! Please, just come for me.' It annoyed George that he had to plead.

Elle slumped back on the pillows. 'Fine.'

'Well. . .' George gestured towards the door. 'Go and get ready.' Why couldn't she just be like a normal doting girlfriend? Someone like Caro, for example, who would go to the ends of the earth for Henry. Who had sat at his hospital bedside and nursed his aching ribs. Who, as if on cue, when the doorbell rang downstairs, came dashing out of her room all dolled up in glamorous red sequins – exactly the type of dress George had wanted Elle to wear.

Caro's hair was only half done, her feet bare. She peered over the banister. 'Did I hear the bell? If that's Henry, I'm not ready yet.' Then she looked at Elle. 'Are you going like that?'

Elle gave Caro the same disparaging look. 'Are *you* going like *that*?'

'Sorry, did you say something?' Caro pretended she hadn't heard and went back into her room to finish doing her make-up.

Downstairs, Lily came out the living room to answer the door.

George went back to finish getting ready and calm his irritation. He saw his *Sunday Times Magazine* cover shot. Held it up and stared at himself in all his glory and remembered whose night this was.

George's self-adoration was interrupted by a sudden thump on his bedroom door which made him jump. Then he heard Henry Bellinger's voice shout, 'George, get in here, Trav's got a fucking medicine cabinet going on.'

George came out of his room to see Henry in Travis's bedroom next door. People had been coming all day to see Travis. One of the rugby boys, Paris Nikolaidis, was currently snorting coke off the mantelpiece, while Anders Black, captain of the hockey team, was counting crisp fifties into Travis's palm.

'Got the best in especially for you boys.' Travis was sitting on his bed. His special edition Harry Potter box set had been taken off the shelf and the doors of the fancy presentation case opened. Inside, rather than housing books, the case was divided up into smart compartments, each full of little plastic bags, beautifully categorized and labelled.

Henry started riffling through the packets. 'You've branched out since I lived here, Trav.'

Travis shrugged. 'Supply and demand, Henry. People ask for it, I get it.'

Paris and Anders left together, Anders slapping George on the shoulder as he went. 'See you later, buddy.'

George watched as Henry took Anders' place on the bed to get a better look at the goods. George was more of a boozer himself, never could handle anything much stronger than a beer. But Henry had the constitution of an ox – *'those years at Eton served me well'* – and was piling up little packets as Travis calculated the tally with more mental alertness than he showed in any other area of his life.

'You sure this is a good idea, Henry?' George asked, tentative because this was not the weeping Henry of earlier but a Henry hyped with nervous energy who already had a touch of mania in his eyes.

Henry smacked him on the arm. 'Chill out, Mumsie.'

Travis snorted a laugh.

George licked his lips. He didn't want Henry here. Already he was killing his buzz.

Henry got his wallet out, checked how much money he had. He said, 'I thought about it, George, and well . . . like you said, my dad's a good guy, he'll get over it, won't he? What do you think, Trav? Reckon you'd forgive this face?' Henry pointed to his own bruised, puffy features.

'In an instant,' Travis drawled, eyes focused on the notes in Henry's hand.

Henry laughed then winced, held his ribs. His breath told George he'd been drinking already, must have been in the bar all afternoon. 'I don't need this shit.' Henry gestured to the house, the surroundings, Oxford in general. 'Who even cares? It doesn't fucking mean anything.'

George wanted to say that it did mean something. But knew better than to say anything.

Henry went on, 'Reckon I might take up boxing. That's

more my kind of thing.' He grinned, came up closer to George. 'Boxing, George? What do you think?' Henry lifted his fists then punched George hard in the stomach before he had a chance to brace himself.

Travis went, 'Whoa!'

George doubled over, coughing, wondering if he might be sick on Travis's carpet.

Henry laughed. 'Sorry, mate.'

George straightened up, hand on his stomach, wincing. 'That's okay.'

Henry went to punch him again but stopped just before he hit; still George recoiled. Henry did it again, then again, goading. Eyes wild. Like with every hit he was reclaiming his status. Hauling himself up from the weak, weeping version of himself that he'd laid bare that afternoon. Intent on showing George who was boss. Who would always be boss. 'Let me buy you something to celebrate *your* race!' Henry said, flashing his big white teeth like a crocodile. 'It all worked out for you, didn't it, George?'

George didn't know how to reply. He swallowed, uncomfortable under the intensity of Henry's wild darting eyes.

Then Henry whacked him again, harder this time. 'Lighten up, man.' Laughing, he went back to the Harry Potter drug box.

George could feel Travis's pity. Could feel the echo of his own meekness in the wake of Henry's power and hated it.

There was a cough from the doorway. Caro appeared. She looked sensational, skin-tight red sequins cascading to the floor like liquid and a slit up her thigh that left little to the imagination. George had never seen her look so good, with her glossy hair slicked back, pouting scarlet lips. But Henry's attention was absorbed elsewhere, he was saying, 'I still can't believe you have half this stuff, Trav.' He cast a quick glance at Caro adding, 'Hey honey, you want anything?'

Caro ran her tongue over her lips. Waiting for the compliment that never came.

George said, 'You look amazing, Caro.' But it didn't have the same effect as if Henry had said it. She knew better than to sulk though, that wasn't the way to appease Henry. Instead she sidled up next to him, slipped her arm round his waist, her hand into his jeans pocket and giggled excitedly down at Travis's stash like she was a kid in a sweetshop.

Henry had put George on edge. Made him stressed. He wanted to get to his party, get back to being the star rather than skulk in Henry's shadow.

But then as if on cue, Elle sauntered into the room looking effortlessly cool in her leather leggings, white T-shirt and a black and red matador jacket embellished in gold. Her hair, pinned haphazardly, fell around her perfect pale face in a cloud of curls. Her letter box-red lips glistened. Henry paused when he caught sight of her. George felt his blood sing with pride. In that one moment, like a parachute snapping open, he was pulled straight back to the top spot.

Next to Elle, Caro looked overdressed, gaudy even. She watched Henry's lascivious gaze with eyes narrowed in envy.

Elle didn't seem to notice the effect she had on the room or she pretended not to. She went over to Travis's box, picked up a bag full of white pills and examined the label.

Travis snatched it off her. 'Can you not touch if you're not buying.'

Elle scoffed. 'Calm down.' She turned away, said to George, 'Are we going?'

By the bed, Henry wasn't finished riffling through the goods. 'All in good time,' he said, like his was the voice of authority.

But George wanted to get out of there as soon as possible. 'We'll start walking, meet you there.'

'Just wait,' Henry said in a tone that made George seem foolishly stressed. 'We won't be long.'

'I have to call a cab,' said Caro. 'I can't walk in these heels.'

Henry pulled a stack of twenties out of his wallet. 'Well call a cab!' he said, irritated at the turn of events. Then to Travis, 'Why aren't you coming?'

Travis shrugged. 'Not a party kind of person.'

Caro, annoyed that Henry had snapped, said goadingly, 'I think he wants a night in with his *girlfriend*.'

'Trav, you're blushing!' Henry whooped.

Caro smiled, pleased with herself for making Travis go red. To George and Elle, her confidence back in place, she drawled, 'We'll take a cab. You two go ahead.'

'Gladly.' Elle sauntered away.

As he went with her, George let his hand rest possessively on Elle's bottom, energized by the obvious envy in Henry's gaze. Glad to get away from Travis's starkly depressing bedroom. This was his moment and no one was going to spoil it. He had Elle. He had the party. Life was good. The best it had ever been, in fact.

CHAPTER TWENTY-SEVEN

NOW
GEORGE

George left Caro's dining room, walked out into the low-lit hallway with its mahogany console table and giant gilt mirror. Once out there, though, he wasn't quite sure where to go. Did he wait? Just stand out here hoping Elle would come? Did he turn and beckon to her through the gap in the door? Christ, was he even cut out for this? Yes. There was that same pumping excitement that he hadn't felt since he was with her. That night she'd suggested they take Henry out of the race. . . When she'd first come into his bedroom and unpeeled her boots. . . The feeling that life could be more than the things he and his wife now fretted about: *The Good Schools Guide*, who could get them Soho House membership, Courchevel 1850 or Gstaad, how much the fucking dog walker charged.

He leant his head against the wall. You can do this, George.

'It can't be that bad,' said Elle's voice behind him, and George felt a rush through his body.

He turned and there she was, ruched red dress, messy

blonde hair, thin coltish legs. It was like he'd conjured her from his memory.

Elle smiled, that wonky, confident grin. She had her jacket over her shoulders and a pack of Marlboro Lights in her hand, fooling the others that she was going out for a fag but instead put her hand on his shoulder and gestured to a room across the hall. He walked ahead of her towards a posh sitting room kept for special occasions. Dark teal walls, plush velvet sofas that weren't covered in sticky fingers. Expensive ornaments and a glass coffee table. George had one too. It was mainly where Audrey watched TV when they'd had a row.

Elle was so close behind him he could feel her breath on his neck as she said, 'I thought this room looked particularly comfortable.'

CHAPTER TWENTY-EIGHT

George couldn't have asked for more. The party was no expense spared. A limitless tab behind the bar. Achingly hip DJ. Food that would either get eaten or hurled in drunken fun. The boat club boys were happily wasted having necked pre-party drinks in the cox, Marco De Poligny's JCR. It didn't take much. Klaus had a bottle of Grey Goose in one hand and sambuca in the other. 'Thank your dad, yeah, George!' he shouted.

George gave him a thumbs-up. JB was at the bar with the others from the crew, all wearing their Blue Boat blazers. Perspiring happily into the woollen signifiers of their status. George had carried his, didn't want to wear it in front of Henry. But now he slipped it on and felt like the god he was meant to be. Girls immediately flocked, preening on the peripheries of the group but seen off by Elle's condescending stare. JB handed round a tray of tequilas, thrust one at George. George passed his on to Elle but she waved it away.

'I've got to work all day tomorrow.'

'Oh come on,' urged George. 'Just one.'

Elle took it, reluctant. George grinned.

JB held up his shot. 'To all of you losers!'

They were about to drink when Henry's voice cut in from behind them, 'Hey, where's mine?' He'd just arrived, Caro tottering by his side. He cast around to see who was standing with a shot, took in what they were wearing; George could almost feel each £200 Blue Boat blazer mocking Henry's failure.

'Oh I see.' Henry tipped his head, bowing out with raised hands, reverent as if in prayer. 'I bring only disgrace here.'

An embarrassed tension rippled over the group.

Elle rolled her eyes and, downing her shot, pushed away from the group to go and stand with some people from her course. George felt the loss of her by his side. He wanted Henry gone. His presence was like a dark cloud over them all. He handed him his own tequila. 'Here, Henry, have mine.'

For a moment, Henry just stared at the glass. George's insides tightened. Somehow the gesture seemed suddenly patronising rather than pacifying. He remembered the punch earlier, could feel the pulse of Henry's coiled-up energy. But then Henry simply took the drink from George's hand and said, 'What are we toasting? How shit you all were without me?'

The laughs were swallowed up by the music.

George felt disorientated. Like he was reading too much emotion where there was none. He ordered more drinks for the group. Henry cut in shouting for doubles, loud and aggressive. Caro hung around next to him, smiling like a plastic doll, not speaking; the music was too loud to hear anything. George searched the crowd for Elle, glimpsed her over the far side of the room. But then Klaus started shouting drinking game rules. Barging between George and Henry, pushing them apart. Shots were lined up five deep. Marco De Poligny was forced to snort the tequila he'd spilled off the bar. George was laughing.

The girls Elle had shooed away flocked back, their hands pulling up George's shirt to stroke his pecs, squeezing his arm muscles, stealing his drinks, pressing themselves adoringly to his side. In the mirrored bar he could see the lipstick marks on his cheek. The drinks kept coming. The whole evening was a blur of lights and colour. At one point, a hockey girl started stripping on the bar. The barman tried to get her down. She slipped in the mess of alcohol and fell on a table of drinks. When they hauled her up, her front was lacerated by glass. Blood ran into the champagne on the table in a river of red. They carried her out crying. George could only see the blood. Everywhere. He thought he saw Elle in the corner but when he pushed through to find her he only came across the captain of the polo team getting a blow job from the women's VIII cox. 'Sorry,' he said, disorientated. The guy grinned.

George was so drunk he could barely stand. The music thumped. The night had no end or beginning, time jumped, got longer, got shorter. He wondered if his drink had been spiked. But it was more likely the shots, one after the other; it was a lot for a body that wasn't used to alcohol. He made his way back to the bar, the rest of the crew still there. Klaus welcomed him, arms wide. 'You're a winner, George!'

George nodded, slurring with satisfaction. 'I *am* a winner.'

Henry appeared. He was fucked. His eyes were huge. His hair a mess. All down his shirt was wet. 'Where's Caro?' he shouted in George's ear.

'I don't know,' George hollered back.

'Good!' laughed Henry. Then he threw his arm around JB's shoulder, and beckoning Klaus inwards, created a huddle away from the rest of the throng. 'I'll tell you who's the real winner, boys.'

Klaus said, 'Who?'

Henry ran his tongue over his teeth and drawled proudly, 'You're looking at him. Yours truly here has nailed the list.'

'Fuck off, you have,' said Marco de Poligny.

'I can give you names and numbers, Marco dear boy.' Henry's mouth stretched into a smug, humourless smile. 'May not have made the boat but I've fucking won this one and none of you fuckers are going to take it away from me.' He rolled his shoulders back, slapped his chest with his hands like the king gorilla.

Klaus tipped his head. 'You got *everything*?'

'Everything.' Henry repeated. The tone of his voice brooked no arguments.

But Marco wasn't convinced. 'Who did you have a three-some with?' he quizzed.

'Some friend of Caro's from her course. Very obliging young woman.'

Marco narrowed his eyes, clearly didn't trust a word Henry was saying.

Henry leaned forward, eyes veined red, drunken spittle flying from his mouth, 'You don't have to believe me, mate, but I know it, up here.' Henry tapped his head. 'I've won your little game, fair and square. And for that, I deserve a fucking medal.'

'You got *everything* else?' Marco asked, just to be sure.

Henry leant forward. 'Everything,' he said slowly and clearly.

George looked nervously around for Caro. Henry was getting louder, mouthing off about his conquests. Bragging about what he'd done where. JB's eyes widened as he listened, hauling his inebriated body from where he was half slumped against the bar so as not to miss a word. Even Marco relented, giggling like a kid as Henry reeled off the contents of his list.

George couldn't believe that Henry had managed to turn the tables, make himself the star of the party. He wanted to kick his legs from under him and go back to being the one heralded by Klaus. Instead Klaus was patting Henry heartily on the back saying in amazement, 'Bloody hell. You are a hero, Henry.' Then he grinned. 'Barman, your best champagne.'

Henry grinned, wet mouth glistening in the spotlights, like he'd redeemed himself of every wrong that had gone before. 'I *am* a hero,' he repeated.

CHAPTER TWENTY-NINE

NOW
GEORGE

George felt like a trespasser in Caro's expensive sitting room that smelt of the shops his wife liked perusing while he stood outside with the pram and his phone. Elle had no such issues; she walked in like she owned the place, chucked her jacket on the sofa and her fags on the coffee table.

'Don't be shy, Georgie.'

George shook his head. 'I'm not shy.' But he was. He was polite and nervous. He'd thought this was a great idea but inside he was quivering. He wanted to touch her but didn't know if he could. She turned so she was facing him, open, inviting, looking up at him through lowered lids, an expression he knew so well, remembered in his dreams. Woke up still with it burned on his retinas. He had never forgotten her. She lived in the back of his memory as the one that got away. Who offered a different path: risk, possibility, excitement. Exactly what was missing in his life. This was what he craved. She made him who he had the potential to be.

In one step he was against her, bodies touching, one arm hard round her waist, one round the back of her neck, his mouth on hers, tipping her head back with the crushing force of it. He wanted to own her again. Have back what had once been his. The regimented sex dictated by his wife's iPhone fertility app was like trudging round Waitrose in comparison to one touch of his mouth to Elle's, the clash of their teeth, the raspberry of her lipstick, the overpowering scent of the perfume on her neck when he wrenched his mouth away and buried his face in her hair.

It was then he realized she was laughing. He pulled back. 'What's funny?'

'Nothing,' she grinned. 'You. The urgency.'

He swallowed. 'You don't want urgent?'

'I don't mind urgent. It's funny, that's all.' She stood on tiptoes, wound her arms round his neck. 'I just didn't know you still had it in you, Georgie.'

And this time, she kissed him. Long and slow, soft like she had all the time in the world. George started thinking about Caro and the others round the dinner table wondering where they'd got to.

'Stop thinking, Georgie.'

'What?'

'I said, stop thinking. They don't care. They don't matter.'

George nodded.

She drew his head down again to meet her smiling lips. He pushed her back onto the sofa. Her jacket crumpled beneath them. 'Hang on,' Elle yanked it away to the side, then said, 'Okay, carry on.' The stop-start made it less carnal than George had imagined. Kept pulling him back into the present. Kept making him remember what he was doing, remember his wife, where he was, but then he was lost again when he tasted her mouth: the red wine and the memory of her, of his youth, of his prime. Her body underneath his was taut and firm, no baby weight. He could push her dress up with one hand, expose her pale thighs, so skinny that he could almost wrap his hand around one of them. Her lace panties. Of course they were lace. He groaned. Moved his hand away, wanted to savour it, reached up, pulled the strap of her dress down, the fantasy of the access; his wife wore layers, shirts, sweatshirts, bras from M&S. This fabric just fell away, taking the turquoise lace of her bra with it. And her breasts, he remembered those breasts. Nestled his head in them. The creamy white flesh. He had never been so consumed by the moment. In his head he was George again, the honed, toned athlete, the Adonis. Not George the office worker with the paunch and the thinning hair. This was who he was meant to be; sex in someone else's house between the dessert and cheese courses, face buried between pert breasts, licking soft white skin, groaning in ecstasy.

CHAPTER THIRTY

THEN
Trinity term, third year
GEORGE

George watched the bubbly liquid dribble down Henry's chin as he gulped champagne straight from the Dom Perignon bottle. All the rowing boys were bent forward, listening eagerly as Klaus pushed Henry for the details of his conquests. 'Who was your fat girl?' Klaus asked.

'Betty Berrycloth,' said Henry between champagne glugs.

Klaus winced. The others laughed. JB faux-retched behind Henry's back.

George knew the list success would go some way to soothing Henry's ego but his slurring brags grated. George wanted it to end so they could move on, go dance or get another drink but he stayed put. Let him have this moment, George thought, as if the least he could do was throw Henry the scraps of the rowing boys' avid delight.

Klaus was just saying, 'And your slut?' when Henry's phone rang. Loud and shrill into a break in the music.

Henry looked around confused. 'Is that my phone? What time is it?'

George looked at his watch. 'It's 2 a.m.'

'Who's calling at 2 a.m.?' Henry asked as if someone standing there might know. Fumbling in his pocket for his phone, he shouted, 'Hello? Henry the Hero speaking!' He winked at the boys, all exaggerated. Then he stopped. 'Mum?'

Everyone stopped laughing.

Henry said, 'What? He's what? No!' And George watched as his face crumpled in front of them. The greatest high plummeted to the greatest low. 'No. He can't be dead.' Henry swayed. Klaus and the others didn't know what to do. George was quicker, held Henry up as his knees gave way. 'Someone find Caro,' George ordered, sobering up immediately. Henry was crying. With his arm round his shoulder, George said, 'Come on, let's get you outside.'

He dragged him through the crowds. Henry started to shake, his whole body trembling. 'I don't want them to follow,' he whispered to George, frantic like a child as he shivered. George was trying to find a coat, something to keep him warm, to stop Henry going into shock. He grabbed someone's North Face jacket from a pile by the doors and made Henry put it on.

'It's okay, let's go outside.' George led him out through the main entrance into the cool spring evening.

Henry stopped, looked left then right and said, 'I have to go home. I have to see my mum,' but stood frozen with indecision.

George said, 'Yeah, tomorrow, I'll drive you back tomorrow.'

Henry shook his head. 'No, I have to go now.'

'No mate, you've lost your licence.'

'Fuck my licence.'

'You can't drive like this. Come back to mine.' George tried to get him to walk.

JB came out of the club. George said, 'Find Caro, tell her I've taken him back to ours.' He hailed a cab, tried to tuck Henry into the back seat but Henry wouldn't comply. 'Come on,' George urged.

Henry shook his head and started to walk away. 'No. I want to be on my own.'

'I don't think you should be on your own.' George grabbed his arm but Henry shook him off. 'Henry, get in the cab.'

'Don't tell me what to do!' Henry hollered. The cab driver pulled away, not wanting either of them in his car. Henry stumbled. George held him steady. They walked on till George found a bench round the back of the club, sat Henry down on it and said, 'Let's just sit here a minute.'

Henry put his head in his hands. 'He's dead. I can't believe my dad's dead and he hates me.'

'He doesn't hate you.' George put his hand on Henry's shoulder.

Henry started to cry.

George sat next to him, rubbed his back, felt like he was soothing a baby. He stared at the graffiti on the wall of the alleyway, the old barrels of cooking oil and plastic crates. This certainly wasn't how he'd envisaged the evening.

Henry sobbed. His body juddered as the sadness coursed through him. He threw his head back up to the black sky and groaned. 'Why is this happening?'

'It's okay, mate,' George said, hand on his shoulder.

Henry screwed up his eyes, his face, his hands. He stood up, paced the alleyway, kicked the wall hard with his foot, smashed his fist into the bricks, grazing his bare knuckles. He raged and tore at his hair. He punched the stack of old boxes, hurled an oil drum at the wall. And when all the violent energy was spent, Henry sat back down, white-faced, exhausted, shoulders slumped and drained. He wiped his eyes, took a deep breath and sat back. Seemed calmer. They sat in silence for maybe a minute, maybe ten. George didn't know. He just waited for Henry to speak. When he did, he didn't say what George was expecting.

'I don't know why you're sitting with me.' Henry looked across sadly. 'You should hate me too.'

'I don't hate you,' said George too quickly.

Henry shook his head. 'I'd hate me if I were you. I was a dick to you. Sorry.'

George shrugged like it didn't matter, but inside he gobbled it up. The apology made him feel like they were back where they were before Henry had asked him to throw the trial race, before he'd made a pass at Elle, back to when they'd just been buddies in the boat. It popped into his head to confess to the poisoning, get it all out on the table. In that moment of raw sorrow it felt like their friendship might handle such honesty. But George knew Henry too well in the light of day to arm him with such ammunition, so kept tight-lipped.

Henry put his head on his knees, sat folded over in a wave of anguish. When he sat back up he'd pushed his hair away from his face. It made him look as he had in their second year, when they had both seemed younger and more carefree. It made George remember their crazy triathlons and blistering Ibizan cycles. The fun, the girls, the friendship.

Henry closed his eyes. 'How can I live with this?'

George didn't know. He thought of the disappointment on Sir Charles's face. Couldn't imagine having to see that every time he closed his eyes.

A rat ran along the damp wall.

The music thumped from the club.

Henry suddenly stood up and squeezed his eyes shut and bared his teeth, clutched at his head as if trying to tear his hair from his scalp.

The moment was too real. The feelings too visceral. George thought he might cry himself.

Henry gave a loud tormented bark then slumped back onto the bench, hands thwacking hard on the wooden slats. 'I don't know if I can live with this feeling.'

George pressed into the corners of his eyes, jabbing at the bud of tears. 'It will get better,' he said. 'It has to.' The words felt pathetically juvenile.

Henry laughed sadly. Then he turned to look straight at him. 'You're a true friend, George Kingsley.'

The sad sincerity of Henry's gaze made George suddenly want to hug him. He remembered what it was like to be Henry's friend. To exist unencumbered in the glow of his aura.

George would never go back to being the underdog. Henry would never be his hero again. But, he thought in that moment on the bench, maybe they could move forward as equals.

George was about to blurt something back, about how Henry was one of the best friends he'd ever had, but then Henry caught sight of the sleeve of the random North Face jacket that George had grabbed on their way out and made him put on. With a puzzled frown, Henry said, 'What the hell is this jacket I'm wearing?' and they both laughed. Cracked up. Maybe it was just something to break the sadness but it felt like the hope of old times.

*

The sun was up when George finally woke. His phone was vibrating. Slivers of beaming light cut across the alleyway. His clothes were wet from dew. He was shivering, his fingers so stiff and white he could barely get his phone out of his pocket. As he sat up, a jacket that had been over him like a blanket slipped to the ground. His head pounded. He could hardly open his eyes to see the screen he was so hungover. Twenty-three missed calls. 'Hello?' His voice was thick and rasping, his breath sour, his mouth dry from the alcohol. Memories of the evening appeared in snippets.

'George? George, it's Caro, where have you been? Where are you?'

George looked around; where was he? In an alleyway round the back of the club on a tatty old bench, probably put here for staff on their fag-breaks. At the end of the street he could see people on their way to work carrying coffee, talking on their phones. The bins stank. 'I'm, er—' He didn't finish, it didn't seem relevant. Instead, he said, 'What's going on? Why so many calls? Is Henry with you?' He looked around to see if he could see him.

Caro choked a sob on the other end of the phone. 'He's dead, George, Henry's dead.'

'What?' George frowned. His head was pounding, he couldn't think properly. 'No, his dad died, Caro. Not Henry.

His dad.' George wondered if he was going to be sick. His brain was a nauseating whirl of confusion.

'No, George, they found him a couple of hours ago.' Caro was gasping through sobs. 'We tried to find him but we couldn't. He wasn't in his room.' She paused to get her breath. 'He didn't answer. He fell from the roof, George. He fell.'

'What? No, he was here, with me.' George did stand now, searched the alleyway as if Henry might be hiding behind the wheelie bins.

Caro was still crying, her voice choking. 'One of the night porters found him.'

George couldn't move. 'Are you serious?' He reached a hand to steady himself against the wall.

'I'm serious, George,' said Caro.

'I don't understand. Did he jump? Why?'

'They don't know. They think maybe he fell. I don't know, George. I don't know if he jumped.'

His friend was dead. It wouldn't sink in. He'd been sitting on the bench with him. He saw the North Face jacket on the floor. They had laughed.

God, what a fool he was. Thinking their little shared joke was enough to counteract that deep-set, hopeless sadness he'd seen in Henry's eyes.

He sat back down on the bench. Head in his hands. All he could see suddenly was the Heineken water bottle filled with the Xylazine. Like a beacon. If he just hadn't given it to him then Henry would have stayed in the race and would have got his Blue and Henry's dad would have died happy and Henry would have dealt with the grief as any other person deals with it. Not fucked out of his brain. Not pumped up on shame and regret. Caro wouldn't be sobbing on the other end of the phone. The guy would still be alive. George's time at Oxford wouldn't be forever shrouded with this. This feeling of shameful horror in the pit of his stomach. The thoughts spiralled through him, faster and faster till he was vomiting his guts out on the cracked concrete, puking till there was nothing left in his stomach.

He rang Elle. There was no reply. He rang again and again. Then finally, when he remembered she was at work all day, he gave up. Somehow he got home, had a shower, pulled on some tracksuit bottoms and lay on his bed till Caro appeared, greasy-haired and ghost-white with tiredness. She curled up beside him and sobbed into his chest.

When she sat up, she wiped her puffy eyes and said, 'The police want to talk to us all.'

George nodded. It was all too surreal.

Travis came out of his room, stood in the doorway of George's room in boxer shorts and a cardigan, and said seriously, 'Can you keep my name out of it?'

For the entire time George spoke to the police, he wondered if they could see the guilt in his eyes. He answered all their questions with polite certainty. Exuded his public school-ingrained emotional detachment. Still, he got out of there as quickly as he could. He sat with the rowing boys in a greasy spoon drinking stewed tea and waiting for Henry's mother, Francesca, who wanted to see them. Marco de Poligny felt bad because he'd told the police that when Henry wasn't racing he was partial to a Camel Light outside his window, sitting on the parapets; he felt like he'd given away Henry's secrets. JB had heard that apparently the cocktail of drugs and alcohol Henry was purported to have taken made it difficult to know if it was suicide or accidental death. Klaus said maybe it was Betty Berrycloth getting her own back. JB said, 'Too soon, mate, *way* too soon.'

There was silence after that.

By the time he came home, having briefly held Lady Bellinger's cashmere-clad body to him, felt the bones of her ribs as she gave a small, harrowing sob, escorted her everywhere she needed to go, recounted Henry's last movements, his last words, saw the grief on her face having lost both husband and son, George was so exhausted he could barely think straight.

Elle was home. Her room was a sanctuary. The white sheets. The sweet-scented air. She held her arms out wide. George clambered over the pillowy softness and collapsed into her warm pink flesh.

The next morning, however, Elle was gone. She'd left him a note saying she had to go home for a while. Something to do with her sister. George read it, perplexed. She was his safe haven. How could she desert him at a time like this?

Lady Bellinger's car drew up outside. There was more to do. More to help with. More questions. More freshly pressed handkerchiefs to pass around. Caro to soothe when Lady Bellinger was too dismissive. Henry's possessions to sift through. His sister, who'd flown in from the States, to meet from the airport. More questions. More questions. George thought his head might explode. He could sense himself getting weaker, the desire to confess his own part in the tragedy bubbling up inside him. He wanted to retch up the guilt. Spew it over the beautiful young Ophelia Bellinger when she stalked through arrivals in her camel trench and oversized sunglasses like a female Henry: same dimpled cheeks, same haughty smile and all-seeing upturned eyes. A willowy vision from the dead.

He had to see Elle. The thoughts were crowding in, threatening to suffocate him.

George searched Elle's room for her address. An action he knew she'd hate in itself. But when he turned up at the concrete block of flats in South London he realized she'd probably hate his being there more. It was one of the most dismal places he'd ever seen, not that he'd seen many; the closest he'd got was when Matron watched *EastEnders* at school. He worried about getting his iPhone out to check the address in case one of the kids kicking a football against the wall jumped him for it. He tried to play it cool but knew he stood out like a sore thumb in his rugby shirt and chinos. The lift stank. There was no way Elle lived here. He found himself hoping she didn't anyway. Part of his brain had fantasized about marrying Elle; he couldn't imagine Douglas Kingsley being happy with whatever family she had who lived here being at the wedding. The thought of it made him cringe.

He thought of Henry's nymph-like younger sister, Ophelia, how she had touched her cheek to George's at the airport, wiped a few quiet tears away with long exquisite fingers, smelt of expensive shampoo and minty-fresh breath even straight off the plane. She was much more the Kingsley type. He hated that he was so much of a snob that he could consider such things when just half an hour ago he'd had to lock himself in the train loo because he'd started hyperventilating, his brain fixated on images of Henry hurling himself to his death.

George knocked on the door, worrying about who might open it. He could see a dead pot plant on the windowsill, glanced down the concrete walkway, had an urge to run away.

A middle-aged woman answered. Blonde hair with dark roots, dressed in leggings and a sweatshirt. Would have been very pretty if she hadn't been so worn around the edges. She gave him a once up and down and just as he was saying, 'Oh hello, I was wondering if—' she shut the door on him and shouted, 'Elle, it's for you.'

A second later, Elle appeared, breathless. She pulled the door open and reared back in surprise.

'What are you doing here?'

George swallowed. Coming here suddenly seemed so obviously a mistake. 'I, er—' He paused under her frowning scrutiny, lost his words. In these surroundings her skin looked somehow shiny rather than dewy. Her ribbed vest with its velvet trim less trendy in its threadbareness. He wanted to pull her away from the door, grab her arm and march her to the hipster café he'd passed on the way from the station.

She was waiting.

He could feel his every thought on his face. He said, 'This is where you live?'

She made a face like surely that was obvious. 'Yeah.'

'Oh.'

She turned back to glance into the flat. 'Look, Georgie, I can't talk to you now.'

He could tell she wanted to close the door. But he put

his hand out to stop her. 'You have to. I'm really struggling. I need you.'

Elle sighed, slipped on some flip-flops and stepped outside, pulling the door to behind her. He felt stupidly overdressed in his collared and discreetly logoed shirt while she had on a crumpled vest and stretch tie-dye mini. She started walking, lighting a cigarette as she went. Took the stairs rather than the lift. He tried not to wince at the acrid smell. She led him to a central playground with a basketball court and swing that had been wound round so many times the seat dangled up by the bar at the top. A kid played on a rocking elephant. Chicken bones and broken glass lay scattered around the hut built into the climbing frame. Elle beckoned for him to sit on the low brick wall.

'So go on,' she said.

He looked around, checked no one could hear. Elle blew smoke away from the direction of the playground.

'I feel like it's all my fault,' he said.

She crossed her arms over her knees. Thin wrists on top of each other. 'It's not your fault,' she said.

He watched the kid going back and forth, back and forth on the springy elephant. 'We shouldn't have done it,' he said, wanting to bury his face in the warmth of her. Feel cocooned and safe.

'Georgie . . .' she looked tired. 'We had nothing to do with what happened. Yes, we might have put something into action but then it took a different path. Like anything can. It's just really unfortunate.'

'It's more than unfortunate,' he said in a desperate whisper. He ran his hand through his hair, wanted to be away from this depressing place. 'Can we go somewhere else to talk? A café or something.'

'No,' she said. 'I have to go back in a minute.'

'When are you coming back?'

'I don't know. There's stuff going on here.'

George said, 'I literally feel sick the whole time. I feel like I want to tell Lady Bellinger. I feel like it would be better if I did.'

Elle put her hand on his knee. It was the first contact they'd had. In those bleak surroundings it felt like the touch of a stranger. 'Georgie, you have to face up to it and move on.'

But George couldn't leave it at that. 'I don't know if I can.'

'Georgie, I can't deal with this right now.' She looked back up at the flat.

He briefly wondered what was going on with her family, but could barely concentrate on anything other than what he was going through.

'I can't do this without you, Elle,' he pleaded.

'Yes you can.' She smiled, placating rather than truly caring.

He could feel his annoyance rise. She should be there for him. They were in this together.

'I need you, Elle. One of my best friends had just died.'

She raised a brow.

That infuriated him more. 'Henry *was* a really good friend of mine.'

'A friend whose drink you were happy to lace with an animal tranquilizer. Come on, Georgie.' She stubbed the cigarette out.

'No. I wasn't happy to do it. I shouldn't have done it. *You* shouldn't have let me do it.'

Elle flinched at the accusation.

The moment George said it he knew it was unfair but there was something infinitely pleasing in passing the blame. Like a child might to its mother. Lightening the load.

He watched her throat as she swallowed. Held his breath, wondered if he'd got away with it. Felt suspended in a moment of relief and terror. He felt like how the girls who cut themselves at school must feel. That sharp, exquisite sting of release. A brief respite from self-loathing.

'I didn't make you do anything, Georgie,' she said, her voice tight with disbelief.

He wanted to say that she had; she had bewitched him. He would never have done anything like that without Elle's influence. He thought again of the tasteful tears of the perfectly groomed Ophelia Bellinger. The monogrammed handkerchief of Lady Bellinger. His own picture on the front of the *Sunday Times Magazine*. He was not some low-rent poisoner. He looked around at the graffitied slide and shards of broken glass on the playground floor. He certainly didn't belong here.

Elle was staring at him like she didn't know him at all. For the first time she looked vulnerable. Wary. It was a shift in power that George didn't totally dislike. He found himself thinking that he could say more, hurt her more, either to make himself feel better or so she felt as bad as him.

Yet at that moment, he realized that most of all he wanted the old Elle back. The one whose confidence he could cling to, so he said again, 'Sorry, I shouldn't have said that. I just . . . I'm really tired.'

She stood up. 'I have to go.'

'No!' he grabbed for her hand. 'This is more important. Please!'

'No,' she said. 'It's not. This is your guilt and you have to deal with it.'

'But I'm *not* guilty!' he half shouted.

The kid stopped rocking on the elephant and stared.

There was a beat of silence.

George hadn't been intending to say that but as he thought about it, it seemed to make sense. He walked them towards the basketball court for privacy. 'I suppose what I mean is, if Henry hadn't taken the steroids in the first place then I wouldn't have had to do what I did, would I?'

Elle tipped her head. 'So?'

'So why do I feel so bad for something that rationally I know wasn't my fault.'

She stared up at him with perplexed exhaustion. 'What do you want me to say, Georgie?'

George didn't know. He looked around, grasped for a train of thought. 'I want you to offer me words of comfort like people do in these situations.'

Her brow creased. 'You want me tell you that it's all okay? That you had nothing to do with Henry Bellinger's death?'

He shrank back a little. 'I don't know.' Was that why he was here?

Her mouth tipped up in its usual, confident half-smile. 'Just take some responsibility, Georgie, and move on.'

'But it wasn't my fault!' he said again, more plaintive, more determined.

Elle looked at him, something in her eyes making it seem as if she were really seeing him for the first time. He worried suddenly that she was going to walk away but then she put her arm round his shoulder, pulled him in towards her and said, 'It wasn't your fault, Georgie. It seriously wasn't. It's going to be okay.'

He inhaled a shaky breath; she smelt of dirty hair and cigarettes. He half wanted to pull away but the desire to let his chest sag, to sink into the hug was too powerful. He hadn't realized how much he had needed to hear that.

CHAPTER THIRTY-ONE

NOW
ELLE

'All right, calm down lover boy, that's enough.'

'What?'

Elle sat up, pulling the strap of her red dress up.

George flailed on the sofa, bamboozled and perplexed against the velvet cushions. Then he saw her phone in her hand.

'What are you doing?'

Elle pulled her skirt down, shifted in position so she was decent. Fluffed her hair. Rubbed any remains of his frantic kisses off her chest.

George almost fell backwards onto the glass coffee table as he tried to right himself. 'What, what's going on? Why is your phone . . .?'

She got some gum out of her pocket, popped a piece in her mouth and started chewing as she pressed the screen and turned the phone round to face him. He watched in growing horror the image of him, nuzzling and grunting in her breasts. He was undignified in his lust. Elle had made sure she captured herself, lying bored and repulsed, waiting for it to stop.

His face was a picture. 'I thought . . .' he stammered. 'I thought you were enjoying it. Why? Why have you done this?'

She bit her thumbnail, thinking. Biding her time, letting him sweat.

And he was sweating. She could see it in speckled patches on his shirt.

'What are you going to do with that video?'

She shrugged. 'Put it on TikTok?'

Elle knew George wouldn't have a clue how TikTok worked but he'd know enough to realize that it could be the end of him. Teenagers would think this was hysterical.

Elle got up to put some distance between them. She perched on the arm of the sofa, crossed her legs, stretched her arms in front of her, the phone held snugly between her palms. 'You haven't changed at all, have you?' she said.

But George was preoccupied with the phone, couldn't take his eyes off it.

Elle said, 'Georgie, stop looking at the phone, the video's on my cloud already. There's nothing you can do.'

'I don't understand why you've done this.' He shook his head, sloping brown eyes indignant. Still trying to get the upper hand even in his dishevelled emasculation. 'Is this fun for you? Are you just trying to cause trouble? Get back at me for something?'

She laughed. He looked so plaintive. 'No, Georgie, not to cause trouble.' She paused, thought for a second. 'Yes, maybe for my amusement. And yes, maybe to get back at you.'

George's appearance matched his confusion; his hair was ruffled, his shirt loose and untucked at the waist. He said, 'I don't understand. I thought we were good together.'

'So did I, Georgie.' She stood up, wandered round the room,

finger trailing over books on the shelf. She slid a leather-bound tome out. 'Do you think Caro's read any of these?'

George didn't answer. He looked very small perched alone on the big velvet sofa.

Elle smiled. 'There aren't many people that I have loved, Georgie.' She slotted the book back into place. 'I find it very difficult to trust people.'

He snorted, like that had always been plain as day.

She let it go. Leant against the bookcase. 'You, though. I don't know what it was. But there was something about you. Your sweetness. You were so eager. So kind.' She walked closer, tried to see in him what was once there. He seemed to recoil from the scrutiny. She sat on the edge of the coffee table in front of him. 'I don't know how you did it, but you got through.'

She could sense him, even then, leaning a little closer into her. Thinking maybe she might still succumb.

'But then I made the stupid mistake of trying to help you. I wanted you to achieve your dream. I wanted you to be as great as you thought you were. I wanted to give you something. That's what you do, isn't it, when you're in *love*?' The word sounded childish, pathetic, as she said it. 'If we're being completely truthful, I was quite happy to get Henry out of the picture. He was a twat.'

George frowned at the insulting of the dead. Opened his mouth to say something.

Elle held up her hand to silence him. 'The worst thing you could do now is defend him. Just shut up and listen.' She carried on. 'It was my mistake really, in retrospect. Helping you achieve greatness you weren't destined for. Fanning your ego.'

'He cheated! I was meant to be in the boat!' He couldn't help himself.

'Oh Georgie. Be quiet.' She sighed. 'Will you ever listen? Do you listen to your wife?' she asked, head cocked as she tried to imagine his home life. 'I bet you don't, do you? I bet it's all George, George, George. Little tantrums that the baby's getting more attention than you.'

He looked at her with righteous affront.

'See, that's the problem. It's always about you. Precious George Kingsley. I thought Henry was bad enough, but at least he made no qualms about who he was. You though, you think you're entitled to everything; that nothing that applies to the rest of us should apply to you.'

'That's unfair.' He smoothed back his hair, adjusted his shirt, tried to regain his managerial authority.

'No Georgie, it's not.' His mock-innocent act still had the ability to make her blood boil.

'I don't have to listen to this. I can't believe you're harbouring a grudge about something that happened so long ago. It's ridiculous. We all have to move on.' He went to stand up.

'Sit down!' she ordered, holding the phone out as if he'd forgotten. She could feel her eyes blazing with fury.

George sat. Eyes glued to the device.

'Don't you tell me to move on,' she said, feeling her indignation rise. 'You have no idea about me. Have you even asked me a question since you got here?'

George swallowed. Then sheepishly shook his head.

'Ask me what I do,' she said.

'What do you do, Elle?' he parroted.

'Me?' she replied, saccharine, hand to her chest as if delightfully surprised to be the object of interest. Then added flatly, 'I'm a lawyer, George.'

He couldn't hide his shock.

'Yes,' she said. 'We can all make it in the City. All drive BMWs if we want to. But I also run a pro bono organisation that helps women, George; provides them with legal advice. Victims of domestic abuse, sexual violence, child support.'

'That's very noble,' he said.

'Isn't it?'

George cleared his throat. 'I still don't understand, Elle. Why you did this,' he gestured to her phone.

She thought for a moment. Stood up, walked to the mantelpiece, picked up a bronze cast of baby feet which she turned this way and that with a scowl of distaste. 'Do you remember that time, Georgie, when you came to my home?'

George paused, squinted as he thought back, clearly feigning lack of memory. 'Vaguely.'

'I can tell when you're lying, Georgie,' she snapped with impatience, putting the bronze cast down. 'There you were, all in a panic, all terrified that you were responsible for Henry dying. All you wanted was absolution. Desperate for it, you were.'

George watched her warily from the sofa.

'You didn't ask me anything then, either. Nothing about what was going on at my house, with me.' She went back to perch on the sofa arm. 'Just thinking about yourself. All needy, wanting my assurance and yet you still managed to look at where I lived and think that you were better than me.'

She saw the expression on his face change. Watched him unable to mask an acknowledgement of the truth.

Elle studied him sitting there, so run-of-the-mill. Thought of her Georgie. Thought of the big adoring eyes he used to look at her with. She still had the gold locket he gave her for Christmas. Could still remember the feeling when he handed it to her. No one had ever given her a gift like it, thought about what she would like, given it to her with such reverence.

Looking at him now, she wondered if she had been more in love with the way he made her feel than anything else. She made a mental note that perhaps it was time for the locket to go.

She would never forget that look on his face, though, when he'd stood on the front door step of her mother's flat. It was etched in her mind. She had known in that moment that it was over. She was no match for the Kingsley pride; especially not one boosted to the godlike status the Boat Race Blue had given him. It was never the same after that. The more the collective Henry grief grew, the more George assumed his new role. Absorbed what Henry left behind. As he was enveloped into the Bellinger fold as the beloved best friend, the gulf between him and Elle grew only wider. If his self-satisfaction after the Boat Race was bad, his overblown grandeur at being Lady Bellinger's substitute son was unbearable.

He started making excuses not to see Elle. He was barely at the house. Spent more time with the rowers – lots of charity events in Henry's name. Time with Lady Bellinger; arranging the funeral, meeting all of Sir Charles's esteemed colleagues. He was pictured walking Henry's sister, Ophelia, out of the funeral. George in his hand-tailored black suit, her draped in crêpe de Chine. The epitome of decorum. There was no more time to laze in Elle's bed, lie in a haze of cigarette smoke, listen captivated as she challenged his inbuilt perceptions, listen to the rain as it battered the leaky windows. He looked at her with different eyes now he'd had a taste of power and success. When she saw him she wanted to ask where her Georgie had gone; where the boy who loved her was. She hadn't realized how much she had loved to be loved until it was gone. And the aching need felt dangerously close to what she had seen in her mother with every boyfriend past. That was what Elle hated the most, that George had got under her skin and she was clutching to keep him there.

When, at Henry's inquest, the coroner recorded a verdict of accidental death, Elle had gone down to George's room and said, 'How do you feel?'

He said, 'Fine.'

She stared at him sitting at his desk, the clean-cut, hard-working student. 'Come on, Georgie, don't give me that.'

He'd chucked his pen down, laughed a little sadly. 'Okay. I feel like I can breathe again.'

Elle smiled. Felt she'd broken the surface. She took a step forward. He reached out and caught her hand, laced her fingers with his own. She couldn't stop her heart lurching at the simple touch, the possibility of going back to how they were. That he would pull her to him and bury his face adoringly in her waist; realize she was worth more than the expectations and aspirations he had inherited.

But then, without looking up, he said, 'I still think it's better, though, that we keep our distance. Just in case.'

Elle stared at the top of his head. 'Just in case what?'

But he didn't reply.

Now, all these years later in Caro's sitting room, holding

her phone with the video of George snuffling at her, she didn't feel as good as she had hoped she would. She had wanted revenge. Wanted to ruin his perfect life. She had intended to send the video straight to his wife. But in the action of filming it, of taunting him with it, she realized how pointless it was. How unworthy he was of her attention. He would never listen. He would always think he was hard done by, owed more, deserved more. It was her fault, really, for allowing him to burrow beneath her surface. She didn't make that mistake nowadays; she had a few men she could call on, but no one who ever stayed overnight, none who she gave more than a few hours of her time. Elle spent most of her time working. As if her day job wasn't enough, the pro bono work filled nearly all her spare time – and did nothing to enhance her opinion of relationships. It probably wasn't the healthiest way of living, she could certainly delegate more, but the work was more fulfilling than any of the annoying vulnerabilities of romance.

Looking at George, plaintive on the sofa, brows drawn down, a red wine stain on his shirt, it only emphasized what a waste of time such fickle devotion was. He didn't need his life upending with a video of his botched infidelity. His own mundane existence was punishment enough. She almost laughed. Felt the amusement of relief twitch at her lips.

'What are you going to do?' he said, quietly. 'With the video?'

She raised a brow. Could see his panic growing.

'Well, Georgie . . .' Elle reached down to retrieve her denim jacket from the sofa, slipped it on. She could feel him watching her as she went over to the mirror, waiting with apprehension. She took her time thinking what she might say, got a lipstick out of her pocket and redid her lips. 'Well to start with,' she said, smacking the newly glossed lips together, 'you're going to understand your place in life. You're a married man now, Georgie. With a baby.' She capped the lipstick, put it back in her pocket, caught his eye in the mirror. 'Do you love your wife?'

'Very much.'

'Then what the hell are you doing in here with me? Jesus Christ, Georgie.' She sighed. Then she moved to sit on the edge of the coffee table, hands in the pockets of her jacket. 'This is what you're going to do. Every time you're tempted to go for something more, something that's not for someone like you, you're going stop. And you're going be pleased with what you have.'

George swallowed.

Looking at him now, his pale office tan, crumpled shirt, the deep lines round his eyes from exhaustion, Elle couldn't believe she had thought his life was any better than hers. That was the danger of Instagram, she supposed.

He went to speak but she'd had enough of him now. She stood up to leave the room. But he said, 'Is that it?' with a hint in his tone that he'd got off lightly.

She paused, narrowed her eyes with frustrated displeasure. Would he never learn? She crouched back down in front of him. 'I can destroy your life in an instant, Georgie.'

His eyes widened.

'When you look at your wife, I want you to see me,' she purred. 'And when you do,' she leant right in close, could feel his panicked breath on her face, 'I want you to know that you are no better. Understand?'

He nodded.

They were millimetres apart now. 'Say it.'

He swallowed. 'I am no better.'

She smiled. 'Good.' Then she stood up and walked out the room.

CHAPTER THIRTY-TWO

NOW
CARO

As Caro walked between the kitchen and the dining room carrying the port for the cheese, she saw Elle standing on the front step lighting up a cigarette, the sequins on her denim jacket glinting in the porch light. The front door was half open and immediately the smell of smoke filled the hallway.

'Can you at least close the door?' Caro asked, stalking over to push it to, resisting the urge to slam it hard and lock her out. 'Where's George, what have you been doing?' They'd been gone for ages. 'Actually don't tell me, I can imagine.'

Elle looked at her for a second, then said, 'Why don't you join me?'

Caro scoffed. 'Why on earth would I do that?'

Elle shrugged, twisted a blonde curl round her finger. 'Just to have a little chat, clear the air.'

Caro glanced behind her; George appeared to be in the bathroom now and she had no desire to sit with just Lily and Travis.

There had always been something about Elle that got under

Caro's skin. While Caro couldn't bear her, she had always been plagued by an underlying desire to be liked by her. Accepted. As if by having Elle's stamp of approval one was elevated to a higher plane in life. It had always peeved Caro that she hadn't been able to achieve that honour. That was why she put the port on the hall table and went to stand on the doorstep with Elle, straddling the threshold, still half in the house, unable to fully commit to the occasion.

Elle flicked ash from her cigarette in the direction of the rose bush. In front of them, just beyond the road, was the river, the water glossy in the moonlight. 'Nice place you've got here,' she said. 'Landed on your feet, didn't you?'

Caro said, 'I thought you wanted to clear the air, not make more digs at me.'

Elle looked lazily her way. 'I don't want to clear the air, I lied.'

'Oh for God's sake!' It was easy for Caro to disguise her disappointment with exasperation, she did it all the time with Brian. 'I'm going in. And can you not flick ash on my roses, please?'

'You know, it's really horrible,' Elle said, gaze fixed out towards the river, 'watching someone ruin the life of someone you love.'

Caro huffed an exaggerated sigh. 'I don't know what you're talking about.'

The look Elle gave her was pure disdain. 'No, I don't imagine you do.' She deliberately flicked more ash at the roses. Caro wanted to snatch the cigarette off her and stomp it to the ground but she stayed where she was, completely still, unsure quite what was going on.

Elle said, 'It was my little sister, you see,' she exhaled a plume of smoke, 'who wrote your essays. Got you your As.'

Caro was confused. 'No it wasn't. I'd have known if she was your sister.'

'Believe me, Caro, she was my sister.' Elle gave her a look like it wasn't worth arguing.

'But you didn't have the same surname.'

'I think you of all people know that's irrelevant.'

Caro felt her stomach tighten. She looked out at the road as a black cab and a cyclist went past. She'd had no idea who the girl was. Just someone who made her life easier.

Elle flicked the glowing fag onto the front path. 'We never knew who it was who gave the university her name. I knew she wrote for you but I didn't think you'd been caught. Figured they'd have chucked you out too. And then there you were at the table, just threw it in casually that you told them everything, didn't sit your final exams. But it didn't mean anything to you, did it? Ruined someone's life to save your own pathetic skin.' Elle ran her tongue over her bottom lip as she thought. 'She was much cleverer than all of us, my sister. Do you remember what her name was?'

Caro did not want to be in this position. Not at the mercy of Elle. The cool expression on her face made her spine tingle. Caro tried desperately to access the recesses of her brain for a name but there was nothing, no memory of it. She had to shake her head. 'I don't, no.'

There was a flicker of fury in Elle's eyes. 'Sarah, her name was Sarah. And she didn't graduate from Oxford and she didn't know enough people for it not to matter. Didn't have anyone rich to bail her out. What was it you said? Quid pro quo? You really landed her in it.'

'I don't think it was completely my fault. She should have known there would be consequences.'

'Oh fuck off!' Elle sneered, walking away seemingly for a moment to calm herself, pulling her jacket tight around her. 'Don't give me your holier-than-thou bullshit, I'm not on your PTA, Caro. I know you. I know what you're like beneath all this bollocks.' She waved a hand at the house, at the rose bush, at the newly laid Indian sandstone paving and black-and-white tiled path. 'She did it for the money. In the same way you prostitute yourself for whatever you can get.'

'How dare you!'

'Oh I dare, Caro.' Elle walked closer. Caro shrank back a touch. Elle's laugh was distinctly humourless. 'My sister wasn't like you, Caro, wasn't the kind of person who could wrangle her way out of anything. She was very clever but had exceptionally low self-esteem. She believed she deserved what she got, didn't fight it, didn't try another path. Some people aren't fighters. Some people give up when they're pushed down.' Elle rolled her lips together, looked down at the creamy white paving for a second and then walked back to lean against the wall and have another cigarette. 'She was very frustrating like that. Once she'd been chucked out that was it for her. Got a job at some shitty accounting firm. All that knowledge and cleverness was spent trying to balance people's dodgy books. Went the same way as my mum in the end. Nasty men, crappy flat, zero self-worth whatever anyone said. But,' she lit the fag and slipped the lighter into her pocket, 'we all have our foibles, don't we? What's yours? Not giving a shit about anyone as long as you're okay?'

'That is not true.' Caro was defensive, her fingers toying

with the velvet of her trousers like her youngest with her comforter. 'I care about lots of people. I'm sorry about what happened to your sister. I didn't know.'

Elle's mouth tightened. 'Don't even try.'

Caro could feel her breath quicken. She looked into Elle's pale blue eyes; they had always unnerved her. She wanted this over with, to go back inside, have the cheese and port and for everyone to go home. She wanted Elle not to be looking at her like that.

'She died last month,' Elle said flatly. 'Liver failure. Drank herself to death.'

Caro gasped. 'Oh Elle, I'm sorry.'

Elle arched a brow. 'No you're not.' She turned so her shoulder was resting against the wall. 'I want you to experience it, Caro. To know what it's like when someone casually destroys something without a care in the world.'

Caro felt a shiver of dread creep up her neck. This was so far from what she'd been expecting when she came to stand on the step. In her imagination they were putting it all behind them by now, maybe even sharing a laugh about Travis's dreadful tattoo or George's cringeworthy letter.

'I know it was Henry's baby, Caro,' Elle said casually. 'I've known since I found the pregnancy test that you hid in the bottom of the bin.' She leant forward, added in a conspiratorial whisper, 'You can't hide anything from me.'

Caro's instinct was to retaliate. 'You know nothing! It *wasn't* Henry's baby!' She could feel the blood pumping fast through her veins, pulsing in her neck. 'It's a complete fabrication. You don't know what you're talking about.'

Elle shrugged, turned so she was looking back out at the

roses, took a long drag on the cigarette. 'I know your stepdad wouldn't have put up with you pregnant and single. I remember him, he was a religious nut. And I presume that someone like Brian would have stepped in, more than happy to take on a child that wasn't his if it meant he got someone like you into the bargain.' Elle rolled her head to study her reaction. Caro obviously wasn't the closed book she thought she was, or else Elle had superhero powers of observation because she suddenly stood up straight and said slowly, 'He doesn't know, does he? Even Brian doesn't know.' Caro couldn't deny it quick enough. Elle laughed, caught by surprise. 'Wow. How the hell did you pull that one off?'

Caro stood very quiet for a moment. She was struck by visions of certain moments in her life, like when stupid fucking Lionel had lectured her on the disgrace of casual harlotry and fornication. He could not have her in the house if she was pregnant. Nor, however, could he condone an abortion; children were a blessing. The catch-22 was solved by Caro's mother who, refusing to compromise relations with her cash cow over something as trivial as a baby, packed Caro off to stay with her uncle in Switzerland. Out of sight, out of mind.

Or when Bethany had sat on Brian's knee and said, 'I think I have Mummy's mouth and your eyes, Daddy.' Caro had sloshed her wine down on the countertop too hard, but Brian hadn't even glanced over. She had wanted to shout, no you don't! You don't have his eyes! Brian had squeezed Bethany tight, 'I think you're the best of everything.' The pair were inseparable. Caro had felt tears welling. She hated that her life was tied to him. She wanted the children for herself only, to be united against him, yet somehow they didn't see Brian the way she did. They weren't repulsed by his weak chin and childish need for constant reassurance. But like it or not, this was the life she had chosen. And for the time being, she couldn't leave him because while he might worship Caro, he also held the purse strings. Money, they both knew, was the tie that bound them. After everything Caro had been through growing up, she made damned sure that her children would never struggle from lack of breeding. Her children would all go to the best private schools, they'd have foreign holidays, ski, surf, sail, eat in nice restaurants. They would live without so much as a whimper of discontent. If they wanted to go to university, they would go to whichever they wanted. If they developed a passion for Mexican street food after their gap year, she'd buy them the van to cook it at festivals. If any of her children wanted to be actors, they had her blessing, although she probably wouldn't be able to help herself steering them towards RADA. They would grow up with the luxury of instinctive entitlement. And it was for that privilege that when Bethany had hugged Brian tight, instead of scoffing at the preposterous idea she had inherited Brian's piggy eyes, Caro had left her wine on the counter and forced herself to go round and wrap her arms round the pair of them, resting her cheek on the top of Brian's head while distancing herself from the moment by imagining how different it would be were it Henry's.

On the doorstep of her house, under Elle's amused scrutiny, Caro was determined to hold the secrets of her life together but it felt like wrapping her hands around a cracking egg. She lifted her chin and said, 'You're mad. You don't know what you're talking about.'

Elle's smile widened. 'Well let's just pretend I'm not mad and this isn't a fabrication. I've been thinking, what does Caro care most about? What would really upset her? Is it her reputation? What people think of her? Maybe I could stand at your kids' school gate, spread ugly rumours about you? That could be fun.' Elle bit her lip as if pondering the thought.

Caro imagined the school playground where she was greeted by practically every parent she met, the PTA meetings she chaired with the Head and even some of the governors in attendance. In the school she was practically famous – that's what happened when one had so many children. The vision of Elle standing smoking at the gate, stopping mothers in their tracks to whisper venomous gossip about Caro's marriage, hinting at the scandal around her eldest daughter's parentage was unthinkable. The Heathfield School grapevine would burn. It would be the end of all Caro's hard work. She could feel her palms sweating but refused to give into any sign of being riled. Instead Caro sighed, 'Surely you have better things to do?'

Elle considered the fact. 'Yes, probably.'

A bus braked loudly on the road. Elle gave it a careless glance. Caro waited, heart thumping, palms sweating. She wondered what the others were doing as they sat waiting for cheese unaware of the catastrophe playing out calmly on the doorstep.

Elle stubbed her cigarette out. 'I bet Henry's mother would be interested.'

Caro thought her legs might give way.

'It would be her grandchild, wouldn't it?' Elle mused. 'And if Henry's sister hasn't had children then it could possibly be her *only* grandchild.'

Caro didn't respond. Everything was suddenly brighter, sharper. The fear heightening her senses.

'That would be a shocking story; an ageing grandmother denied the chance to hold the child of her dead son. It would certainly spice up the grand unveiling of the Bellinger statue, wouldn't it?'

Caro swallowed. Heat rushed to her cheeks. In her mind, Henry's mother had given up any rights to knowing about the baby when she told Caro she'd never be good enough for her son. No way was Caro having her anywhere near her child. She'd had nightmares about Lady Bellinger and her lawyers somehow branding Caro an unfit mother, demanding access or visiting rights. She could just imagine the old cow taking Bethany for high tea somewhere and whispering lies about Caro into her impressionable teenage ears.

Elle was watching, eyes sparkling with mischief.

Caro took a deep breath and said, 'What do you want? If you need money, I can help you.'

'Oh don't be ridiculous.' Elle dismissed her with a huff. 'I don't need your money.'

Caro didn't know what to say. Money was the only thing she had to offer. 'Elle, just tell me what you want. If it's an apology, then I give it willingly, I really am sorry about your sister.'

'You couldn't care less about my sister as long as you save your own skin,' Elle replied. She walked forward, picked a petal off a rose, rubbed it between her fingers then let it drop to the floor. 'Only you could pull off a torrid affair with Brian Carmichael.' When Elle turned, her face had softened a touch. She was smiling, offering in that look a vague détente. 'Even by your standards you must have worked super quickly. But I don't see how you got him to think the baby was his?'

Caro exhaled, suddenly exhausted. She moved to perch on the windowsill. 'The chlamydia affected Bethany's birth weight. She was born tiny and with pneumonia.' Caro shrugged. 'I told Brian it was because she was premature.'

Elle laughed, a mix of respect and surprise on her face. 'Bloody hell, Caro. Only you could make an STD work in your favour.'

Caro looked up at her. 'What are you going to do? I don't want Henry's mum knowing about Bethany. I'll do whatever you want to stop it.'

Elle tipped her head as she thought. 'I'd like you to get a taste of what it's like to watch some bitch destroy your life. That would make me feel better.'

Their eyes locked. For a moment there was silence. Caro tried to force herself to feel something for Elle's sister. To feel for a fraction of a second an emotion about the mousy nondescript girl that she had picked up a USB memory stick from every couple of months in exchange for an amount she couldn't even remember – though she did recall that she had often paid less than agreed when she came to collect it; Caro had a good nose for desperation. Did she feel bad? Not particularly. Had Elle succeeded in giving her a taste? Without doubt. 'I've felt it, Elle. I can feel it,' she said. 'I promise.'

Elle rolled her eyes at Caro's sudden earnestness. Then she bent and smelt the rose. 'Don't worry, I'm not going to do anything to upset your precious family. Not tonight anyway.'

'What do you mean "not tonight"?' Caro gripped the windowsill. What did this mean? Could she relax?

'It means, I'll be keeping watch, Caro, with all your little secrets in my pocket,' Elle said calmly. 'And you, like me, can see what it's like to live with the consequences of someone else's selfish whim for ever.'

Caro tried to keep it together, hold herself tall. 'Okay.'

Elle said, 'I don't need your agreement, Caro.'

'No, of course not.' She hated this; being at the mercy of Elle's condescension. 'So you're not going to tell Lady Bellinger?'

Elle shrugged a shoulder. 'No. Not right now. But one day I might go to one of the memorial ceremonies. Or pop in for a cup of tea.'

Caro pursed her lips. She could just imagine it, Elle sauntering past all the precious Bellinger heirlooms, delivering her bombshell over a cup of Darjeeling and a Scottish shortbread.

Elle came and sat on the windowsill next to Caro; she smelt so familiarly of Elle. 'There is one thing I'd like you to do.'

Caro eyed her warily. 'What?'

Elle grinned. 'Be nicer to Brian, Caro. I liked him, he was in one of my zoology classes. He deserves better than you.'

Caro felt her insides contract. 'What do you mean by be nicer to him?'

'I mean,' said Elle, hint of glee in her voice, 'act like a loving wife.'

'How do you know I don't?'

'Come on, Caro, you've got escape fund written all over you.'

Caro swallowed. She had indeed been squirrelling money away over the years with the intention of getting the hell out of her marriage as soon as the youngest was safely ensconced in university – or a Mexican taco van. It was one of the main things in life she had to look forward to; she woke every morning aware the countdown clock was ticking. And now they had all started school, time positively whizzed by. The sadness of her children growing up was only made bearable by Caro's taste of freedom on the horizon.

As if she'd been a friend of the family for years, Elle said, 'I'm sure Bethany wouldn't be too happy, would she, to learn about naughty Mummy's lies and deception?'

It didn't bear thinking about. Brian and Bethany were like two peas in a bloody rugby club pod. Always siding with each other against Caro. Listening avidly to each other's opinions. Laughing at their in-jokes and memes that Caro couldn't fathom, excluding her however hard she tried to prise them apart.

Caro tipped her head back against the window, appalled but resigned to her hideous new fate.

Elle patted her knee. 'You don't have to go overboard, Caro. Just be nice. Hold his hand once in a while. Snuggle up to him in bed. Take him to the memorial tomorrow and show him off. And, you know, it's never too early to start planning a little retirement cruise together; I've heard the Nile is fabulous.' From the laughter in her voice, Elle was very much enjoying herself. 'I think it might be time for me to look Brian up, reacquaint myself with my old zoology pal.' She stood up, brushed down the back of her dress. 'Don't look so glum, Caro. It could be worse. You could have ended up with Henry.' She winked.

Caro wanted to grab her, haul her back, pummel her face, bash her head into the Indian sandstone paving, anything to keep her out of her life. Knowing that she'd bloody won, that every decision Caro made from now on would have Elle's laughing eyes in the back of it.

'Oh hello, Georgie,' Elle said as she went into the hall. 'Having a good listen, were you?'

Caro whipped round. Through the open front door she could see George standing in the hallway, his cheeks red. Their gazes locked but he looked away down to the floor and hurried off to the dining room.

Elle turned back to Caro, grinning, 'Don't worry, he won't say anything. Doesn't have it in him.'

Caro had to steady herself with her hand on the window-sill, felt all her adrenaline draining away, wondered if she might tumble forward and smash her own head on the Indian sandstone.

CHAPTER THIRTY-THREE

NOW
LILY

Cheese: Brie de Meaux Dongé, Comté extra vieux and a vintage Lincolnshire Poacher (vg. A smoky vegan cheese alternative)

Lily had helped Caro serve the cheese, unwrapping all the expensive packets that George had brought from his local deli. They came with cards explaining each flavour. Caro had all the proper cheese accoutrements: a silver knife with a tiny mouse on the handle and holes in the blade that no doubt served a purpose but had been fashioned to resemble the holes in Emmenthal, a heavy white marble slab for serving, grapes, fig jelly, and small plates decorated with pictures of French cheese labels. Not for the first time, Lily was very glad they had not had the dinner party at her flat; she did not have cheese accoutrements.

She was trying to keep herself busy. Laying the table, clearing plates, folding new clean linen napkins. It stopped her thinking about Caro and Travis having sex while Travis was meant to be in love with her. It stopped her thinking about anything that had been said.

George came in looking particularly ashen. His hair was damp; clearly he'd been splashing his face with cold water. When he sat down, Travis said with a sly grin, 'What have you been up to?'

'Nothing,' said George immediately and Travis laughed, a deep rumble that Lily could feel inside her. She concentrated on the table; his vegan cheese had its own small wooden board.

The three of them sat waiting like stuffed birds at the table. George started reading the cheese labels intently then unable to sit still, he jumped up and said, 'I'll just see where the other two are,' before leaving the room. Travis had closed his eyes and looked like he was meditating, his dark lashes fanning his slim tanned face. Lily wanted desperately to say something but couldn't think of a thing to say.

Instead the thoughts started. Wormed their insidious way into the gaps that weren't filled by observations about the best way to serve cheese. She looked at Travis's bronzed hands on the table and thought about when George had announced his post-Boat Race party and Travis had said to her, 'Do you want to go to the party? I don't really.'

She'd said, 'Me neither. I'd rather stay in with you.' The way she had said it, she'd tried to convey an underlying message, a deeper meaning that perhaps their relationship could move on a step. She saw the glint in his eye when he grinned. 'Great minds, Lily.' Lily had felt a flutter like wings through her body. Nervous excitement fizzed in her fingertips. She hadn't gone out and bought a dress, she'd gone to Boswells department store and bought underwear. Black lace. The type Elle dried on the radiators. Lily told her mum she needed money for books and instead bought new sheets and perfume. On the day itself, her heart beat like she was reading her nan's books, anticipating the clashing and the pounding and the shuddering in ecstasy. She thought she might pass out from expectation. All the others made a big fuss about getting ready and leaving, while Lily waited. Did her make-up, shaved her legs twice, waxed, buffed, moisturized, poured herself into the frilly scraps of underwear.

Travis strolled in wearing an old long-sleeved T-shirt with holes like laddered tights at the cuff. He looked around. 'Smells nice in here.'

Lily tried for sultry but nerves meant she couldn't keep a straight face.

He'd picked her flowers from somewhere – tulips, one petal with bird poo on it. 'Sorry about that,' he said, pointing to it. Lily put them in her water glass. 'Adds to their charm,' she said.

'Exactly what I was thinking,' Travis grinned. He hadn't shaved, his jaw was covered in thick stubble. His hair stuck out at wild angles like he'd just woken up. Lily reached to stroke it down. He moved his head, either bashful or not wanting to be preened, she wasn't sure.

There was dithering; what music do you want? Shall I turn down the light? Are you thirsty, hungry, hot? No, I'm fine, fine, fine. The room seemed to shrink. The lace underwear got caught in her bum when she moved; she tried unsuccessfully to subtly tug it free. Travis said again how nice the room smelt. Then suddenly they were kissing, as if neither of them could bear the tense small talk a second longer. Travis drew her close, pressing her against the soft threadbare cotton of his T-shirt, his hands spread wide on her back. He started to lift her top, said, 'Is this okay?' She nodded, then when he pulled it off she stood embarrassed in her black bra.

'Nice, very unexpected.' He grinned, cupping her lace-clad breast, smelling her skin.

Lily was half enjoying it, half dying inside. She could feel her whole body start to tremble. She felt more exposed semi-dressed than she thought she might naked. Nerves were clouding her thoughts, making her worry that the door wasn't shut properly or wonder if somehow her brothers had bugged her room and were watching. Travis lay her down; she sank into the duvet with his weight on top of her, she closed her eyes and breathed in his scent of weed and soap, she ran her hand over his roughly chopped chaotic hair, his spiky stubble, she opened her eyes and stared straight into his light green ones; all of it exactly what she wanted, who she wanted. She would write books about him if she could. She wrapped her arms around his neck and held him tight against her, inhaling him. She thought of all the others at their party when she was here living what might just be the best moment of her life. Travis and Lily. She loosened her hold and reached her hand down so it slipped underneath his top, his skin was warm. He laughed, ticklish. She grinned shyly. He yanked the T-shirt off over his head so they were skin against skin.

He tried to get his hand underneath her to unzip her skirt, got caught up with the duvet, feigned annoyance. She lifted her hips and did it herself. He skimmed it down over her legs, whistling through his teeth at her flimsy, scalloped-edged pants. The corners of his mouth tipped up. 'Lily, you have excelled yourself.'

When he reached to touch her, she realized she was shaking.

'Are you cold?' he asked.

'No,' she said, shaking even more.

'You're shivering.'

She bit her lip. Felt her face redden. She couldn't stop the shaking now, it was a violent tremble engulfing her. She couldn't even try to hide it. Cursing her body, she whispered, teeth chattering, 'Travis, I've never done this before.'

Immediately his hand stilled. 'What?'

She had to repeat herself.

This time he laughed. 'You're joking, right?'

She shook her head.

'But the underwear, the—' He paused, frowned in confusion.

Lily clasped her hand across her chest, felt like a child.

'You're shitting me?' Travis laughed again. Eyes alight like he'd been caught on candid camera. 'You can't not have had sex? I don't believe you.'

Lily felt the humiliation burn through her cheeks, down her neck, all over her body. In her mind she glowed as red as a tomato. She felt the prickle of tears behind her eyes as she tried to drag the duvet round to cover herself but it was caught between the bed and the wall. 'Well believe it.'

When it finally dawned on Travis that she was telling the truth, that this was no big joke, he physically recoiled back off the bed. 'Whoa,' he said, hands held wide like he was avoiding touching something repulsive. He laughed again, this time more horrified than amused as he pushed his hand through his dishevelled hair.

Lily was struggling to put her top on, her arm was caught in the sleeve. 'Can you stop looking at me like that, please?'

'I'm sorry.' Travis tried to get his face back in order. 'I just didn't know anyone . . . I just can't believe . . . Are you really serious?'

'Yes, I'm serious,' Lily mumbled, wrestling with her clothes, wanting the bed to fold inwards and swallow her whole.

Travis was pacing. 'Shit, Lil, shit. Why didn't you tell me?'

Lily didn't say anything, just pulled her legs up, wrapped her arms round them. 'Because it's embarrassing.'

'Too fucking right.' Travis grabbed his T-shirt, started to yank it back on. 'You knew I wouldn't do it if I knew.'

'That's not true.'

'I feel like I've been tricked.' He shook his head, exhaled like he was lifting the weight of the world. 'I don't want to be responsible for this. Getting wrapped up in something that intense. No way. Christ, what, for all I know you'll want to get married next?'

She couldn't speak. Her heart actually hurt. 'Are you serious? Can you hear what you're saying?'

'I don't know what I'm saying. I'm sorry.' He stood with his thumb and forefinger on his forehead, eyes closed, brain running through it all, then he laughed again in disbelief before opening his eyes and saying, 'Lily, I'm not who you want me to be. I can't be this person for you. You've saved yourself for someone. Me, it seems. That's a huge responsibility. It comes with stuff I don't want. I don't want to be saved for. I don't want to be that person. I don't even read Harry Potter. I couldn't give a shit about Harry Potter. Honestly, I'm just not cut out to care about people like that. I care only about myself. I'm fucked for most of my waking hours, fucked so I don't have to deal with this stuff. I'm an arsehole.'

'No,' Lily shook her head. 'You want to be, but you're not.

261

Not really.' Her breath hiccupped. She just about stopped herself from saying, 'You're a Hufflepuff,' because she realized suddenly that he'd made that up.

He sighed, looked at her like she was a wide-eyed child dressed up in her mother's underwear. 'It's not Cinderella, Lily. This is not your happy families farm. I have no blueprint for this. I promise, I'm an arsehole. I don't want the responsibility of this.' He gestured to where she was sitting on the bed.

There was a pause.

'So what have we been doing it for?' she asked, her voice small in the cavernous silence.

'I don't know, Lily. Just a bit of fun,' he said, shaking his head, backing out the room. 'Nothing this serious.'

In Caro's dining room, Lily tried to focus on her breathing. The smell of the cheese was overwhelming. She could feel the urge to vomit. The idea of Caro's face if Lily were sick over all the beautifully laid out cheese briefly made her smile but then the dizziness got worse and the room started to spin in a haze of artfully curated décor.

George reappeared and silently took his seat. Something had clearly happened between him and Elle.

Lily steadied herself, gripping on to the sides of her chair.

Then suddenly the quiet of the dining room was shattered by Elle bursting in, denim jacket slipping off one shoulder, flushed cheeks and a giddy expression on her face. She came over to the table, unhooked her bag from the back of her chair and said, 'Right, I think my work here is done.'

Travis's eyes flew open. 'What? But we're just having cheese.'

Elle grinned, blonde curls tumbling round her face. She

popped a grape into her mouth. 'I'm not a massive fan of cheese.'

No. Elle couldn't go. Lily's panic started to rise again, tunnelling her vision, heightening the sounds. 'You can't go.' She wanted to talk to Elle, to try to get her alone. Her chest tightened. *You're stronger than you think, Lily.* She was caught in the waves of nausea. She begged herself not to be sick on the table.

'Elle absolutely *can* go!' snapped Caro who had appeared in the doorway looking the exact opposite of Elle: pale and tired, red hair now scraped back, make-up smudged.

Travis looked between them confused. 'What's going on? What's happened?'

Elle was trying to hold in her giggles as she backed out of the room. 'It was lovely to see everyone.'

George stood up quickly and in so doing pushed the big table back towards Lily, squashing her chair against the large French dresser behind her. When she tried to stand up there wasn't enough room. The leg of the chair caught on the rug, hitching it up, trapping her where she was.

'Wait, Elle, I—' Lily called but her voice didn't carry above George's booming, 'Sorry you can't stay!'

And Elle's jaunty, 'No you're not.'

Travis gave the table a shove so he could get out and that only succeeded in wedging Lily in further.

Caro was doing her best to usher Elle out, 'Thanks for coming.' But Travis stopped her, insisting on a goodbye hug. 'Are you sure you have to go, Elle?'

The lip of the table pressed hard into Lily's stomach making her breath shallow as she pushed against the wood, the awkward angle increasing her feeling of panic like a dream when nothing would move how it should. Her ears started buzzing. Her arms felt weak. Elle was leaving, strutting out of the dining-room door in her red dress and sequinned denim jacket. Caro followed. George stood with his hands on his hips next to Travis, blocking Lily's view. She had to stop Elle. She couldn't let her leave. You're stronger than you think, Lily. Her breath raced. She squeezed her eyes shut as sparks appeared in her vision. Then she heard a voice shout, 'I had chlamydia!' and realized it was hers.

CHAPTER THIRTY-FOUR

THEN
Trinity term, third year
ELLE

Christ, the party was dull. They were all such imbeciles. Couldn't handle their drink or their drugs. Puking in the corner. Jumped-up schoolboys with their games and their forfeits. Girls hovered around them with their expensive highlights and shrill laughs, in their strappy silk dresses that cost the same as Elle had watched Henry casually blow on drugs. The boys in their ugly navy blazers puffed up like royalty until they got too pissed to speak without slurring.

This was not what Elle considered a good time. She was about to leave, slip away unnoticed when she saw a familiar face getting squished by the crowds. 'Lily?' she shouted above the noise. 'What are you doing here?' Elle held out her hand and pulled her through the mass of people.

Lily rearranged her hair, flustered, jittery. She pulled awkwardly at her plain black dress. 'I was invited,' she said, her eyes so thick with liner they filled her face like an anime character.

Elle laughed. 'I know. I thought you were home with Travis, I was jealous!'

Lily shook her head. 'No,' she said, the music getting louder, people shoving them from either side, a song coming on that made Henry Bellinger holler, 'Tune!' and Elle wince and Lily say without – to Elle's disbelief – a hint of irony, 'I'd rather be here.'

CHAPTER THIRTY-FIVE

THEN
Trinity term, third year
LILY

Everything Lily wished she'd said to Travis ran through her head on a loop. She thought how the Japanese had a name for that, or maybe it was the Germans, she couldn't remember; it was something she usually wouldn't have any trouble recalling. When Travis had stood on the landing and asked, 'Where are you going?' when she came out of her room and ran down the stairs, she wished she'd said, 'Anywhere that you aren't!' She wished she'd paused, taken a step back and said right up in his face, 'There's a person inside here, Travis. It's not just for you to decide what happens to her. *"Can't take the responsibility? Can't love if you've never been loved?"* That's a pathetic excuse. You can try, you can learn. You can do anything if you want it enough.'

He would have said, 'Maybe I don't want it enough,' defensively glib.

And she would have looked him straight in the eye and said, 'Except you know you do.' Then she would have spun away and stalked to the party high on her own assertive self-assurance. She would feel how Elle must feel all the time; the certainty of having the upper hand. He might even have followed her to the party. Grabbed her arm, spun her round and kissed her passionately in apology. And Lily would be the one to decide whether to kiss him back or push him away.

As it was, she didn't say anything to Travis when he asked, just ran away down the stairs in her little black dress without looking up, out into the cool outside where it felt like a different world from the oppressive humiliation of her bedroom. She had to walk fast, outrun the thoughts, the look of horror on his face. 'Don't think about it,' she repeated to herself but when she got to the party, pushed open the door of the dark, loud, sweaty club she didn't need to think about it. The music pushed all thoughts out of her head. It smelt of alcohol, sweet and sticky. The lights, the noise, the rising chatter engulfed her, swept her up. She tried to find a place to hang her coat, then a guy just grabbed it and flung it to the back of a booth full of people where it got thrown further, disappearing from sight.

The crowd was out of Lily's league. Every jock from campus was there, every radiant Verity and Fionnuala with their condescending stares, expensive blow-dries and figure-skimming, spaghetti-strapped dresses. She just needed to find someone she knew, hopefully Elle. She headed over to the bar, just so she could take a moment, get her bearings. The noise was crazy.

She was surrounded by strangers; the athletes she could decipher from their sport-emblazoned leisurewear. She could tell the rowers from their blazers; they weren't the best-looking bunch but together they morphed into one being greater than the sum of its parts, radiating success. In the midst of them was Henry Bellinger, Adonis-like. It was hard to take your eyes off him when he was near, he was so beautiful. Chiselled and aloof while cheekily good-looking. She didn't realize she was staring till he saw her and said, 'You're here!'

Lily turned, just to make sure he was talking to her, because even though they had shared a house for a year, she didn't think he knew who she was. He had never once registered her presence in the time she had known him. Once, when he'd bumped into her on the landing of the house, he'd said, 'You here to see Travis?' and she'd said, 'No, I live here.' Henry had looked at her most perplexed. Now, in the club, when she glanced over her shoulder she saw that the person behind her was looking the other way and realized with some bemusement that Henry was talking to her. Then to make it completely clear, he bent down and gave Lily a kiss on the cheek. He smelt heady, of aftershave and tequila.

'Hi,' Lily said, nervous. She almost laughed because of all the people she thought she'd talk to tonight, Henry was not one of them. Maybe he had registered her presence in the house after all.

'Champagne?' he asked.

'Okay. Yeah. Okay.' Lily was so bamboozled by his attention she added, 'Are you sure you've got the right person?'

He laughed. 'You're very sweet.' Then ordered her a glass of champagne which she gulped too quickly.

Caro came over, enviably confident among the boys, and dragged everyone to the dance floor. Lily hung around by the bar but then Caro grabbed her hand too. Lily didn't normally dance but the rush she got from being included allowed her to be swept up in the throng, buzzing and light-headed from the champagne. That was when she saw Elle; her clear displeasure at having to endure the party pulled Lily out of her reverie. Immediately she was back with Travis, lying exposed and rejected on the bed. On the dance floor, Henry hollered, 'Tune!' and she let herself slip away from Elle, be pushed under strobing lights with the rugby boys, sweat glistening on the hockey team, the rowers, everyone shiny and golden. The music made her bones rattle. JB Watson was jumping around like a lunatic next to her. Henry nuzzled Caro's red mane adoringly. It was all loud singing and big smiles, hands in the air and thumping beats. The music got louder. The ground shook. The lights pulsed. Lily didn't know if she was enjoying herself, part of her felt like she was about to have a seizure, but whatever it was, she wasn't thinking about Travis, so that was good.

CHAPTER THIRTY-SIX

NOW
LILY

They all paused mid-action. Elle half out the dining-room door, almost out of sight. Caro tersely shooing her away. Travis and George side by side like sentry guards. The collective gaze turned and fixed on Lily, trapped between the table and the dresser.

George was holding in an embarrassed schoolboy snigger, the word chlamydia still echoing in the air between them.

Elle took a cautious step back into the room, eyes firmly on Lily. Expression wary of what might follow.

In the doorway, Caro folded her arms across the velvet ruffles on her chest and said haughtily, 'See Travis, I knew you were to blame for the chlamydia. Don't try to wriggle out of it now.'

But Travis shook his head, said to Caro while pointing with dawning puzzlement between himself and Lily. 'We never—'

Caro huffed, 'Oh please.'

Lily gave the table a shove, freeing herself enough to stand up. The attention was smothering, made her legs wobble and bright sparks fleck in her vision. But she could feel a strange out-of-body confidence wash over her. Her therapist had once said, 'Sometimes, Lily, in times of trauma, our body and our brain can disassociate,' and she wondered if this was what she meant as she watched the ensuing scene from outside herself. She shook her head and said, 'We didn't.'

While trying to glean what was going on, Caro was redoing her hastily scraped-back hair, as if realising the stresses of the evening were not yet over and needing to primp herself back to her hostess glory. She glanced to check her reflection and said, confused, 'I don't understand. If not Travis, then who . . .?'

What had been a beautifully stylish, on-trend dining room, suddenly felt like an interrogation room. The smoky grey walls oppressive, the sparkling chandelier glaring in Lily's face.

Caro stood with her arms crossed on the other side of the table, flame hair now in a smoother low ponytail, and laughed, brash and incredulous, 'You're not about to suggest this is something to do with you and Henry?'

They were all staring at Lily. This was not the same as being in her therapist's office with the white walls and box of Kleenex. When the therapist had asked Lily if there had been any other special relationships in her life since Travis, Lily said, 'No, just a really jealous cat.' The therapist had replied with gentle authority, 'Lily, we can keep on like this. You can keep paying me. You can keep avoiding questions with flippant asides. That's fine. We can go on like this for years, in fact. But I want to remind you that you came to me for help. That's what I'm here for: to help. I'm not the one you need to try to evade.'

Lily had looked down at the floor, at her scuffed shoes on

the rug. She wondered what she was trying to prove. That she was smart enough to outwit the therapist? That talking was overrated? That none of this would work anyway because there was nothing wrong with her? Or that however hard they tried to crack her, she'd prove she was impenetrable? But who were they? she wondered. This was surely only a battle with herself.

The therapist said, 'I promise, all I'm here to do is help you.'

It was on the tip of Lily's tongue to say, 'I really do have a very jealous cat.' But she had a sudden picture in her mind of her childhood running through the woodlands, feeding baby lambs with a warmed bottle, lying on the grass as a fat chicken pecked by her head, her dad's strong hand on her shoulder, her mum's soft kiss when she fell. She could remember that girl, her freckled face and unruly hair, but the happiness was unfathomable. She couldn't imagine the lightness behind the smile. To feel that safe, that easy with life, was a mystery to Lily. She wondered how it was possible to be jealous of yourself.

The therapist said, 'I want to talk about relationships, Lily. Relationships since Travis.'

Lily nodded.

Silence.

Lily said, 'There haven't been many,' feeling like her voice was not her own. 'There's probably only been one person I've liked. There *has* only been one person. His name is Peter. He works in my local bookshop.'

'Tell me about Peter.'

Lily crossed her arms tight over her midriff. 'There's not much to say. We got on well. I think we had the same sense of humour. He would have laughed, you know, about the jealous cat.' She herself laughed, nervously. 'We went for a few drinks, to exhibitions. He'd read my book.'

'And why are you no longer together, Lily?'

'It's complicated.'

Silence.

Lily brought her thumb up to her mouth, nibbled the skin by her nail. 'He talked a lot about wanting a family, kids, you know. And er,' she paused, gnawed at a hangnail. 'I can't have children, so . . .' The skin tore on her thumb, hot pain seared like a knife slice, she tasted blood in her mouth.

The therapist pulled out a Kleenex and handed it to her. 'How do you know you can't have children, Lily?'

Lily wrapped the tissue round the bleeding cut on her thumb, felt the calming throb of pain. 'Because I had something called pelvic inflammatory disease and I wasn't diagnosed early enough. It developed from chlamydia I caught at university.'

'I'm sorry to hear that, Lily.'

Lily shrugged. 'It's okay.'

'It's not okay, is it, Lily?'

Lily pressed hard on the tissue round her thumb. The wound burnt.

The therapist said, 'Can I offer you another way of looking at your relationship with Peter?'

Lily nodded. 'If you want.'

'Could it be that you removed yourself from the relationship in order to avoid physical and emotional intimacy?'

Lily ran her tongue over her lip. That wasn't at all the focus she had expected. She had assumed they would move into a tangent about coping with infertility. 'That is certainly another way of looking at it,' Lily replied, uncomfortable with the new direction. 'But I don't think it's true because I would have always felt guilty, about the children. And him being stuck with just me.'

'Firstly, there are other ways of having children and a family, Lily,' the therapist said frankly. 'It doesn't have to prevent you from having relationships. But more important, Lily, is your use of the phrase "stuck with just me". You don't think you're enough on your own?'

Lily laughed. 'No.'

The therapist didn't laugh.

Lily felt suddenly as though, while trying to do the exact opposite, she had exposed her innermost self, her jelly-like core was on raw display right there in the room. She wanted to curl over into a ball, protect herself at all costs. Her eyes darted to the door.

There was a pause.

Lily's thumb was bleeding through the Kleenex.

'Who did you catch chlamydia off, Lily?'

Lily wasn't thinking straight. She was unbalanced from her stupid laugh, confused by thoughts about why she had ended it with Peter, wanting to go back and dissect that yet still fighting the urge to flee. She had another vision of the little lambs with their bottles and their fast beating heats, her easy laughter and excited eyes. She couldn't speak. She felt unmoored. Defenceless.

'Who did you catch chlamydia off, Lily?' the therapist asked again.

Lily squeezed her eyes shut and shook her head. 'I don't know,' she said, and immediately burst into tears. That was the first time Lily cried in the stark white office.

CHAPTER THIRTY-SEVEN

NOW
ELLE

Elle stared at Lily standing in front of the French dresser, the shelves behind her filled with Caro's paraphernalia: a white porcelain cockatoo ornament, a neat pile of glossy books, a hand-blown glass vase. She took in the brave lift of Lily's small, pointy chin. Those giant eyes. Sometimes she saw them in her dreams. Tried to forget them. Made the mistake of thinking that Lily was so quiet perhaps things didn't actually affect her.

'My drink was spiked at George's party. I was raped in the toilets by someone. I don't know who. I have no memory of it happening.' Lily's detached mechanical tone cracked at the last minute. She rolled her lips together, pressing to quash the emotion. Picked up a napkin, dabbed her eyes. Then stood staunchly, breath tightly controlled.

Elle closed her eyes, unable to stop the memory replaying in her head. All she could see was Lily stumbling as she came up the stairs from the bathroom of the club, tripping over her own feet. Only one shoe on. Dress twisted. The weight of her as she collapsed, fragile like a bird, in Elle's arms. The normality of everything around them: the music, the laughter, the sweaty drunk faces as Lily sobbed silently, barely able to breathe.

'Lily, what's happened?' Elle urged, as Lily's weight got heavier, her legs buckling under her grip. 'Tell me what's happened.' Elle could taste her own fear. Eyes darting round the club, taking snapshots of the grotesque faces in the bright lights.

But Lily just shook her head, pale and disorientated. 'I don't know,' she said, voice like a child. 'I don't know.' Then she was sick on the floor, right over Elle's shoes and those of a girl next to them who screeched and backed away, shouting, 'You're disgusting.'

Elle held Lily tight to her chest, one hand cradling her head, trying to keep her upright, trying to get her to walk. She could see the blood on her legs. Brain rewinding to the moment she'd seen Lily all wide-eyed on the dance floor. Where the hell was Travis? Elle pushed through the crowds of people, every leering face a suspect. Someone reached to grab her, she smacked them hard away. 'Ow! Crazy bitch.'

Now, in Caro's dining room, Elle couldn't find the words to speak, consumed by the memory of Lily trembling like a dog in her arms.

That was how Caro swooped into the silence unfettered. Striding across the room to face Lily, she drew herself up to her full, imposing height and said with patronising faux-sincerity, 'I'm very sorry this happened to you, Lily. But I really hope you're not implying it was Henry. He's not here to defend himself. And, if we're honest, that whole place probably had chlamydia!'

CHAPTER THIRTY-EIGHT

NOW
GEORGE

There was something niggling George. He couldn't quite put his finger on it. He moved away from the dining table, into the portion of the room that had a couple of low leather armchairs, a sideboard with a collection of pastel-hued glass candlesticks and a large green marble sidelight. He stood by the armchair, stared at the beaten lines in the leather.

His memory of the party was hazy. He had never been good at drinking shots. Most of what he remembered of that night came after Henry had got the call from his mother telling him his dad had died. George remembered vividly their time on the grubby bench together. A moment out of time that rekindled their friendship and made him remember the good in Henry Bellinger.

But now he was reminded of something else.

'I'll tell you who's the real winner, boys.'

George could see Henry's face, the jittery coked-up eyes, the wolfish grin. He could smell the acrid dryness of his mouth when he spoke. *'Yours truly here has nailed the list.'*

'*Fuck off, you have.*'

For a moment George couldn't remember the name of their cox. God, tonight had ruined him. He could barely believe what had happened with Elle in Caro's sitting room. It made his skin crawl with humiliation. Imagine if Audrey found out? Imagine if the video went viral. He looked down at the sheepskin rug on the floor between the armchairs, felt woozy and off-balance. It was too much.

Behind him, Caro was jumping to Henry's defence, bristling and high-pitched.

Marco! That was the name of the cox. He remembered him clearly now, his small neat features grimacing as he baited Henry over his claims.

George remembered the smug, violent pride in Henry's voice when he bragged, '*I can give you names and numbers, Marco, dear boy. May not have made the boat but I've fucking won this one and none of you fuckers are going to take it away from me.*'

George remembered when Elle had seen the criteria for the list on his phone. He'd dismissed it as a tradition. 'Just a little harmless fun.' They'd had a massive row about it.

Now all he could see was Henry's face. Right up close, spittle glistening on his chin, eyes triumphant as he mouthed off his conquests. All the rowing boys baying for names. Gleeful, jeering. George preoccupied with wanting to be the star, annoyed Henry was stealing the limelight.

'*Just nailed the last one in the toilet. Virgin, tick!*'

Klaus slurring, 'Bloody hell. You are a hero, Henry.'

All George could hear, ringing in his ears, was Henry shouting, 'I *am* a hero!' at the top of his voice.

Now, in the dark lushness of the dining room, he said, 'Christ, I think it *was* Henry.'

He could see his own face, ashen, in the round gold mirror above the sideboard as he told them in awkward stutters, his voice getting posher like a disgraced politician, ashamed to be in Lily's earshot, what Henry had said.

Caro bashed the table, making the glasses rattle. 'No!'

CHAPTER THIRTY-NINE

THEN
Trinity term, third year
LILY

Elle ran the shower, took Lily's clothes off carefully, stood her under the water. Lily remembered thinking Elle was getting her new leather leggings wet. She kept her head down. Watched the water as it ran red. Elle dried her, walked with her to the bedroom. 'Don't let Travis—' Lily said and Elle said, 'I won't.' Then she put Lily to bed. Her eyes were damp. Lily had never seen Elle cry before. She said, 'It's okay.' Elle said, 'No it's not.'

Lily didn't know after that. She was so tired. She closed her eyes hoping she would never wake up.

But she did. When the sun came in through her open curtains. And all she knew, apart from the pain clamping round her head, was that she had to get away. It felt like all eyes were on her. That everyone knew. Everyone at the party had seen what she hadn't seen. There was blood matted in her hair, she saw her torn black pants folded on the floor. 'You should keep them, as evidence,' Elle had said.

Evidence of what? Lily asked herself. She had no memory.

Nothing. A void where anything could have happened. One minute there was dancing and the lights. And then the toilet cubicle. Double vision, blood and the feeling she had left her body behind.

She had to get out of her room. The house. Those people. Were they all laughing at her? Stupid, naive Lily.

Someone knocked on her door. She flinched. Pretended she wasn't in. Kept silent. 'Lily?' It was Travis.

She opened it a crack.

'Wow, look at you. Someone had a good time.' He was on his way to the bathroom, towel slung over his shoulder.

She didn't say anything. He didn't seem to notice.

'I was a twat last night. Sorry. I shouldn't have laughed. I shouldn't have said what I did. It just caught me off guard, that's all.'

She thought about what she could say. *It's okay, I'm not a virgin any more.* Some voice inside her cackled. Was she splitting in two?

She couldn't look at him. Instead she said, 'I feel a bit sick.'

'Too much to drink?' Travis laughed. 'Poor Lily.'

Lily left as soon as she could after that. In the street she moved from the pavement to the road when she passed people. She couldn't stop looking behind her; felt like she was being followed.

At home on the farm, she couldn't sit still, couldn't sleep. She watched the sunset and sunrise and all the stars in between. Her mum said, 'Lily, love, what's wrong?' And she said, 'Nothing, I'm fine.'

There was a black hole in her brain. But her mind loved a puzzle; kept trying to fill in the blanks. Kept imagining horrors that made her whole body flinch.

When they were out checking the fences, her dad watched silently as she was sick in the hedgerow. Retching till her throat burned. When she walked back to the quad bike, he said, 'You all right, Lil?'

'Fine, Dad.'

He paused before starting the ignition and said, 'You don't have to go back, you know.'

She wanted to curl up on his lap and sob into the soft wool of his sweater that smelt of bonfires and childhood. She wanted him to hold her tight and tell her she couldn't go back, that she wasn't allowed. That he'd make it all go away.

But he just looked at her with his sad, kind eyes and nodded when she said that she did.

Lily knew she had to go back. The books were the only thing that would stop her going mad.

She was so tired. She just wanted it to disappear. She reasoned that if she couldn't remember, she must be able to forget.

She went to the doctor. He'd known her since she was a child. She asked for pills to sleep. Pills to get her through the day. He prescribed exercise and meditation and suggested that if she was feeling anxious, she should see a counsellor. He said Oxford could be a very stressful place. She went back another time when the locum was prescribing; she gave Lily all the pills she needed.

Lily stayed at the farm for as long as she could bear, but in the end the kind claustrophobia drove her back to Oxford. Thankfully, Elle wasn't there, she'd gone home for some reason. Something to do with her sister. Henry had died and George and Caro were wrapped up in their grief. To them, Lily went unnoticed. Not them to her, though. She felt like they were looking and laughing. That they knew. She wasn't sad Henry had died. They could all die and Lily wouldn't care. She imagined her name on a list in some locker rooms somewhere; she felt people point and whisper when she walked across the quad. The library was the only place she could breathe, where she felt herself disappear into the books. She barely left. In the house, Travis tried to put his arm around her once but she moved away so fast she smashed her leg into the coffee table. She wasn't having anyone touch her.

Elle came back. Lily did her best to avoid her but she caught her in the hallway really early one morning. Elle stopped and said, 'Lily . . .'

And Lily said, 'Yes?'

'How are you?' Elle asked, reaching very tentatively to touch her shoulder.

Lily moved away from her hand on the pretext of picking up her bag. 'I'm fine.'

She felt Elle's eyes searching her face and stared blankly back.

Elle said, 'Do you want to talk?'

'What would I want to talk about?' Lily asked, because already she wasn't sure herself. Her brain filling in the past like cement.

Then the police broke the front door down and Travis was arrested for possession with intent to supply. Which in a way was good because it meant Lily didn't have to avoid him any longer.

CHAPTER FORTY

NOW
LILY

'Oh God, Lily, I should have known.' Elle came round the edge of the table, reached for Lily's hand and held it warm in her own. Lily could smell the cigarettes on her skin. 'Fuck. I'm so sorry,' Elle said. 'Henry almost did the same to me and I should have reported him. Oh God, I could have—'

'You're lying,' Caro snapped accusingly from the other side of the table.

But George was striding over, frowning as if this was information he should have been privy to. 'What do you mean, the same to you?'

'Rape, George,' Elle said with a frankness that made George flinch. 'That day he was in my room.' She gave him no more than a withering glance before turning back to Lily. 'Here look, Lily, why don't you sit down? Do you want some water?'

Caro put her hands on the back of the dining chair, leant forward readying for battle. 'Why didn't you say anything then?'

Elle poured Lily a glass of mineral water. 'What was I going to do?' She half laughed, turning to face Caro, sleeves of her denim jacket pushed up. 'Go up against Henry Bellinger? Please.' She shook her head. 'No chance.'

George was still looking hurt. He said, 'Why didn't you tell me?'

'Because I thought I could deal with it on my own,' Elle retaliated, hand on her hip, braced and defensive.

'Oh, and how did you *deal* with it?' asked Caro, mocking the very idea.

'I got George to poison his drink before the Boat Race,' Elle replied, snarky and cool like a teenager with a smart answer that no one expects.

'What?' shrieked Caro.

George reared back, flustered. 'I don't know what you're—'

'Give it up, George,' scoffed Elle, giving her hair a flick. 'It's done. Nothing anyone's going to do about it. And more important things are happening.' She gestured to Lily.

Caro was flapping. Hand fluttering in front of her chest like she might be about to faint. 'You poisoned Henry?'

'No, absolutely not!' George denied quickly.

Elle took a few steps towards where Caro was standing and said, matter-of-factly, 'Yes. George poisoned Henry. And it damn well served him right. The guy was a fucking bastard.'

Meanwhile, on the other side of the table, Travis took the opportunity of the furore between Elle, George and Caro to slip over to where Lily was sitting quietly sipping her water and crouched down to gently take her hand. He said, 'Why didn't you tell me?'

Lily didn't want this attention. Didn't want him this close. She could see his tattoo moving when he swallowed. She wanted to push him away. But she was exhausted. It had taken everything she possessed to say what had happened to her out loud. The only other person she'd told was her therapist. Now she felt like her insides had been sucked out. And it was an effort to move her hollow body.

Travis put his hand on her shoulder. His fingers warm and possessive. Lily wanted him to stop touching her. Travis was thinking back, running through events. 'I knew there was something wrong with you,' he went on. His face was close, she could see the piercings in his ear, the pores in his skin. She looked away, down at her plate, her eyes tracing the fancy pattern.

'Lily, you could have told me. You should have told me,' he said in the annoying voice he used when he was talking about his meditation and life coaching. Patronising, like he could have told her the answer if only she'd paid to hear one of his talks.

Across the table, George was blustering, justifying himself. 'Can we please stop saying the word poison? It was just a sleeping drug. It was Henry who cheated!' He made desperate eyes at Elle who watched, hands on her hips, expression reeking of disdain.

Caro was having none of it; she shook her head, emerald earrings flicking back and forth. 'I'm going to report you both!'

'I don't think that's a good idea, do you, Caro?' Elle shot back, tone warning, eyes narrowed like a prowling cat. 'You never know what secrets might come out.'

Caro's shoulders sank a touch. Her nostrils flared.

George cut in, his fingers pulling uncomfortably at his collar, 'I, er . . . I think the focus now should be on Lily.'

Caro dragged out a chair, sank down defeated, her voice welling with tears as she said, 'You're all just trying to blame Henry to make yourselves feel better about what *you* did. It's lies. All of it.' She shuddered, starting to sob, head in her hands so all they could see was the top of her copper-red hair. 'He would never have done anything like that.'

Across the table, Lily felt like her story was being taken and pulled in different directions; everyone making it about themselves. She wanted it back in its box. Back to when the therapist had said with calm assurance, 'Lily, you have been denied control of your own story all these years. You need to reclaim it. Make it yours to own.'

When Travis said again, 'Why didn't you tell me, Lily?' She wrenched her shoulder from his touch. The patronising sympathy with which he looked at her, with the same eyes that had once dared be so simultaneously amused and horrified by her confession that she'd never slept with anyone, was like a match to the anger that simmered low inside her. She could feel her cheeks prickle. She thought of the therapist saying, 'Do you ever feel angry, Lily?' And taking a moment to think, to put a name to the constant gnawing tightness that lived red-hot in the pit of her stomach, Lily had looked up and said, 'I feel angry *all the time*!'

The relief of admitting it out loud, labelling it, made her carry on and say in a breathless flurry, 'It's there when I'm on stage and have to talk about my book, I sometimes get an overwhelming urge to scream. And sometimes when I'm in the supermarket. Or when I'm lying in bed . . . It's burning so viciously inside me I think I'm going to have to tear my hair out just to make it stop. It's not anger. It's more than anger. It's rage.'

It was this internal ball of ever-burning fury that led Lily to push back her chair so it banged hard against Caro's French dresser, toppling the white porcelain cockatoo ornament to the floor where it bounced on the rug, and shout, fists clenched, teeth bared, 'You rejected me!'

Travis paused, stunned. He almost stumbled in his crouched position, staring open-mouthed at Lily like a bomb had gone off. His tattoo and shorn hair looked suddenly ridiculous, like props for a costume. Everyone was quiet. Lily could hear her heart like a drum in the silence. No one moved. Only Caro's vintage wall clock ticked on regardless.

Then suddenly, out of nowhere, Travis bashed the table with his fist and said with a laugh of resigned condescension, 'I knew it was you.'

CHAPTER FORTY-ONE

NOW
LILY

'*What* was me?' Lily looked to see if anyone else knew what Travis was talking about but no one seemed to have a clue. Even Caro had forgotten her self-pity to stare, eyes wide like a startled chicken.

'Don't pretend you don't know.' Travis's fingers drummed on the table as he stared contemptuously at Lily. 'I always suspected but was never sure. I wondered when I saw you tonight if I'd find out. You called them out of revenge, didn't you?'

'*Who?*' Lily was so discombobulated by the turn of events she didn't know what was going on. She wanted to shrink back but the chair was already pressed against the dresser.

'The police!' he said, emphasising it clearly like she was an idiot for not understanding.

Lily swallowed.

In the glinting chandelier light, Travis's eyes looked black. He stretched his arms above his head as if trying to escape his own frustration. 'You messed up my whole fucking life.

All just to get your own back because I wouldn't bloody sleep with you.'

Tears pressed against Lily's eyes. 'You said it was the best thing to happen to you!'

'Yeah, well I was lying!' Travis huffed. 'You think I want to spend my time teaching this bullshit to people? Telling people sitting where *I* should be sitting about how to calm their pathetic, anxious minds – do you know how demoralising that is?' He held his hands out as if posing the question to the group. 'All the while my dad sits on millions that should by rights be mine by now. I was owed that money!' He jabbed the table. Lily stared at his blunt, neatly trimmed nails. 'That should have been my life. And you know, I'd have got it but oh no, some prick of a judge has to tell him that I brought shame on my family, validates his every criticism. Gives the pompous bastard the ammunition to really make me grovel. Best thing that happened to me?' Travis scoffed, ran his hand irritatedly over his shaved head, sweat patches under his arms. 'How can you *still* be so naive?'

Lily was too dumbfounded to speak.

Travis got right up in her face and muttered, 'I hope it felt good because I can assure you it did the trick, it fucking ruined my life.'

Over the other side of the table, George tried to add some calm by saying, 'Steady on, Travis. This doesn't seem entirely fair.'

'Shut up, George.' Travis didn't even glance his way.

Lily couldn't believe this was happening. That after everything she'd said, everything she'd been through, Travis still had the power to kick her when she was down. To make her feel like nothing. The air filled with a buzzing white noise. 'I didn't call the police, Travis. But God, I wish now that I had.'

'Don't bother,' he said, arrogantly assured, 'I always knew being with you was a mistake.' He gave Lily a disparaging once up and down before shoving his chair out the way so his path was clear to stalk away.

'She *was* the best thing that ever happened to you and you know it.' It was Elle speaking. Her blue gaze fixed, voice tightly controlled like she would rather be shouting. 'You were just too much of a spoilt, self-pitying brat to realize it at the time. You ruined your life long before Lily came into it, Travis.' Elle yanked the table hard away so she could stand by Lily's side. 'It was me who called the police.'

Caught unawares by the confession, Travis stopped. He turned, didn't know where to look, who to believe. He came back round the table, his eyes darting between them. 'No it wasn't.'

Elle laughed, humourless. 'Yes it was.' Then she moved past Lily so she stood between them. All Lily could see were the sequins on her jacket. 'Come on, Trav, shout at me,' Elle said, unflinching. 'Get right up in my face. Let's see what you've got.'

But the air had been knocked out of Travis. He stepped back, stumbling on his tipped up chair. 'Why?'

'Because, Travis,' Elle's disdain was evident in the curl of her red lip, '*I* found her. *I* walked her home. *I* saw the state of her. Not you. You were nowhere to be seen. Hiding out in your sad little bedroom. And do you know what I thought?' Elle raised her chin in question, waited until Travis shook his head.

'I thought you sold them the drugs. It was all there in your little box of tricks, the Rohypnol, the GHB, the ketamine all nicely labelled, catalogued for all your discerning customers.' Elle couldn't have looked at him with more contempt. 'I thought it was a little unfair for you to get away scot-free.'

Travis couldn't believe what he was hearing. He stood with both hands on his head, elbows jutting out, muscles tensed as he processed what she'd said. On a huffed outbreath he hissed, 'You bitch.' Then, when Elle didn't falter, he moved closer, stood legs apart, jabbed the table hard with his finger to emphasize his point. 'If Henry wanted it, he'd have got it from anyone.'

Lily wanted Elle to move out of Travis's way. His angry eyes made her worried for her safety.

Elle raised a brow. 'But he got it from *you*, Travis.'

Across the dining room, Caro whined, 'Henry would not have bought anything like that!'

No one listened.

George cut in with, 'Maybe we should all sit down, talk this through calmly.'

But Travis kicked the table leg in his frustration. 'This is not my fault! People were asking for it.' The bottle of port tipped onto the cheese, glistening red all over the tiny labels and the oozing Brie. Caro swore, immediately patting the spillage with a napkin.

Elle made a face like Travis was the stupidest person she'd ever met. 'That didn't mean you had to sell it!'

'What they did with it was their responsibility!' Travis shouted.

'Oh yeah,' said Elle. 'Tell *her* that.'

Elle pointed to Lily who felt suddenly the glare of a spotlight. The voiceless victim sitting while Travis grabbed Elle by the scruff of her denim jacket, hauling her forward, her head snapping back at the force, blonde curls tumbling, and spat, 'What happened to her had nothing to do with me!'

Lily didn't know if Travis was going to hurt Elle. She was pretty certain Elle could defend herself, or even perhaps George would step in and yank Travis away. But something happened in Lily's mind the moment he put his hands on Elle's jacket.

Maybe it was the knowledge that Travis sold Henry the drugs. Or the memory of him humiliating her at her most vulnerable. Maybe it was a fuck you for laughing. Maybe Travis had warned her who he really was but he also led her on with the belief there might be more beneath the surface. Maybe it was the realisation that Travis was exactly who he always said he was, that the only one he'd really been in thrall to was his father because they were so damn alike, and Lily had been stupid enough not to see that he was rotten to the core. Maybe it was anger at her former self. Maybe it was defence of her former self. Maybe it was that she had spent fifteen years knowing that every time her own dad looked at her with his tired, worried eyes, he knew there was something awfully wrong with his daughter. Or that she hadn't slept properly for what felt like a lifetime. Or that Travis had so viciously accused her of informing the police of his petty dealing when she had just put her life-shattering secret out there for all. Or maybe it was just that she could finally put faces to names and in the absence of Henry Bellinger, Travis was the next best thing. Her therapist would work out the finer details. But right then, watching Elle be dragged off her feet in Travis's grip, Lily's disassociated brain and body fused, she picked up the fancy cheese knife with its faux-Emmenthal holes and, with the force of fifteen years' repressed rage, she plunged it hard and fast into Travis's abdomen.

CHAPTER FORTY-TWO

NOW
LILY

Caro screamed.

George barked, 'Oh Jesus Christ.'

Travis dropped his hold on Elle and grasping at the bleeding wound on his side, shouted, 'Oh my fucking God! You stabbed me! I can't believe you fucking stabbed me! Fuck. I'm going to die.'

Elle stumbled to regain her footing. 'Don't take the knife out!' she ordered.

Travis was hopping from foot to foot, hands clutched where the cheese knife was sticking out of his body. The loop of the handle curled to mimic a mouse's tail.

Lily sat down. She couldn't believe she'd done it. It felt so good. Powerful and strong and entirely satisfying. Her eye caught the print on Caro's wall that said, *We'll go dancing. Everything will be all right*. In her head she scoffed.

'Call an ambulance!' Caro shouted, running round to stem the wound with a linen napkin.

George got his phone out and called 999.

Travis staggered back, supported himself on the chair, clutching his bleeding stomach while his disbelieving eyes stared at Lily. 'Why would you do that?' His skin was white and clammy.

Caro helped Travis to the floor, her expensive linen soaked red, trying to make him comfortable as he writhed and kicked in angry agony.

George said, 'Ambulance is on its way. What can I do?'

Ignoring everything going on with Travis, Elle turned to Lily. She held her by the shoulders and said, 'Lily, I'm so sorry for everything that happened.'

Lily looked into her beautiful blue eyes and said, 'That's okay.'

Elle said, 'It's not okay. I wanted to talk to you about it at the time but I had to go home and then Henry was dead and you had your head in your books. It was weak of me not to push you, to try to help and that's something I am not proud of. I'm sorry.'

'What the fuck are you talking about?' Travis shouted. 'I'm dying over here. I've been stabbed!'

Elle glanced over her shoulder. 'You're not dying.'

George said, 'He might be dying.'

Lily stared down at her hands in her lap, at her bitten nails and the thumb that she kept a plaster on all the time now.

'Well google how to treat a stab wound!' Elle snapped curtly to George and then to Lily she said much more softly, 'I should have reported Henry at the time he tried to assault me.'

Lily looked up from her hands into Elle's sad, guilt-ridden face and said, more sharply than she'd imagined she might, 'Or maybe Henry shouldn't have done any of the things that he did.'

Elle smiled, blinked her watery eyes and wrapped her arms

around Lily, pressing her tight to her chest. Lily closed her eyes, inhaled the sweet perfume and let herself be held.

'This is not the time to be hugging! Jesus Christ!' Travis snapped.

'He looks very pale,' said Caro, cradling Travis's head in her lap, keeping his body folded forward so the wound stayed closed, her hand pressing down on the napkin. George was scrolling on his phone and saying things like, 'Gentle pressure, Caro. Raise his legs, we have to stop him going into shock. Is it a sucking chest wound, Caro?'

'It's lower than that, George.' Caro had gone into efficient mode. 'Elle and Lily, could you do your hugging later and help, please?'

George said, 'Keep him warm!'

Caro called, 'Can someone get me a blanket?'

Elle sighed. She let Lily go and walked over to the leather armchair in the corner and pulled the decorative throw off the back. When she threw it to Caro, she said, 'He doesn't deserve this attention.'

'Elle, he's been stabbed,' Caro stated firmly as she tucked the blanket round Travis who was becoming more subdued as the initial shock wore off and the pain kicked in.

'It really hurts,' he groaned.

'Why don't you meditate?' suggested Elle with sardonic disinterest. She pulled a chair over to sit by Lily, smoothed Lily's hair back over her shoulders.

Like she was directing a PTA meeting, Caro said, 'George, could you get me one of the clean towels from the downstairs bathroom cupboard, please? Preferably a brown one as the pistachio ones are new.'

George hurried off.

Travis moaned and writhed on the floor.

George came back with three brown towels and went to kneel by Caro who swapped the linen napkin for a towel and said, 'I think that's all we can do for now. He's comfortable and we're keeping the pressure on the wound.'

Travis muttered, 'I'm not comfortable.'

Elle went and got another blanket, this one she draped over Lily's shoulders. When she sat down again she said, 'What are we going to tell the ambulance people?'

'We tell them I was fucking stabbed!' Travis groaned.

Elle ignored him. Leaning forward, elbows on her crossed knees, hands clasped in front of her, she said, 'We're going to have to make something up.'

Caro frowned. 'I'm not lying to the police.'

The candles flickered on the table. Wine glistened on the cheese.

Elle said, 'I don't think you'll find it too hard.'

Caro's lips pursed. 'It's perjury.'

Elle rolled her eyes. 'Like you care.'

George hid behind his phone, scrolling for more information. 'Check his pulse. Elle, I really don't think lying—'

'You don't need to think, George. I'm doing the thinking.' Elle sat back, arm draped along the back of Lily's chair.

George lowered his head back to his phone and nodded.

Travis tried to sit up, wincing in pain, pupils dilated. 'You're not making something up. I want fucking justice.' Caro soothed him back down again.

Lily couldn't face any more animosity and confrontation. She wanted it over. She said, 'You can tell them I did it. I don't mind.'

Caro adjusted her position so she was sitting more demurely. 'I think that's the best plan.'

'It damn well isn't.' Elle stood up so fast her chair toppled. Her hand shot out to catch it, barely looking at what she was doing as she said firmly, 'Lily's been through enough.'

Lily could see a furious tremor in Elle's hands as she righted the chair then fumbled in her bag for a cigarette.

'You can't smoke in here,' Caro ordered.

Elle lit up regardless. She went to stand at the end of the table, pacing back and forth, smoke billowing in clouds, clicking her fingers as she thought. Then she stopped, leant against the table and said, 'Okay, Travis, these are your options. First is we say it was self-defence. I'll say I did it because you had me in a threatening hold. This is not an ideal solution for a variety of reasons, and I don't really want to take the blame for something I didn't do.'

Travis narrowed his eyes, listening but pretending he wasn't.

Elle went on, 'The second is Lily says she did it.' She held her hands out. 'The truth.' She flicked her ash into an empty wine glass. Caro visibly flinched. 'But let me warn you, I will make sure Lily's defence team know about everything you've ever done; everything that ever happened in this group will come out. You hear me, all of you? Travis, your dad will find out about a lot more than a little Harry Potter box of drugs on your shelf. He'll know it all, every consequence, every detail. Understand?'

Travis glared at her as best he could with the pain pulsating through his body.

Caro's face had gone pale as she clutched tightly at the towel.

Trying to maintain his composure, George mumbled, 'And what's the other option?'

Elle dropped her cigarette into the glass. 'We say it was an accident.'

'How the fuck do you get stabbed by accident?' Travis grunted.

They could hear a siren in the distance.

'I don't know,' said Elle. 'But the ambulance will be here soon, so we're going to have to come up with something.'

Everyone was more invested now in finding a way out without criminal blame. From the floor, Caro said, 'I read a thing the other day about middle-class injuries. Avocado hand and pizza-oven forehead. Maybe this is cheese-plate tripping or something like that?'

George said, 'What's pizza-oven forehead?'

'You know, when you burn it on the bit at the top when you're checking.' Caro released pressure on the wound to demonstrate to George.

'For fuck's sake!' Travis shouted. 'Stab wound!'

'Sorry, Travis.' Caro put her hand back.

Lily had to fight the urge to laugh.

Elle said, 'Good. Cheese-plate trip. George, stand up and come over here.'

George was on his feet in an instant, stumbling over himself to do what he was told.

Elle picked up a spoon that was on the table for coffee later. 'Just so we don't make the same mistake twice,' she said with an amused glint in her eye as she brandished the blunt cutlery. Then she scooped up a bit of Brie and said, 'Here, try this amazing . . .' and fake tripped into George's stomach.

George recoiled. 'Ow.'

Travis muttered, 'Imagine how it feels not with a spoon!'

Lily looked at the gloopy Brie dolloped on George's shirt. She bit her lip. 'There was no cheese on the knife.'

'Oh for God's sake!' Elle chucked the spoon on the table annoyed.

'Can we put some cheese on it now?' Caro asked.

'No!' Travis shot back, his hand going protectively to his abdomen.

The siren was getting closer.

George was trying to wipe the sticky Brie off his Paul Smith shirt.

Elle squeezed her eyes shut as she thought.

Lily cleared her throat and said, 'Maybe I was showing Travis the knife. With its little holes and the mouse and the mouse-tail handle and then I tripped?'

Caro said, 'Does it have a mouse tail handle?'

'Yes, look,' said Lily.

They lifted the blanket and all had a look at the mouse-tail handle sticking out of Travis's stomach.

'So it does,' mused Caro.

'Great idea, Lily!' Elle congratulated.

The paramedics banged on the door.

'About bloody time,' Travis muttered.

George hurried off to answer it.

Lily watched it all from her chair. She looked at Travis on the floor, writhing to try to find a more comfortable position, Caro fussing with his blanket, Elle's eyes fixed on the door, waiting, her professional mask slipping into place as she formulated the story. As the paramedics bounded in, Lily was overcome by absolute exhaustion. But underlying that was an unfamiliar sense of satisfaction. The understanding of what it felt like to be heard. To have found her voice.

CHAPTER FORTY-THREE

NOW
CARO

Digestif: Hennessy XO Cognac

Caro's husband, Brian, came home from the rugby club dinner with her daughter Bethany as the paramedics were strapping Travis to the stretcher.

Travis was sobbing into his mobile phone to his father, 'I might be dying. I'm so sorry. Will you come to the hospital?'

They didn't catch the answer because Travis was carried out to the ambulance.

George walked back from the front door. 'What do you think? Do you reckon his dad will turn up?'

But Caro wasn't listening, she was too distracted watching Elle greet Brian and Bethany.

'Brian Carmichael! Oh my goodness. It's been *so* long! I can't believe it.' Elle threw her arms around Brian as enthusiastically as if he were a long-lost husband. 'So great to see you! And who is this ravishing beauty?' Elle turned her attention to Bethany. 'Wow, you're stunning! And you look so alike!' Her smile was so wide it split her face in two.

Bethany blushed, delighted at the attention, as was Brian, his cheeks a rosy, bashful red.

Caro felt her hackles rise. She was desperate to tear them apart. To send Bethany immediately to bed and frogmarch Elle out the house. But she could only watch, even found herself bristling with annoyance as Brian lit up under Elle's gaze. While Caro didn't want him, she certainly didn't want him thinking he was worthy of such fawning attention from the likes of Elle.

To make it worse, Elle had wrapped the usually disparaging, somewhat surly, Bethany round her little finger. Ushering her to the leather chairs like a new best friend to find out everything about her while they waited for the police, throwing Caro a little wink as she went.

For something to do, Caro started to clear up. She cling-filmed the cheese and put it in the fridge. Brought out the fancy chocolates she'd got from Waitrose.

When the police arrived, Elle dealt with them with quiet authority. Used hushed lawyerly tones and complicated legalese.

Caro made coffee. All the while, she tried to find Brian's presence less of an irritant. Could his smile seem sweeter, his hair less dull, more neat? His cheeks less rosy, more ruddy? His money something to be saved for their old age together rather than frittered away on expensive things just to irritate him? It was early morning when the police finally left; birds had started to sing in the garden. Bethany had gone up to bed.

They were all in the kitchen. Brian came back from showing the police out and said, 'Well goodness gracious, what a night. Anyone need a brandy?'

But Lily already had her jacket on. 'No, not for me, I'm going to go.'

With her most ravishing smile, Elle said, 'I'd love one, Bri.'

Caro tensed, she didn't think she could bear any more.

Elle smiled, her big, laughing eyes glancing briefly to Caro, as she added, 'But I think I should make a move. We'll have to catch up soon.'

George said, 'Me too, actually. Get back to the wife.' Then he paused, looked nervously at Elle and rephrased. 'Need to get back to Audrey and the baby, explain what's happened.'

They all walked through to the front door. Caro checked her reflection in the hallway mirror: pale and wan, hair flat, horrible dark circles under her eyes. 'Well, it's been interesting,' she said, standing in the open doorway, just wanting them gone now.

George shook hands with Brian. 'Indeed,' he said. 'Funny old evening.' Then he paused and asked awkwardly, 'I, er– I take it we're not going to Henry's memorial thing, are we? I mean, if you still wanted to go I could drive back after I've had a sleep and go with you, if you want? I just, I suppose Lady Bellinger will be expecting us.'

Elle snorted with derision.

Caro said calmly, 'I'm not going to Henry's memorial, George. Not after this.' She felt Brian put his hand supportively on her shoulder and tried not to shrug him off.

'No,' said George. 'No. Right. You're right.' Three Ubers had been called and were now in a line at the kerb waiting. George picked up the overnight bag he had never unpacked. 'Well, thanks for having us.' He kissed Caro on the cheeks, shook Brian's hand. Lily did the same.

Elle said, 'Brian, I'll give you a call, yes?' Then leaning in on the pretext of giving Caro a kiss on the cheek, whispered, 'You be good now.' And they all walked out into the dusky pre-dawn.

Caro shut the door with a sigh of relief.

'Quick brandy, my love?' Brian asked.

Caro did her utmost not to flinch when he called her my love. 'Yes, why not?' she said, testing out a smile. Brian seemed momentarily taken aback by her niceness. Maybe it didn't have to be so bad.

She could but try.

CHAPTER FORTY-FOUR

NOW
GEORGE

George and his wife sat side by side on the sofa, Raffy happily feeding for apparently the tenth time that night, guzzling away content in his tiny yellow towelling Babygro.

George had come up with a whole host of lies to explain events of the evening away, cut out any mention of his own wrongdoing, but the minute he had walked in the door, seen Audrey familiar and sleep-deprived, Raffy in her arms, eyes wide with whatever emotion babies felt, he had burst into tears. George always tried his best not to weep in front of people, not to weep at all if possible. Ever since his father had whipped him on the back of the legs with his belt for breaking the glass in the Victorian greenhouse with a cricket ball; he'd had to snivel his tears away quick smart because his dad had threatened to tell everyone at prep school his son was a crybaby.

'So go on, tell me what happened,' Audrey said, stroking the baby's downy head.

'I don't want to,' admitted George, tears dripping down his cheeks. 'You're not going to like it.'

Audrey looked at him from under lids hooded with exhaustion. 'George, neither of us would say we were in the best place right now. If anything is going to change, you need to get it all out now.'

The revelation that she was no more satisfied with their marriage than him put George even further on the back foot. It hadn't occurred to him that Audrey might leave him. Might not be blindly devoted.

'No lies, no messing. Just tell me,' she said, losing her patience.

So, like a snivelling child wanting absolution from its mother, George told her everything from beginning to end, including the Xylazine poisoning and his desperate nuzzling of Elle's breasts while being secretly videoed and lying to the police about who stabbed Travis.

Audrey listened, occasionally looking away in displeasure. By the time George had finished, Raffy was fast asleep, making the noises a snoring mouse might.

Audrey shut her eyes for a moment, took a deep breath to compose herself. 'Wow,' she said.

'I hate myself,' said George.

She looked at him like that was not something she wanted to hear just then.

George reached to touch her. She jerked away. Raffy woke up and began to wail. Audrey sighed.

George had to get away from the look of pitiful repulsion on her face. 'I'll make us a cup of tea,' he mumbled and sloped out to the kitchen, hoping the time alone might give her the chance to think things through and abhor him a little less.

But when he came back, Audrey had fallen asleep. Leaving

George stranded in a desperate purgatory, alone with his thoughts and terrified about what might happen in the morning.

He pulled a blanket over her and Raffy and sat on the sofa next to them, feeling like everything Elle had said about him was true. He had walked around his whole life seeing only himself. And now, just when his eyes had been opened, he was in danger of losing the people that meant most to him.

George forced himself to stay awake as long as he could, aware this may or may not be the last time he sat close to his wife, depending on what she planned to do with what he'd said. One thing he knew for certain was that the part of his life built on his emotionally supressed, bulldozing self-assurance had come to an end. If he was lucky Audrey would forgive him, and in time he might not feel such a weak, pathetic fool. The alternative didn't bear thinking about. Right now he simply wanted to sit in the dark with his wife and child and watch her, beautiful and unencumbered, as she slept.

CHAPTER FORTY-FIVE

NOW
LILY

Lily closed the curtains on the breaking dawn. She took off the floral shirt, navy trousers and grey blazer that she wore to every book party and event and would likely never wear again. She tied her hair up in a neat ponytail and took a shower. Just that little bit too hot so her skin went pink and the mirror fogged. She put on the cotton pyjamas that her mum had sent her for her birthday and her slippers. She could hear the whir of the milkman's van outside as she went to feed the cat. The calendar on the fridge reminded her she would see her therapist on Monday. The idea of it felt different. She wondered if she would say Lily'd had a breakthrough. She put the food down for the cat and imagined the therapist leaning forward, gently touching her hand and saying, 'I'm proud of you, Lily.' Or perhaps Lily was just proud of herself.

She went to the bedroom thinking how she would describe how she was feeling. Like a weight she had lugged about for years had diminished. Not gone, just less heavy. Yes, that was it, she thought as she climbed in between the white cotton sheets: less heavy.

She knew she would have to unpick it all at therapy. Go through all the intricacies. To talk about it out loud was to move on. But she was fairly confident the worst was over, the hard work had been done, that her story was now hers to own. Lily had found it among the hellfire.

As her head rested on the soft pillow, it occurred to Lily that she might pop in and see Peter at the bookshop, just to say hi. Maybe she wouldn't do it straight away. One step at a time. But the idea was definitely worth some thought. And she could always just buy a book if it was weird.

The cat jumped onto the end of the bed and curled up by Lily's feet. The milkman's van disappeared off up the end of the road. The cacophony of birdsong rose with the sun. And for the first time in forever, Lily slept.

CHAPTER FORTY-SIX

NOW
ELLE

At work, Elle always enjoyed the organized comfort of her varnished ply desk and Eames chair, the subtly tinted window where birds flew at eye level, all her neatly labelled papers. But there was a coil of energy inside her she hadn't felt in a while that couldn't be sated with her caseload.

Midweek, she made the journey to her sister's flat after work. A lifeless layer of dust had formed over everything. She went into the bedroom, sat on the bed, opened and shut the drawer of the bedside cabinet that housed things too personal and too innocuous to bear considering, a punched-out packet of paracetamol, a half-finished paperback. She smelt her sister's perfume, ran her hand over the clothes in the wardrobe, wrote her name in the dust. Her mum had taken the photograph albums but in the living room Elle found on the floor a couple of photos that had obviously slipped out of their plastic cover. Some innocuous shots of a Brighton beach visit. Her sister at a work Christmas party in a paper crown. But the last one was of the two of them, Elle and

Sarah. A first day back at school, when their mum had made them pose side by side in their green uniforms. Sarah with her white socks pulled up and hair scraped back. Elle with non-regulation black tights and badly bleached curls. Sarah grinning, Elle pouting. She could see the outline of her mum's then boyfriend's arm in the picture so holding it carefully she tore the strip off the side and let it fall to the floor. Then she lifted the photograph to her lips and gave her sister a soft, last kiss before slipping it into her bag. On the train home she rang a house clearance and cleaning company to take care of the rest.

There were birthday drinks after work on Friday for one of the partners, Fiona McNeil, a fearsome divorce lawyer with an obsession for karaoke. She popped her head into Elle's office on her way out. 'You coming? It's a tiki-inspired private booth with themed lighting and a cocktail button!' Fiona said, like that might be enough to tempt Elle from her office.

Elle watched the work crowd go with a flicker of unexpected envy.

It occurred to her that she'd actually had fun at Caro's dinner at the weekend. Despite poor Lily and everything else that happened, she had enjoyed being out, being that version of her former self. More and more she had kept people at arm's length. The decision to stay detached had become a habit.

She caught sight of her reflection in the office glass, hair swept back, thick tortoiseshell glasses, crisp white shirt. All work and no play had made Elle a dull girl.

She got a taxi to the tiki-karaoke.

On the way there a notification popped up on her phone from her fake Instagram account – the innocuous belinda. bakes.cakes – to say that George's wife, Audrey, had accepted her follow request. Elle felt a rush of guilty excitement. Ahead were potentially hours of judgemental fun down a forensic rabbit hole of George and Audrey's life. She itched to open her Instagram app.

But then she thought of his pathetic face as he quivered with fear after Elle had taken the video of him nuzzling her skin. Leave him to his little life, she thought. And at the same time chastised herself for her shameful, clichéd habit of lurking on Instagram, believing the air-brushed lives of others compared to her own. She should know better. She deleted the app.

The cab pulled up at the Soho karaoke bar.

'Oh my God, it's Elle!' Fiona shouted from up on the platform, microphone in one hand, pina colada in another.

Elle ordered a Manhattan and took a seat on a leather banquette next to Xavier Jones-Wright, who wasn't a lawyer but worked in advertising on the top floor of their building and had been coming out with them for years. Dark and brooding, he was one of the star players on Elle's Rolodex.

They drank. They danced. Elle even sang, which was fun but not something she needed to repeat in a hurry.

As the night started to wind down, she turned to Xavier and said, 'You coming back to mine?'

He tipped his head like he'd very much like to.

She bit the sweet cherry off her Manhattan cocktail stick. 'You can stay over if you want.'

Xavier nearly spat out his drink. 'Stay? Bloody hell, Elle. What's come over you?'

She raised a brow. 'Do you want to stay or not?'

He sealed his smiling lips. 'Absolutely.'

Elle shrugged like the deal was done. She'd give the possibility of intimacy a little road test, just to check she hadn't been missing out.

CHAPTER FORTY-SEVEN

NOW
CARO

Caro would have killed for one of Elle's cigarettes. Brian was snoring in post-coital bliss. She had tried but failed to enjoy herself.

She stared out the window at the river, tinfoil silver in the moonlight. She imagined the two rowing crews steaming past, blades carving up the water. All that fuss, all for a race. She remembered Henry's face, livid, as he lay in the hospital bed and watched it on the TV. She thought of Lily standing up at the dinner table in her neat blouse, bravely announcing what had happened to her.

The water glistened. Sleeping swans drifted past. A fox jogged along the towpath.

Standing at the bedroom window, Caro's eyes lost focus. She saw only her own ghostly face in the glass.

She remembered the taxi journey to George Kingsley's Boat Race celebratory party.

To her relief, Henry had finally managed to flag down a cab but she'd had to walk far further than expected in her new shoes which were already rubbing the back of her heel raw. The waistband on her dress was digging in and her hair was frizzing the more flustered she got. All in all, she did not feel every inch the glamour puss she had been aiming for, and Elle in her grunge chic, sparking Henry's obvious appreciation, had not helped Caro's ego. When Henry got in the taxi without even checking on Caro, or opening the door for her, it felt like it didn't matter to him if she was there at all.

Henry sat back against the leather seat. The car smelt sickly, of air freshener. Caro had to ask to open the window.

Henry said, 'So what's going on with Travis and . . . whatsername?'

'Lily, Henry. You lived with her, remember?'

'Yeah I know, but it doesn't mean I have to remember her name. I don't think I've ever heard her speak. What does Travis see in her?'

Caro was enjoying the cool breeze on her flushed cheeks. 'She's a virgin,' she said, dismissively, 'that's what he sees in her.'

Henry almost choked. 'You're kidding?' He turned to Caro wide-eyed and enrapt. 'How do you know?'

Caro didn't know for certain but she was pretty damn sure. And she enjoyed finally having Henry's avid attention. 'Women know these things, Henry.'

Henry slung his arm around Caro's shoulders, drawing her in tight against his side. 'Well, well, well. Isn't Travis the sly dog?'

Caro had taken the pregnancy test the day before. Had been mulling over when the right time to tell Henry was; preferably when she was past twenty-four weeks and he couldn't tell her to get rid of it. Caro had always wanted a baby; something to love and that would love her back in equal measure with no strings or judgement.

She hadn't paid much attention to what Henry had bought from Travis for the very reason that she wouldn't be partaking. When she got to the party, any shot of tequila or similar she chucked onto the already sodden floor. But actually it was the smell of the alcohol that got to her; made her spend nearly the entire party throwing up in the toilets.

That was when she saw him. She'd heard something going on in one of the stalls but she'd been preoccupied with her head down the disgusting toilet bowl. It was his shoes she recognized, from where she was sitting getting her breath back on the cubicle floor. She stood up, pressed her nose to the crack in the door. Henry was in front of the mirror, checking his hair, looking awfully pleased with himself. She knew that look; she'd seen it when he'd successfully bullied a waiter or cut someone down to size who was in his way. He gave his reflection a gun salute and bounded out of the bathroom, checking his fly was done up as he left.

Caro didn't want to know what he'd been doing. The thing about going out with Henry was you turned a blind eye to a lot of things. She wiped her face on some loo roll, unlocked the door and planned to slip unnoticed out of the bathroom. But she couldn't help herself, she had to look. To see what bimbo was currently flumping her hair and straightening her dress. It helped to always be aware of the competition.

But there was no bimbo, just a leg sticking out of a half open-door and a lost shoe. Caro dared to reach out and push the cubicle door open a fraction more. She gasped out loud when she saw her. Black dress hoiked up. Slumped, out cold. Lily.

Caro ran back to her own toilet cubicle. Retched and retched. It added up in an instant. She knew about the list. She'd seen his spreadsheet when she'd gone through his phone. Yet one more thing she had turned a blind eye to. But there was a difference between some harmless seduction and a fairly humiliating threesome to drugging and raping someone he'd just found out was a virgin. Who Caro had told him was a virgin.

As soon as she knew there was nothing left in her body to throw up, Caro fled as quick as she could from the bathroom back out into the club. Anything to get away from the sight of Lily like a ragdoll, broken and bent out of shape.

She saw Henry over by the bar, arms thrown over the rowers' shoulders, holding court as they listened enthralled.

She kept thinking of everything she'd put herself through in order to keep him happy. What a waste that had been. There was no way on earth she was having a rapist as the father of her child. Her tiny, precious baby.

She could see the scenario play out in all its stifling glory; she would have to stay with Henry, have his hands – that now repulsed her – all over her body, cradling the baby, off doing God knows what with God knows who, otherwise he and his vile mother would crush Caro for custody. Would snatch her cherished child and make it their own, cut her out of the picture with malicious disregard. What were Caro's other choices? Persuade Lily to testify against Henry? Really? Lily, who wouldn't say boo to a goose. The Bellingers and their expensive lawyers would annihilate them both. No one got done for rape anyway.

Caro stalked the party in a fury. Why couldn't he have just been decent? Just ten per cent more decent and that wouldn't have happened.

He'd ruined everything.

She couldn't let that version of the future play out.

CHAPTER FORTY-EIGHT

THEN
Trinity term, third year
CARO

It was tricky to navigate the route in the dark. The dust underfoot. The death trap wires and cables. At one point she tripped on a loose board and almost fell through a hole, scrabbling on her hands and knees to safety. There was rubble on the floor, broken tiles, lethal-looking tools. Her hands were shaking. The speed of her heart made her worry she might black out as she felt her way along the upper corridor, past steel poles, plaster flaking under her fingertips. She tried to calm her breathing. She was scared and strangely excited. There was no reality to it. Everything heightened: the sounds, the dirt, the dust. She saw faces in the shadows. Then nothing. Just her imagination. She kept going in the darkness, had to be careful as she climbed out the back window onto the scaffolding. She could see the whole city glimmering in the night. Her fingers gripped the cold metal as she forced herself not to look down. What was it Henry said about winning races? Don't think, just do it. From the scaffolding she had to reach to grab on to the castellated roof edge and haul herself onto the parapet, scraping white lines onto her legs. She thought about the little baby inside her. Could fear hurt it? Less, she told herself, than Henry Bellinger as a father might. She edged her way along the lead flashing, a makeshift balcony for this ancient stone castle. Her heart on fire, almost giggling with nervous terror and disbelief. Don't think, she told herself, just one step after the other until she got to the first dormer window. Focus on something else. The view from here was incredible.

A desk lamp was on inside Henry's room. Smoke curled from the ashtray. She could see him sitting there on the bed, top off, head back against the wall, eyes closed.

It was now or never. Ten minutes and she could breathe again. Adrenaline made her muscles flinch. She forced her hand steady as she tapped gently on the glass. Then stood up and pulled her top down so all he'd see was a creamy white breast. A sure-fire way to get Henry to the window. He was up like a shot.

She stepped back into the shadows, drawing him out the window like a fish on a hook. She could taste the fear in her mouth. It was almost too easy. He was so predictable.

Henry climbed out of the window, stood on the narrow ledge, fag hanging from his mouth. It wasn't happening. She wouldn't do it. He said, 'My dad's just died so I'm not in the mood for games. You either fuck me or fuck off, yeah?' Then flicked the cigarette out into the ether.

'I'm not here for games,' she said, voice amazingly steady, moving closer, wondering if he touched her whether he'd feel the racing of her heart. She placed her hands tenderly on the muscles of his chest, stroking his skin like she was smoothing the creases from fabric. He watched her fingers caress him, grinning. He was so stupid. So self-adoring. Believed all his own hype. That was what made him both so dangerous and so susceptible; the arrogant belief that everyone wanted him.

His features loomed above her; he was all nose and eyes and lips in her vision. A different Henry to the one she'd looked at in the past. What had been so handsome was suddenly monstrous. He tried to yank her top down but she said, 'Uh-uh, this is your treat.' She doubted suddenly that she would actually go through with it as she made as if to get on her knees. It wasn't happening, she would walk away. But then she thought of the baby. She thought of Lily on the toilet floor, her bloody legs akimbo. Of herself telling Henry so casually of Lily's innocence.

Henry put his hands delightedly behind his head, dimpled cheeks grinning. 'This gets better and better.'

Caro smiled, flicked her glossy red hair. 'Doesn't it?' And without allowing her thoughts the chance to object, she pushed Henry Bellinger through the gap in the parapet.

CHAPTER FORTY-NINE

NOW
CARO

How easy it had been. One shove. Firm and sharp, like a good push of a child on a swing. Sometimes it scared her how easy it was. As innocuous as putting a chicken in the oven. When she and Brian walked over Barnes railway bridge sometimes Caro's fingers tingled with possibility.

She had often thought that it would be nice to share her secret with someone, release it like a belly held in all day. She'd fantasized about telling Elle, shocking her with her bravery. It would gazump Elle's casual admittance that she'd master-minded a poisoning, while at the same time revealing them to be more alike than Elle ever imagined. Caro would revel in Elle's admiration. She imagined her being so impressed that it would be the start of an unlikely friendship, Caro welcomed into Elle's inner circle. Finally accepted.

Caro hadn't expected the sister revelation, though. Hadn't anticipated something so minor throwing a spanner in the works. Since leaving Oxford, Caro hadn't given the essays she'd paid for a second thought, but there were only so many times she could kick herself for mentioning them at the dinner. Hoist by her own inexorable desire to always have the upper hand.

And now she was trapped.

Brian did a giant rattling snore and woke himself up. He rolled over in the bed like a walrus on the beach. Patting the empty space beside him and finding Caro absent, he looked up and yawned, 'You coming to bed, my love?'

Caro forced a smile. 'Yes, dear.'

She moved away from the window and slipped back beneath the sheets. His arm flopped over her stomach, pinning her to him with sleepy content.

Caro lay with her eyes wide open staring at the patterns in the wallpaper. She had many a long night ahead to devise a way out.

ACKNOWLEDGEMENTS

Huge thanks go to my editor, Kate Mills, and my agent, Rebecca Ritchie, who were instrumental in making this book the best it could be. I'd also like to thank the incredible team at HQ – Editorial, Design, Production, Marketing & PR, Sales – who work so hard on every book they publish.

ONE PLACE. MANY STORIES

Bold, innovative and
empowering publishing.

FOLLOW US ON:

@HQStories